I0678689

DESTINY
BLUES

HAND OF FATE BOOK ONE

DESTINY BLUES

HAND OF FATE BOOK ONE

SHARON JOSS

AJA PUBLISHING
USA

DESTINY BLUES
Copyright © 2013 by Sharon Joss
All rights reserved.

Published 2013, 2015 by Aja Publishing
www.ajapublishing.wordpress.com

Book and cover design Copyright © 2015 by Aja Publishing
Cover art & design by Lou Harper
Heraldic Griffin Design Copyright © by Buch / Dreamstime

All rights reserved. This is a work of fiction. All characters and events
portrayed in this book are fictional, and any similarity to real persons, living or dead, or incidents or events is coincidental and not intended by the
author. This book, or parts thereof, may not be reproduced, distributed, or
transmitted in any form or by any means, or stored in a database or retriev-
al system, without prior written permission of the publisher.

PRINTED IN THE UNITED STATES OF AMERICA

SECOND EDITION

ISBN: 978-1-941544-33-4

Also by Sharon Joss

Novels:

ARUM
BROTHERS OF THE FANG
STEAM DOGS

(HAND OF FATE SERIES)
DESTINY BLUES
LEGACY SOUL
CHAOS KARMA

Novellas:

STARS THAT MAKE DARK HEAVEN LIGHT

Short Story Collections:

DREAMS OF FLESH AND BLOOD (HORROR)
SOLACE AMID THE PLANETS (SCIENCE FICTION)

CHAPTER 1

IT WAS A stretch, but I just managed to slide the parking citation beneath the wiper blade of the white Freightliner refrigerator truck. I'd never had to crawl across the hood of such a big-assed truck to issue a parking ticket before. I half-fell, half-jumped to the ground, and dusted the grime off the front of my uniform.

"Give him another one, Miss Mattie," Mr. Yousef insisted. The truck was parked directly in front of Mr. Yousef's Paradise Garden Cafe, taking up three parking spots, which Mr. Yousef liked to think of as reserved for his customers. "Give him two more! He's ruining my business!"

He was right, of course; I should write two more tickets. But I wasn't altogether certain that Mr. Yousef wasn't trying to get another look up my culottes while I sprawled across the hood of that truck again. I'd barely started my shift, and I was already dirty and sweaty. Upstate New York is especially humid in July, and beneath my helmet it was like a sauna.

"How long has the truck been parked here?"

He flapped his apron; his chin jutted toward at me like a bulldog's. "It was here when I arrived at six this morning. That's five hours without paying! I am certain it was parked there all night. Why you won't tow it? What are you waiting for?"

Mr. Yousef was usually such a jovial man; I'd never known him to be this agitated. The Paradise Garden Café was a popular spot for lunch in Picston. They served the best Greek-Middle-Eastern-North-African food in town. Most of the crew from Parking Control were regular customers. His home-made Koshari in particular was legendary. I sure didn't want to upset him any further.

I walked around the truck again, looking for an oil leak or problems with the tires, but couldn't spot anything obvious. The truck was in rough shape. A couple of gashes appeared to have compromised the insulation, and there was a lot of rust. The refrigeration unit wasn't working. The rank aroma of rancid meat was already beginning to overwhelm the good smells emanating from the café. I could see Mr. Yousef's point.

"He's got twelve hours to move the truck. If it's still here tomorrow, we can do something then."

The scowl on Mr. Yousef's face deepened.

I began to fill out the second ticket. I should have filled out all three citations from the get go; that way, I'd only have had to crawl over that stinking truck once.

"Wait! Please, miss; I've got the money right here." The parking violator jogged toward me; jaywalking across the street from the Buzztown Café.

The guy in the summer linen suit was blonde, tanned, and fit. No socks. He looked like he belonged behind the wheel of a sleek Italian sports car. He flashed me a mouthful of the most perfect set of chompers I'd ever seen, and slammed a quarter into the meter. No kidding, this guy could have been in toothpaste commercial.

No way he was the driver of this beat-up hulk.

He glanced at my nametag. "Officer Blackman. Does the "M" stand for merciful, by any chance?"

I blushed; glad for my helmet and mirrored shades. I recognized him.

I didn't exactly know him, but I'd seen him at my gym. Older guy, maybe early forties, but in great shape. As in, really great shape. Underneath that business suit, lurked the broad-shouldered body of a gymnast. I'd been trying to catch his eye for weeks, but this wasn't how I'd imagined our first meeting. I hoped he wouldn't recognize me, parking control officer uniforms being what they are. My formerly crisp white shirt and navy culottes were already damp with perspiration, not to mention truck grease.

The odor of rotted meat wafted over me. He'd probably already lost the whole shipment. A couple of fifteen dollar parking tickets would be the least of his worries. Somehow the suit and the meat truck didn't seem to go together.

"This your vehicle, sir?"

He glanced up the street. "Ah, I'm helping out a friend. The truck conked out early this morning and he left to get another. He asked me to come and wait for the tow." He held up a Styrofoam coffee cup. "I stopped for a coffee; didn't realize the time. This is my fault, officer. Please don't write that ticket. The tow guy said he's on his way."

Up close, he was even better looking. I echoed his grin, with interest.

Mr. Yousef flapped his apron and glared at me.

Focus, Mattie. Technically, I was obligated to write

three tickets, but with a tow truck on the way, maybe a little leniency was in order.

I nodded my head to the ticket on the front windshield. "I've already issued the first citation, sir. But I'll give your friend a break on the others this time." I gave him my best professional smile. "I hope your friend doesn't lose all that meat,"

He gave me a quizzical look. "What meat?"

"Isn't that what's inside the truck?"

"No, pretty lady. It's flowers. From the flower market. Tear up that ticket, and I'll give you a whole armful."

I rolled my eyes. What a flirt. Maybe I liked him better from a distance. "No thank you." I recognized the truck coming up the street and waved to the driver, Chad, who worked for my brother. "Here's your tow. You have a nice day, sir."

I left Mr. Wonderful and Chad to their business, nodded to Mr. Yousef, and walked back to where I'd left my scooter. The distinctive smell of rotten meat and licorice seemed to trail after me. Flowers my ass. It didn't take a detective to know he was lying through his teeth. I told myself it wasn't my concern.

Don't get me wrong, most of the time; Parking Control is a good gig. It's just that sometimes my Scooby detective hormone goes into overdrive. I have to remind myself that I'm not paid to investigate; I'm paid to write tickets. Then again, maybe it wasn't the detective hormone at all. I hadn't even kissed a man in six months.

With my thoughts still so preoccupied by Mr. Wonderful, I didn't notice my three-wheeled scooter until I was practically standing next to it. I stopped in my tracks and stared at the transparent apparition seated just behind the driver's seat.

It was no larger than a three-week-old kitten; grey-brown and hairless, with yellow bulbous eyes and a face like a gargoyle.

The bottom fell out of my stomach. Suddenly, the extra-strength dose of putridity in the air made sense. I groaned. They call it teratosis, or, 'breath of the demon'. That was no cat. That was an un-materialized demon. And somehow, he'd attached himself to me.

CHAPTER 2

MY LEFT EYELID began to twitch. Not only did this thing smell bad enough to strip the chrome off a hubcap, but its stare gave me the creeps. I'd never actually seen one before, but along with all her other problems, my mother had been plagued by a series of demon spirits for most of her inebriated and abbreviated life. Or *djemons*, as they're called, before they materialize. Her doctors thought they contributed to her mental decline and eventual suicide.

Of course everybody knows Shore Haven, New York is the spirit capital of the northeast. Located some forty miles east of Rochester, along the lake Ontario shoreline, the neighboring towns of Picston and Shore Haven sprawl around the base of Sentinel Hill, one of North America's few demon portals. Legend has it that a horde of djemons were imprisoned beneath the hill in ancient times, and that the local Senequois tribal magic keeps them there. Every once in a while, though, one of them gets out and attaches itself to a human. They're invisible to everyone but their new host at first, but readily identifiable by their ugly appearance, glowing yellow eyes, and putrid smell.

I glanced around, but nobody seemed to be watching me. I threw my ticket pad at it, and it went right through the thing. It didn't even move. Yup. It was a djemon, all right. The only thing I knew about un-materialized demons is you have to get rid of them. Fast. Before they attach themselves to you and become *materialized* demons. Because once they materialize, they're with you forever. And as if that wasn't bad enough, after 9/11, the government required all demon masters to register their demons for tracking purposes. Say good-bye to your passport, airline travel, or your government job. And that includes Parking Control.

Sweating now, I picked up my ticket pad, and waved it in the direction of the demonic mirage. The apparition slowly dissipated. Gone for now, but he'd be back. I glanced at my watch. It was a tad early for lunch, but there was an extermination company just a couple blocks from here. Visitors from all over the world come Shore Haven every August to be blessed by the ancient spirits and healed at the Spirit Festival. They come to get their auras read, their chakras cleansed, and their fortunes told. It's also one of the few festivals in North America where you can get your demons banished.

With any luck, I'd be rid of this thing in less than an hour.

Five minutes later, I turned down Empress Street and was stopped by a police barricade. My heart sank when I saw four sheriff's cars and the county coroner's black van parked outside Four-Starr Pest Abatement. A crowd of onlookers from the neighborhood gathered on the sidewalk, watching the proceedings. From the weighty silence in the air, I knew it must be bad.

I motioned to the sheriff's deputy assigned to crowd control. Picston has their own Police Department, but Shore Haven has a contract with the Monroe Country

Sheriff's Department.

"What's going on, Lenny?" I asked. Lenny Dawson was the Sheriff Department's best bowler.

"It's the owner's wife, Mrs. Starr."

"Heart attack?"

He glanced around. "More like shark attack."

A shiver ran up my spine, in spite of the heat. Not another one. I shook my head. The local press had christened him 'The Night Shark'--as the wounds were described as generally similar to that of a great white. No traces of DNA had been found at the crime scenes, and the murder weapon hadn't been identified yet. Mrs. Starr would be the fourth victim in four weeks--the first in Shore Haven. Whoever it was, the guy was extending his territory.

Lenny asked me a question.

"Sorry, what?"

"I said what are you doing here, Blackman? Why aren't you patrolling the streets like all the other little meter maids?"

As I pondered my snappy comeback, the aroma of baby demon washed over me. Most likely, this place would be shut down for days for the investigation. I'd have to find another exterminator. And soon. The stink was so strong; I could barely draw a breath. I choked out a flimsy excuse to Lenny and got out of there.

CHAPTER 3

THREE DAYS LATER, I fought back another wave of nausea as I stood next to my scooter in the parking lot in front of Picston City Hall. I clamped my jaws shut; determined to keep the Lucky Charms I'd eaten for breakfast where they belonged. I swear, the fetid stink was growing worse by the minute. If I didn't get rid of this djemon soon, I'd go stark ravers for sure.

The nights were the worst. I couldn't breathe through my nose, and if I tried to breathe through my mouth, I could taste it. I couldn't sleep or keep food down. Olfactory hallucination or no, I imagined the toxic fumes were strong enough to melt my brain calls. I took a deep hit off the Springtime Fresh dryer sheet crumpled in my hand. The scented sheets offered only short-term relief.

I glared at the demonic illusion seated on the asphalt beside me. "This is all your fault."

Blix replied with his one and only expression, a yellow-eyed stare.

"Same to you, buddy," I sneered. In just a few short days, I'd come to hate him with everything in my sleep-deprived being. "Your remaining hours are now in single digits." I glanced up at the clock face on City Hall, and checked my cell phone for the fourteenth time to make sure the darn thing was turned on.

11

By six o'clock this evening, my demon hallucination and the corresponding reek would be gone, and my little *teratosis* problem would be extinct, thanks to the capable folks at Merle Shine's Pest Control. After three nights of misery, life would be sweet again, and I'd be back to my usual self with no one the wiser. If only they'd call to confirm.

"Come on guys, it's after nine already." I'd been counting the minutes. I'd waited in the parking lot at Merle Shines this morning, waiting for the first person to show up for work. Lucky for me, it was the receptionist. I'd told her I couldn't wait until next week for my scheduled appointment, and begged her to squeeze me in today.

They were short-staffed and busy, she'd told me.

I lost it. Burst into tears like some blubbery six-year-old. I hated myself for being such a wuss, but I couldn't help myself.

She reluctantly agreed to ask Merle to get me in as the last appointment of the day. No promises, but she could see my desperation.

I was still shaky from the experience. I flapped the front of my white uniform blouse, hoping for a cool breeze. My shirt was already sticking to me. Moisture from an early morning shower rose from the pavement in steamy waves; the mute air hovered, thick with tension. My tension. I hated waiting. I felt like Wile E. Coyote clinging desperately to the receiving end of an Acme rubber band, just before the anvil made the return trip.

The front glass doors of City Hall opened, and a dozen somber men and women in crisp blue uniforms approached. How I envied them. They strode as a unit down the steps and passed by me with neither a word nor glance in my direction, a first. The chief had been under a lot of pressure lately to solve the Night Shark murders, and after the most recent victim, his men had showed up today to support him at the press conference. It's what cops do.

Picston's finest climbed into their air-conditioned cruisers and leisurely circled the lot before heading out on patrol. Lou Scali gave me a grin and a mock salute as he drove by with his new rookie partner, Wesley Zigo. The kid looked like he didn't even shave yet. The rookies were getting younger every year. That should be me riding with Scali. I was way better than that string bean Zigo any day.

I tucked a strand of limp hair back under my helmet, tightened the strap, and then swung my leg over the seat of my three-wheeler. I straddled the clammy pleather seat, and pulled down the legs of my culottes, hoping for some air movement, but no luck. Between the relentless weight of the stuffy air and the eerie silence of the men, I had that hinky feeling real cops sometimes get when all hell was about to break loose.

My gorge rose again, and I forced myself to swallow. The line of black and whites exited the lot as I fired up my scooter. Ten seconds later, all six patrol cars hit lights and sirens, and six powerful engines thrummed up Seneca Avenue. A silent alarm, or maybe another body. I hoped not. Things were bad enough with the FBI running the show now. Any other day, I might consider following them, but not today. Nothing was going to keep me from my teratosis extermination appointment with Merle.

Focus Mattie. I waited, tapping my fingers against the handle grips for a last tardy civilian to pass by, before I eased the trike out of my parking space. My route today covered the northeast part of the city, and the sooner I reached my quota, the sooner I'd be out of this heat. After my appointment, I might mosey over to McGill's tonight for the Dart 'N Drown tournament. Every cop in town, and most of Parking Control would be at the bar. I'd hang with the gang and get the four-one-one then.

I'd cruised to within twenty yards of the exit of the lot when I spotted a large brown toad emerge from the landscaped shrubbery and begin to crawl across the pockmarked asphalt. The kudzu summer weather brings them out. I did a double take when I caught sight of the three-inch fangs.

I shuddered. That was no toad, that was another stinkin' djemon. What I was seeing was impossible. I already had a djemon. Once you had one, you couldn't get another. I looked around, but there was no one else nearby. I shouldn't be able to even see this guy.

Angry frustration tore through me in an instant, and raw adrenaline shot through my veins. White-hot fury surged, kicking me into action. I goosed the gas on the three-wheeled scooter and veered directly for it.

I knew it wouldn't do any good, but the smug expression on the thing's ugly face goaded me like the flag on an expired parking meter.

"Eat this, grease spot!"

My cell phone began to ring. I ignored it. My grip on the handlebars slipped, but didn't deter my resolve to squash the disgusting creature flat. My chin dropped, my arms braced rigidly against the handles, the throttle wide open. The scooter whined in protest, but we were approaching warp speed now: nothing could stop me.

I didn't see the pedestrian until almost too late. My life flashed before my eyes as I jerked on the handlebars to avoid him. *Idiot!* The front wheel hit a pothole and the steering wobbled. Queasy prickles of uncertainty stung my cheeks. The scooter wasn't made for quick maneuvering. The left rear wheel achieved lift-off, and the machine started to tip. I slammed my weight back, but the momentum was too strong. Unable to let up on the throttle, I was no longer in control of the scooter. Images of bumpers, metal rims, and tires flew by as I careened unchecked across the parking lot, accompanied by the shrilling of the darn phone. This was not going to be good.

The trike smashed headlong into a fire hydrant. With a crunching jolt, I was airborne, and continued on my trajectory, weightless and screaming toward inevitable disaster. Instinctively, I put my hands up and braced for impact as I slid over the trunk of a parked car. I hit the street hard, rolled and tumbled to a stop in the westbound lane, the demon breath knocked clean out of me. My phone gave a final ring and was silent.

I crouched on hands and knees, gulping for air in the roadway, fighting like a landed eel, all my cocky bravado melted to a puddle of mortification on the asphalt. My heart raced with unspent adrenaline and I shook uncontrollably. The realization of my own idiocy descended with the weight of impending doom.

Cars swerved around me, honking. People came running from all directions. My instincts screamed to run and hide, but my body responded slowly, each vertebra in my neck answering to roll call individually, as my inner TIVO reran the highlights of my humiliating flight and four-point-landing over and over and over in my mind. *Stand up, Mattie. Get out of the street.*

"Miss, do you need help," somebody asked me.

I choked on the foul stench that engulfed me, unable to answer. I rubbed my forehead; avoiding eye contact. I needed time to figure out how to deal with this. You've really done it this time, Mattie. What was I thinking? More than anything, I wanted to slink off without being noticed.

"Is anybody hurt? Call nine-one-one."

I looked around, but the crowd hemmed me in with their concern. I never liked being the center of attention. When you come from the wrong side of the tracks, you strive to keep a low profile.

"It's one of the meter maids."

Tendrils of shame curled around my neck. *Parking Control Officer.*

"I saw the whole thing."

My cheeks burned in humiliation. I didn't remember colliding with anything other than the hydrant. I was pretty sure I hadn't hit anybody human. Wouldn't I remember if I did?

"Check out the scooter." I instantly recognized the nasal whine of Lacey Lippman, followed by the sound of sniggering laughter.

"Oh no, Mattie." I cringed as the Honorable Sylvia Jefferson ran toward me, pearls askew, sensible pumps clacking authoritatively against the pavement. She waved her arm at the crowd. "Get back, give her some room! Are you okay?"

The whoop-whoop of an approaching ambulance added to the chaos. I gritted my resolve, pulled off my helmet, took a deep breath, and clambered to my feet unaided.

"I'm good, thanks." Hands reached out to me, but I avoided them, and took a few stiff steps toward the curb. A headache pounded at the base of my skull. I brushed myself off, straightened my collar and tucked my shirt back in. I'd grown up a tomboy; raised mostly by an older brother who'd taught me to take my licks as they came. Besides, I'd already lost it once this morning. *Walk it off.* Mattie Blackman was nobody's princess.

CHAPTER 4

Two hours later I sat opposite my red-faced supervisor in his City Hall office. My scrapes stung like crazy, and I had a booming headache of mythic proportions. The EMTs had taped big white squares of gauze to each of my knees, the palms of both hands, and one elbow. My white Parking Control shirt had a torn sleeve, a lost button, and a big oil stain on the left boob, but miraculously, I had managed to avoid hitting the mayor. My shirt was the only loss. Oh yeah, and the trike.

Of their own accord, my eyes drifted to the corner of Mike's office. I gulped down a horrified giggle. Teratosis was a rare condition, but the symptoms were well documented. Once you acquired an un-materialized demon, you simply couldn't get any more. It was not possible.

"Mattie, at least give me the courtesy of pretending you're paying attention, would you? I swear you've got the attention span of a gnat. This is exactly what I am talking about."

"Sorry."

I felt more like a four-year old facing her first spanking than a grown woman in her late twenties. Poor Mike. He probably felt worse than I did. Along with being my boss, he was a good friend. For the last six years, I'd eaten all my Thanksgiving dinners at his house. I'd helped him shop for his wife's birthday presents. Hell, my brother was his mechanic.

"How about explaining to me how the hell this happened?"

Of course the harder I tried not to look, the more fascinating the vampire toad became. My glance flicked to the corner again. This particular demonic hallucination smelled strong enough to curl my nose hairs. Its yellow eyes compelled my attention. I struggled to breathe without gagging. Thank goodness, Mike was unaware of the smell. *It's not real, Mattie.*

"Mike, you know what a nuisance those feral cats are. The darn thing ran right in front of me." I didn't like lying, but more than anything, I wanted to keep my job. City employees are specifically prohibited from fraternizing with teratozoids, heteroclites, demons, ghosts, or spirits of any kind. Especially during business hours.

"You're a lousy liar. The mayor called me to give me the blow-by-blow. I'll tell you, he's pretty shaken up. He is demanding that you be tested for drugs. I received emails from two other witnesses who will swear you jumped the curb and rammed that hydrant for no reason."

"I guess I got distracted for a second. It could have happened to anybody."

The turd-colored toad sat right next to Blix. I'd never heard of anyone with two. Absolutely not possible. Yet there they squatted, a few steps away from where Mike and I sat at the cramped conference table. Neither one would be much of a threat to a decent-sized guinea pig, yet both gave me the creeps in a gut-sickening way. I dragged my eyes back to Mike.

"How the hell did you manage to wreck a three-wheeled scooter? My maintenance budget for the whole year is out the window, thanks to you. Our budget was already stretched to the max. The parking division is supposed to be profitable. We can't do our jobs without scooters now, can we?" Beads of sweat glistened between the sparse dark hairs on his scalp. He looked like he was about to cry.

"I'm sorry, Mike. You know I didn't plan this, I can ride rings around anybody."

All the air went out of him. He shriveled into a balding little man before my eyes.

"Mattie, are you going to tell me the truth here or not? Why the hell did you try to run down the mayor?"

He was breaking my heart. I wanted to tell him, but there was no way. I only needed to hold things together for a few more hours.

"It was an accident. I give you my word, it won't happen again."

"Parking Control is a plum job. The list of people waiting for the next opening here is longer than my arm. You guys may all think I'm part of the gang, but I take my responsibilities seriously. In case you forgot, we owe our jobs to the taxpayers of Picston."

"I know; I love this job. Parking Control is my life. I'll do anything to fix this. I'll pay for the damages." Of course, I'd just hocked my bike to come up with the rest of the green I needed for Merle Shine. My employee badge lay on the Formica surface between us. I chewed my lower lip. I was going to need a second job.

"This isn't just about you. This reflects badly on the entire department and me personally. Come on Mattie, you've got to give me something to tell the mayor. Anything."

I couldn't tell him the truth. Two months ago, my landlady had been arrested for harboring an unregistered demon. Neighbors said her ex-husband tipped off the FBI. The SWAT team showed up at dawn with dogs and conducted the search while the local news station covered all the lurid details. Weeks later, a steady stream of gawkers still cruised by the house every day. Everyone in Shore Haven knew Patty. She'd worked the breakfast shift at Dave's Killer Burgers for more than a decade. After the arrest, the guys on the force turned on her with a vengeance that appalled me. I couldn't let that happen to me. Not when I was so close to getting rid of Blix. And now, with the toad guy showing up, there's no way I could tell him. It would be all over City Hall by lunchtime. I'd make it up to him. Starting tomorrow.

"Okay, have it your way." He tapped my badge. "This is a policy violation. I can't let it go."

The blood drained from my face and I froze. Oh man, he wasn't kidding. He was going to fire me. What would I do? I'd never get another job as good as this one. I sent out a silent prayer. I'll do anything, please!_

"I'm suspending you for two weeks without pay, starting right now. With this trike out of commission, we don't have enough vehicles to support the shift anyway. I'll figure out something to tell the City Manager and finance folks." He slumped back in his chair and closed my personnel folder.

I stifled a hiccup as relief surged through me.

"Thanks Mike," I croaked. "You're the best. You

won't be sorry." At least I still had a job. I bit my lips shut to stop them from trembling. If I said one more word, I'd lose it.

"I'm not done yet. I'm putting you on six months probation. When you come back, you'll be subject to random drug testing. Any violations, or missteps and you'll be out."

I trembled as the delayed shock of the morning events hit me. I studied a bloody scrape on the back of my knuckles.

He leaned forward and chucked my chin. His earnest face searched mine. "Hey. I'm worried about you, Blackman. Are you all right?"

I didn't know how to answer such a loaded question. Mike knew about my mother, the whole town did. Once you get that tar on you, it sticks in people's minds forever. Not telling him made my heart hurt. I didn't want Mike thinking I was nuts, but there was no way. Teratosis was somewhere below having crabs on the social acceptability meter, and law enforcement had about as much respect for paranormals and demons as crackheads and lepers. If anyone on the force or in the department found out about my demon problem, my life would be over. I swallowed hard.

I could see he'd already made up his mind. I couldn't stand the pity on his face.

My eyes filled and I looked away.

He sighed and gave my arm a gentle squeeze. "You're like the department mascot, Mattie. Everybody around here loves you, but you haven't been yourself lately. I'm not the only one who's noticed, either. Use this time constructively. Talk to someone. Get your head straightened out."

I nodded. "Yeah." I tried not to breathe.

"Maybe the universe is trying to tell you something."

At that moment, the security officer arrived and I blushed furiously. My ex-boyfriend Kip here to escort me out of the building. How thoughtful of him to volunteer for the job.

Mike dropped my badge into the center drawer of his desk. "I'll see you back here in two weeks. Try to keep the excitement to a minimum, okay?"

Of all the people to usher me to my ultimate humiliation, no worse choice came to mind than Kip Bruckner. I wanted to slap the smirk right off his face, but I didn't dare. What a winner this day turned out to be.

Kip ogled the oil stain on my shirt. "You've been a busy girl."

I gritted my teeth and embraced my hostility. Being pissed off was a lot better than being pitied; and nobody irritated me quicker than Kip. He couldn't help himself, he was naturally obnoxious, and it was one of the reasons I broke up with him. Or I guess you might say it had been a mutual parting of the ways. Or would have been if not for that oversexed Public Information Officer, Lacey Lippman, the mouth-breathing Queen of Lookatme. I was conscious of the stares as we made our way to the exit. The worst thing I could do was to give Kip any more ammunition. I squared my shoulders and walked toward the stairs.

"There was a reporter here earlier, trying to get a statement from the Mayor's office."

"Shut up." I picked up the pace and entered the exit stairwell. My stiff knees protested in silence as we descended two flights to the lobby. I wasn't about to let

Kip see me hurting. I reached the front doors and didn't look back.

No one followed me as I walked down the steps of City Hall into the oppressive noon green. I unlocked my Trusty Rusty red Honda and got in. But I instantly detected the presence of my two followers by the distinctive licorice-and-raw-sewage reek that accompanied them. Sure enough, two pairs of lidless golden eyes stared at me from the back seat of the car. Goody, goody; my very own entourage mirage.

CHAPTER 5

"WELL, WHOOP-DE-freakin'-do." I scowled into the rearview mirror. I lowered each of the car windows, grabbed a fresh dryer sheet out of the pink box sitting on the passenger seat, and inhaled deeply. I don't know why I bothered.

Suspended. I closed my eyes, and Mike's face flashed before me. I'd never seen that expression on a friend's face before. Anger, embarrassment, pity, and hurt--all in one place, and all because of me. I'd make it up to him, somehow. In a few more hours, everything would be back to normal again.

Frickin' inner demons. I jerked the seatbelt across my chest and snapped the buckle into place.

My cell phone vibrated, and I jumped. I checked the caller ID, and relief flooded through me as I answered.

"Matilda Blackman?"

My lips quivered. "Yes, yes, I'm sorry I missed your call earlier. It's been one of those days. Are we still on?"

"This is Jackie over at Merle Shine's Pest Control. I'm calling to confirm your five-thirty appointment for this afternoon. "

I choked back another wave of nausea. "I'll be there. The stink is killing me. You have no idea--"

"Please be prompt, Miss Blackman. Merle's made a

special exception for you. He needs to be home early for his daughter's birthday party tonight. You are the last teratosis treatment of the day."

I glanced furtively around the parking lot to make sure no one could overhear our conversation. "No problem. Thank you so much for squeezing me in. I don't think I can stand it much longer."

"Yes, well business has been a bit busier than usual."

"I had no idea djemon infestations were such a big problem."

"They aren't normally. We rarely treat more than few local cases in a year. Most of our teratosis business is tourists in town for the Spirit Festival, but that's not until next month."

"You have my word, I will not be late," I promised, and disconnected. The tension in my shoulders eased. I'm all set.

I scrunched around in the driver's seat to better examine the new guy. Even with their physical differences, they appeared to originate from the same place. They had the same eyes. They both wore dull brown skin with an ashy bloom to it that chocolate got when it sat on the shelf too long. Where Blix was skin and bones, the fanged toad was a slick blob. I'd named him Blix, after a goblin character in a movie I'd seen once. He even resembled the one in the movie, a little. Sort of a forlorn hairless kitten, with big bat ears, and a face like a gargoyle. Pitifully ugly, but Blix was strange in other ways, too. His eyes glowed in the dark, and that was pretty creepy. I'd started leaving the light on at night.

I'd never seen a real live demon before, but if you didn't count the stink, these two certainly didn't live up to expectations. From the beginning, the odor came and went in waves--a noxious blend of licorice with a little after-zing of eau d' poop. If I kept the windows open and the fan on, I could almost pretend the stench didn't bother me too much. Yeah right.

Good lord, what if another one showed up? I'd lose my job for real, that's what.

A nervous tic vexed my right eyelid, and I held my finger over it. I loved my job. I was proud to say I worked for the city. A government job is respectable. I loved my uniform. When I put it on, I felt confident; I liked the feeling of authority it gave me. But more than anything, in spite of the circumstances of my birth, my job made me legitimate. My job made me a person of substance. I couldn't lose that.

With a shaking hand, I slipped the key into the ignition, and started the car. I sure hoped the exterminator people could handle both these guys.

"You two better hope Merle gives me a discount."

☾

I drove to my apartment in Shore Haven, a lakeside suburb about three miles from Picston City Hall. As I changed out of my uniform, I remembered a Laundromat located a couple blocks from Merle's. It would be an easy to do a few loads while I was at my appointment. Clever girl, Mattie.

With Four Starr Pest Abatement shut down for the foreseeable future, here were only two other places in town to go to get rid of demon breath. Tourists preferred the local fortuneteller experience of course, but I wanted a professional. Merle Shine had been in the pest control business for more than fifty years. They were a member of the Better Business Bureau and had a strict customer privacy clause right there in the contract. The best part was that they were located in Picston, so I faced less chance of running into anybody I knew.

The neat chignon I always wore to work now resembled a squirrel's nest, so I brushed it back into a tight ponytail. I piled the laundry into the basket, and headed out to the car. I had almost an hour to kill before my appointment with Merle. This was going to work out just perfect.

❦

I drove with the windows rolled down and the radio turned up, determined to recover from my disastrous morning, singing along with Credence Clearwater Revival. Bad Moon Rising is one of my all-time favorites. Glancing in the rearview mirror, I thought I saw Blix bobbing his head to the beat, but couldn't be sure.

"Won't be long now, boys," I warned them.

The car behind me honked, and I swerved back into my lane, red-faced. *Focus Mattie*. The trip back to Picston wouldn't take long. Shore Haven is geographically separated from Picston by Sentinel Hill, which rises some six hundred feet above the lake shoreline. In the green months, my twenty-minute commute past dense woods and parkland was one of the highlights of my day.

I drove past Merle Shine's Pest Control on Seneca Avenue, about a mile past City Hall. As I cruised by, I checked out the parking lot, which looked pretty full. I still had twenty minutes before my appointment, plenty of time. I zipped past four more blocks to the Spanky Kleen Laundry, situated in a tired strip mall on the seedy edge of an industrial neighborhood. This was not a great part of town. My knees had stiffened up on the drive over and I hobbled inside with my dirty laundry.

I'd never used this place before, and it wasn't as nice as my usual spot, Tidy Whiteys. I debated leaving my undies unattended, but beggars couldn't be choosers. I filled the washers, added detergent, and fed my quarters into the slots. I was ready to go meet Merle.

I limped back out to my car, put on my seatbelt, and started up the engine. I released the parking brake and put the car in reverse before checking the rear-view mirror. I'd barely touched the gas pedal when I noticed a third djemon staring at me from the backseat.

I froze, my body clenched into a rigid spasm of revulsion. My foot stomped the pedal to the metal, and Trusty Rusty zoomed backwards across the parking lot. My hands gripped the steering wheel in a white-knuckled vise. A nausea of disgust washed over me, petrifying my foot on the gas. I prayed there was nothing behind me.

With a loud bang, the car collided with something solid and bucked me right out of my seat. For the second time that day, velocity held me airborne. My stomach rolled and my foot slipped off the gas pedal. The car jerked to an abrupt stop beneath me and I slammed back to earth. The engine died without a whimper. The silence was deafening.

CHAPTER 6

MY HEART POUNDED with a sick sensation. "Enough already, I can't take this!" I shook myself against the steering wheel.

No one seemed to have noticed anything. Fortunately for me, the strip mall did not appear to offer much in the way of commercial viability, as the parking lot appeared mostly empty, and no one had come running out to investigate. I checked the side mirrors, but didn't see any bodies.

I couldn't believe how narrowly I'd escaped killing anyone. Twice. I forced myself to unclench and made a quick physical inventory. No new injuries, thank you very much. I rubbed the sweat off my face with a jittery hand.

"Look what you made me do, you little shits." I glared at the stupid things behind me. The new guy reminded me of the bearded dragon lizard Lance kept as a pet when we were kids. Heavily-muscled jaws sported a wide reptilian smile. A regular Larry the Lizard. A fit of hysterical giggling came over me. In no time, I was cackling like a mad rooster. I clamped my hand over my mouth and closed my eyes. *Get a grip*.

I climbed out of the car and gingerly walked around to inspect for damage. We hadn't crashed or anything, but the Honda now straddled a cement parking block, and poor old Rusty had a flat. Dang.

I gave the tire a couple of halfhearted kicks, but it was kablooey. A nasty hole bloomed where the bald tire had blown out. I thought about the spare in the trunk, but I was worried about the time. An auto parts store stood two doors over. I debated going over and asking for help, but decided I didn't need to mess around with this right now. If I didn't start walking, I'd be late. That flat wasn't going anywhere.

"Looks like you could use some help," my brother's voice sounded behind me.

My heart sank. Lance strolled toward me from the direction of the Vinnie's Auto Parts. Oh boy, this was perfect.

We have different fathers, and except for our smiles, don't appear related. I'm dark-haired with a natural tan. Lance is ten years older than me; tall and lean, with slicked-back blond hair curling around his ears. When he smiles, he gives Brad Pitt a run for his money. Most women tended to overlook the work-stained mechanics overalls and black fingernails. He carried a box of parts carelessly under one arm. What was he doing here?

I looked around. "Where's your car?"

He nodded toward the sleek torpedo shape of a vintage yellow Jag convertible. Must be a customer car. Lance had practically raised me, and had been appointed my legal guardian when I was sixteen. Any other day, I would have been glad to see him, but not today, and definitely not at this particular moment. I had to get out of here.

"What happened?"

A trickle of sweat rolled past my ear.

"Ah, nothing. Just a little accident." I choked back a giggle. "I ah, guess my foot slipped."

Lance set the box down on the pavement and leaned over to inspect my rear wheel; hung up on the wrong side of the parking block, and noted the flat. He took the keys out of my hand and opened the trunk without saying anything. I fidgeted impatiently as he lifted out the jack and tire iron.

"Do we have to do this now? I'm kinda running late for something."

Lance gave me a sharp look. Too late, I shouldn't have said anything. If he suspected what I was up to, I'd never hear the end of it. I glanced down the street to where Merle's sign beckoned to me.

"What are you doing here, Matt?" He appeared calm, his movements slow and sure as he loosened the lug nuts on Rusty's rear wheel.

I blew my breath out my cheeks.

"Laundry." I squeaked, and pointed to the Spanky Kleen. "I figured I'd try this place. What are you doing here?"

"This is not a good part of town. The police found another Night Shark victim half a block from here this morning."

So that was what sent them off in such a rush. "I had no idea. Thanks for the tip." I edged closer to the sidewalk.

Lance slipped the jack under the rear bumper and gave the lever a few slow pumps. I could tell he had something on his mind. I hoped he'd get to the point pretty soon.

"Listen, I've got an errand to run. Do you mind if I, ah--"

"I talked to Kip."

I kicked at the asphalt in frustration. "Why does he keep calling you? He's not my boyfriend anymore." I could feel destiny slipping though my fingers.

"You want to tell me about it?"

"No." I struggled to keep my emotions off my face as I gave him my highly-edited short version, and he pretended to believe me.

"Suspension isn't so bad."

Before I could answer, a black and white cruised up beside us. I gazed over into the grinning faces of Picston's finest, Bart Kitterman and Jason Jaekel, better known as Heckle and Jeckle. Bart was a second-generation policeman, and the first boy I ever kissed. I'd known him all my life. Jason was a loudmouth jerk and Kip's best friend.

I groaned. Any chance I had of getting to Merle Shine's today had just about left the station. Sorry Merle. All that begging to get that appointment down the drain. Man oh man, could this day possibly get any worse? Of course the whole police department must have heard about my suspension by now. Probably the fire department, too.

"Hey look, it's Mad Mattie," Kitterman said. "What's the problem, beautiful? Need some driving lessons?" They both hooted with laughter. I rolled my eyes and grinned in spite of myself.

I used to wish Bart's dad was my father. Hank Kitterman was the neighborhood cop who showed up when people complained about the noise every time Mom's s drug-dealing 'boyfriends' beat the crap out of her. To me, police officers represented everything noble and respectable; they brought order to chaos. To a kid growing up on the wrong side of the tracks, Officer Kitterman was Superman. He'd inspired the dream in me to become a cop. I wanted to be just like him.

"Very funny." I smoothed my hair. These two would show me no mercy.

"Hey, maybe all you need is some training wheels. I'll ask my four-year old if you can borrow hers. You'll like 'em, Mattie, they're pink." Bart winked at me.

"Don't you two have crimes to investigate or something? Bad guys to arrest?"

"I'm lookin' at you, Blackman," Jason answered. "You wreak havoc and mayhem wherever you go."

The smile faded from my face. "No donuts for you, Jerkle."

"Is that the best you can do? You're losing your touch."

"Now now, kiddies, play nice." Kitterman nodded to Lance. "Hey McNair, how's it going?"

Lance stood and casually draped an arm over my shoulder. I leaned into him. I had to give Lance a lot of credit. He looked out for me, but never tried to make me feel like an idiot when he did so. Most of the time he hung back until I worked things out on my own. We both knew these guys enjoyed yanking my chain, but at this particular moment, I was glad to have Lance around. He raced motorcycles when he was younger, and in addition to being the best mechanic around, my brother was way cool.

"We're just about done here, fellas, but thanks for asking." He let go of me and went back to the wheel. With an easy movement, he lifted the old tire off the axel and laid it on the ground, then picked up the spare and placed it into position with no apparent effort.

"Lance told me you guys found another body today."
Jason nodded. "Not a pretty sight."

"We're stepping up patrols in the neighborhood, looking for any suspicious activity." Kitterman watched Lance with a speculative expression. The police radio bleeped out a garbled message, and then both officers went to work.

"Okay Mattie; we'll leave you to your knitting. See you in the funny papers." Kitterman grinned like the madman he was, and gave me a little toodle-oo finger wave. He gunned the engine and they sped off with lights flashing.

I sighed and crumpled to the pavement next to Lance.

"Cop groupie."

"Shut up, grease monkey."

"Every time one of those guys shows up, you go all gaga."

"My life is in the toilet and you call me names. Why can't you do something constructive?"

"I'm fixing your flat, lady. And you're welcome. What's the matter with you?"

I shook my head. "I'm sorry. Thanks." I rested my chin on my hands. "What time is it, anyway?"

"A little after six. Why so grumpy?"

I groaned and struggled to my feet again, knees as stiff as cardboard. "This day is a total loss." My stomach growled in agreement.

Lance squinted up at the late afternoon sun. "I don't know. You up for some Shanghai Palace? I'm buyin'." He picked up a lug nut and screwed it tight.

Kung Pau at Shanghai Palace is my favorite meal, but Lance never, ever paid. "What do you want?"

"I need a favor." He grinned at me as he tightened another lug nut.

"Of course you do." We grinned at each other.

"I need you to stay with Mina for a few days." He tightened down the last nut and reached for the tire iron.

Surprise, surprise. Lance and Violet had split up when Mina was three, but Violet got full custody. A compulsive gambler, Lance spent a couple stays in rehab before he'd been successful in persuading Violet and the courts to allow him shared custody. Since then, Lance had not once left town or stayed out late or even had an overnight guest whenever Mina stayed with him. Violet remarried last year, and Lance worried his ex-wife would try to gain sole custody again.

"As it happens I've recently become available for full-time babysitting. What's up?"

"Thanks. By the way, they brought the remains of your scooter into the shop today. Bang-up job there, Mattie."

The city has their own mechanic, but Lance and his partner Doc have a contract with the city for major bodywork. His blue eyes stared into mine. I wondered what was important enough to make him decide to leave town when he had Mina.

"Har-dee-har-har, funny-man. I told you it was an accident. End of story."

"I'll bet." He picked up the tire iron and tightened the wheel nuts.

"How long will you be gone?"

"You'll need to take her to summer school and back every day."

I rolled my eyes. "I remember."

"Both hands on the wheel. Make sure you're both wearing seatbelts."

"Duh. Give me a break, Lance. It's just a run of bad luck."

"Well, whatever it is, stop screwing around while you've got Mina with you." He leaned over and braced himself at the back bumper. "You ready? Let's get you unstuck."

All three of my inner demons were still sitting in the back, stinking up my car. I got in and started the engine. With a bit of steady pressure on the gas and a push from Lance, Rusty scooted off the jack, over the concrete backstop and bounced to the pavement with a thump. Lance packed up my dead tire and tools.

I scampered back in to the Laundromat and moved my clothes into dryers. With the day a total shambles and my big plan shot to hell, I decided to make the best of a bad deal. I dumped my remaining quarters into the big dryer, and walked back to my car.

"You're all set. No more accidents or I'll give Kitterman a call about those driving lessons. I mean it."

"Oh you're hilarious. Thanks for the help, but I'm not sharing any of my Kung Pau with you."

"Meet you there, brat." He sauntered over to the Jag and folded himself in. He started the engine, and I followed him back to Shore Haven. Five minutes later, I realized he hadn't told me why he was leaving town or even where he was going. That wasn't like Lance. That made two of us with secrets.

CHAPTER 7

I HAD BARELY finished unloading my wad of clothes from the dryer at Spanky Kleen when my phone rang.

"Abbot's in five," was all Karen said.

"I'm in Picston, make it fifteen." I grabbed the basket and threw the whole shebang into the backseat. Rusty fired up on the first try, and off we zoomed.

Karen and I had been solving the world's problems at Abbott's Frozen Custard since fourth grade. When the summer steam bath weather hits upstate New York, the humidity doesn't give up when the sun goes down. To escape the oppressive evening mugginess, folks headed either to an air-conditioned bar or Abbot's Drive Thru.

I glanced in the rearview mirror at the row of bulbous yellow eyes staring at my back. Sheesh. This wasn't an embarrassment anymore, it was a collection. The new guys brought their own eye-squinting blend to my olfactory misery. The fanged toad added a gorge-grabbing touch of dirty cat box, while Larry spiced things up with a not so subtle twist of sulphur. The three of them together combined to make an aromatic essence which neither the open windows nor a hit from a fresh dryer sheet could disperse.

Karen and I arrived at the same time, and settled at a picnic table beneath the hazy night skies and neon lights of Abbots. Karen is a willowy blonde with blue eyes, a pixie haircut, and freckles that cover every square inch of her anatomy. As kids, we were as inseparable as twins, as teens, partners in crime, and now that she had a husband and children of her own, bosom friends who didn't get to spend nearly enough time together. She gazed at me expectantly.

"What's up?"

I took a deep breath. "You have to promise not to say anything to anyone. Not even Martin."

"Ooh, I'm intrigued." She hunkered down and leaned forward. "Do tell."

"I mean it. If this gets out, I'm moving to another state."

"Oh come on, how bad can it be? The boys came down with head lice again last week. I get the icks just thinking about it." She scratched her neck. "I have been doing laundry for days. And will you look at what that shampoo has done to my hair?"

"This is a lot worse than a bad hair day, believe me."

"What? Is it rats? I thought you said you were going to get a new cat--"

"No, shush." I glanced around to make sure no one else was close enough to listen in and leaned forward. "I've got teratosis."

She grimaced and pulled away, her eyes as big as walnuts. "Ew!" She caught herself and apologized immediately. "Oh Mattie, I'm sorry, I just never expected to hear you say that."

"Oh, I shouldn't have told you."

She grabbed my hand. "Oh you know I'm here for

you."

"I missed my extermination appointment today at Merle Shines. It's going to take me another two or three weeks to get rebooked." I started to tell her about the accident, and she cut me off.

"I already heard. I work with Lacey Lippman's sister, remember?"

I groaned. "Oh I'm sure everybody's heard about my suspension by now. I'm never going to live this down. That's why nobody can find out about this. Gossip spreads like an oil fire in this town."

"Why are you always so worried about what everybody else thinks?"

"Easy for you to say, you're not the one with an un-materialized djemon trailing around behind you, stinking up your life. And I think I must've caught a really bad case. I've got three of them."

She snorted. "You're talking crazy."

"I thought so too, until today. When the second one showed up this morning, it made me wreck the trike. The third one showed up when I was at the Spanky-Kleen."

She shook her head. "You can't have more than one demon. Everybody knows that. What makes you think they're demons?"

"What else could they be? These things are real. The only other explanation I found for hallucinations was schizophrenia." My voice faltered, and I fought to blink back my darkest fear. My mind flashed on a secret memory of my mother, her eyes wild, her manic face ravaged by years of alcohol and drug abuse as she screamed incoherently at Lance and me. Doctors debated whether or not schizophrenia was inherited.

"You poor thing. Why didn't you tell me?"

"I was hoping I could get this cleared up before anyone found out, and I would have, except for what happened today. I can't take much more of this. This is serious. If I don't get rid of these soon, these demons will show up for real. Either that, or I really am going crazy and I'm going to end up like mom. I'll lose my job for sure. My life will be ruined."

She ran her fingers through her cropped hair. "I shouldn't have said that. I don't think you're crazy, but if they're demons, you can't have more than one. What do you think they are?"

I shrugged. "How would I know? They're too small to be scary, and so ugly, I kind of feel sorry for them. I saw a picture of a baby aardvark once, that's what these guys remind me of." I studied them for a few moments. "All they do is sit and stare at me. And yes, I do realize how stupid that sounds."

"They're here now?"

"Yeah." I gestured toward a neighboring picnic table. "There's a cat, a toad, and a lizard, but they don't look like they're supposed to. They're hairless, and they've got these weird yellow eyes. It's hard to explain."

"And they follow you around."

"Yes, but not like you think. When I'm busy, I don't notice them."

"Maybe they're trying to tell you something."

I shook my head. "I don't think so."

She pointed her spoon at me. "But if they were trying to tell you something, what do you think they would be trying to say?"

I always thought Karen would end up as a psychologist. She'd majored in sociology in college, but dropped out to work full-time while her husband Martin finished his master's degree. After he finished and they got married, she went back and finished her bachelor's in library science.

"I don't know. If the only choice is demons or schizophrenia, then there is no good choice."

Karen snorted and squeezed my hand. "Mattie, you're the smartest person I know. If you don't think you're losing your mind, then you aren't."

"Thanks." Hearing Karen say that to me was like getting the Good Housekeeping Seal of Approval. "You always know just what to say."

"I think these things are trying to tell you something. What if they're speaking to you from your subconscious? What if they're some sort of messengers? Like spirit guides?"

I rolled my eyes. "Give me a break."

"No, really. Think about it. Shore Haven is built on Indian land, and the local Native American tribes revered animal spirits as an important part of their culture."

"Need I point out, I'm not Native American?"

"You can't be certain. Your mom never talked about who your dad was. She was an orphan, right?" She frowned at me. "And you have those killer cheekbones. And what about your hair? Weather like this and your hair looks like the 'after' photo in a commercial for Frizz-Ease. Why couldn't you be Senequois? Maybe you're becoming sensitive to the local spirits."

I thought about what she said. It sounded strange, but a whole lot better than schizophrenia. In the absence of any other explanation, I was willing to consider the idea.

"So you're saying I might be psychic? I've never been psychic before."

"Shore Haven is a hotspot for the supernatural. The library has a whole section on local history and legends and paranormal phenomena in the Finger Lakes region. I know of at least one book on animal totems."

"Animal totems."

She grinned at me. She was having too much fun with this. "Otter is my power animal." She batted her eyelashes. "Each animal totem is associated with different characteristics and meanings when they appear."

"You mean like astrology? And you think these creatures might be some sort of mystical animal messenger." I couldn't keep the skepticism out of my voice.

"I can look up their meaning and see what it says. Maybe once you get the message, they'll go away."

In spite of my doubts, the idea was beginning to grow on me. "What if they don't?"

"You get tested and registered as a paranormal. A lot of people have psychic abilities. I'll bet there are even support groups now."

I pictured myself standing in front of a roomful of people saying 'My name is Mattie Blackman and I'm a psychic.' Gag me. "My landlady got hauled off to jail for harboring a demon. She was registered."

"That's different. Patty Vincent never registered her demon."

"Can you blame her? You might as well walk around with a big 'D' for demon branded on your forehead. I mean, for the rest of your life, you're on some list somewhere. People with demons are forced to live with the stigma for the rest of their lives. I heard they put you on a permanent no-fly list, and after that train crash in Portugal last year, the anti-terrorism folks are talking about requiring passports for trains now, too. As soon as you catch a demon, your life is ruined. I've got to get rid of these things before they show up permanently. Before it's too late."

"Hel-lo, earth to Mattie. You don't have teratosis, you're psychic. You register. It's nothing. Don't you pay attention to the news?"

I shifted in my seat uncomfortably. "What if I don't want to get registered? The guys at work would never understand."

"Oh come on. Don't be such a baby. Anyway, I'll check the books tomorrow, and see if I can find a local expert who can tell us about Senequois spirit messengers. Remember my yoga instructor, Sonja? She has a couple of paranormal clients. Actually, the politically correct term is Anomalous Individuals. Or what about that lady I used to go to? Madame Coumlie. She's the real thing. She must be registered."

The name sounded familiar, but I drew a blank.

"You know, the Hand of Fate."

I remembered a horrid old witch with black-stained hands, shouting at us to get off her porch at Halloween.

"The dwarf? I'd rather dance buck naked down Third Street than be caught dead anywhere near that old fraud. That stuff isn't real; it's just a show for the tourists. I need real help here, not some cheesy fortuneteller. No way."

"First of all, she's not a dwarf, she's a midget, and the correct term is 'little person'. Secondly, Herbert Hoover recognized her as a national treasure and gave her a presidential pardon. They even made a movie about her. She is definitely not a fake."

I frowned. Hand of Fate my ass.

"Look, I told you I don't want anyone else to hear about this. Not Lance or Mike or anybody at work. They already think I'm nuts. And even if I am psychic, how does that get rid of my problem? I can't live like this."

"Stop worrying so much about what other people think. I think it's cool!" She laughed, but it was a good laugh, and I knew she was trying hard to make me feel better.

I sighed. "Okay, maybe you're right. I hate the idea of all the voo-doo woo-woo stuff, but at this point, it doesn't make much difference to me whether these things are demons or spirits."

"I will check those books tomorrow morning, and call you as soon as I find anything. Things will work out, you'll see."

"I hope so. I just can't lose my job over this. I want my life back."

CHAPTER 8

INSISTENT KNOCKING ROUSED me from a dead sleep. I cracked an eye in the direction of my bedside clock, which said nine-thirty. I experienced a momentary flash of panic when I thought I'd overslept for work, but then I remembered. Oh yeah. I closed my eyes and savored the pleasant whoosh of the fan oscillate a wave of soft air across my exposed skin. I winced as a fresh surge of pseudo stink assailed my sensibilities. I cracked another eye in the direction of the foot of my bed, where four putrid creatures stared back at me.

I groaned, and threw my pillow right through them.

"Oh for Pete's sake." I closed my eyes, renewed in my determination to get rid of these little stinkers once and for all. Nothing was more important.

The knocking turned to pounding. It couldn't be Lance; we agreed he would take Mina to school this morning, and I would pick her up this afternoon. Karen would be at work at the library, and my landlady Patty was locked up, unable to post bail. I lived in the apartment over her garage, but I'd noticed a FOR SALE sign on the front lawn when I got home last night. Probably a realtor.

The banging continued. I grabbed my robe from the

hook on the bathroom door. "Just a minute," I yelled, and the infernal noise stopped. Yay.

I padded downstairs. A very large man stood on my very small porch. He was wearing a western-cut suit, white shirt, black string tie, and cowboy boots. The military haircut enhanced his receding hairline. Alert blue eyes stared back at me without expression. Cop eyes. Definitely not real estate.

"What do you want?"

"Matilda Blackman?"

Must be official business; no one else would use that name.

"Who wants to know?"

The guy was big. Not fat, but barrel-chested. Probably played football in college. He looked like a cop, but I knew everyone in the police department. I braced my bare foot behind the door, knowing it would be useless if he decided to use those boots.

He handed me his identification. FBI. My heart skipped a beat. The photo matched the guy's face. Special Agent Frank Porter.

"I'm a Paranormal Control Investigator, attached to the FBI Counterterrorism task force. I received a report that you may be the victim of a psychic attack. May I come in?"

My bladder tweaked at me. Oh lordy, I was so not ready to deal with this. I should have gone to the bathroom before I answered the door. And coffee. I needed lots of coffee. I had the feeling I wasn't going to like what Porter had to say, but I asked anyway.

"Where did you hear that?"

"We conducted a raid on Merle Shine's Pest Control yesterday. We had a court order to shut the place down for tax evasion and engaging in deceptive business practices, among other things." Hard eyes stared directly into mine, searching for the slightest reaction.

My heart fluttered like a trapped moth, and I gulped hard against the first tremors of a giggle. Focus Mattie. The guy couldn't yank my chain unless I let him. I hadn't done anything wrong.

"In the process of conducting the search, we discovered several unregistered demons on the premises, and your name in their appointment book. When we looked up your address, we realized we already had your landlady in custody on a similar charge. May I come in?"

An involuntary shiver shook me. Porter's blue eyes narrowed.

"Um, this is a bad time. Can you come back later?"

"This is standard procedure, Ms. Blackman. You are not under suspicion of anything illegal. I'm here to follow up on a report that you may be a victim of a paranormal terrorist attack by demons. I am required by federal law to debrief you within twenty-four hours of such notice. You are of course free to have your attorney present during the interview, but I assure you that unless there are extenuating circumstances, the matter takes a few minutes and is entirely routine."

Here he was giving me serious cop face, and I hadn't even had coffee yet. This guy was starting to get on my nerves. I didn't want to talk to him at all, least of all now. My bladder protested, throbbing with the rhythm of my nervous heartbeat.

"This must be some mistake. I'm not being attacked. It's just—um, hard to explain."

"I must warn you, there are laws against invoking

or fraternizing with demons or other teratozoids. The penalties are severe."

Holy moley, he was making a big deal out of this, and he was a whole lot better at the stone-face game than me. Under his sharp stare I felt as vulnerable as a water balloon. I thought of the horde of baby demons sitting on my bed upstairs. This was my opportunity to come clean, but all I could think about was increasingly urgent need to pee. I had to get rid of him.

"Can't we do this some other time?" I looked down at my robe. "I'm not exactly ready for uninvited visitors." It came out sharper than I intended. "No offense."

"I will have your statement by end of the day today or a warrant will be issued for your arrest." Porter took a half-step closer, and I nearly slammed the door on him. He was crossing the line here, and we both knew it. But if I got arrested, I would lose my job for sure.

Alarm flooded through me, fueling my panic. "What kind of statement? What do you want from me?"

He must have seen my distress, because he backed off a little. "I assure you, it's just routine. A few questions and a couple of quick diagnostic tests. Depending on the results, you may have a few extra forms to fill out."

"What if I fail the test?"

He gave me an irritated smirk. "They're not that kind of tests. It's more like getting your blood typed. The test procedure merely records the body's involuntary response to stimulus. It detects psychic sensitivity and helps determine the type and magnitude of your ability."

I pulled my robe up around my neck and wondered if Agent Porter had any psychic abilities, and if he did, whether he could read my mind. What if he was able to detect my animal-spirit-demons? Goosebumps raced up my arms. Get a grip, Mattie. I took a deep breath. Maybe I was making a bigger deal out of this than it deserved.

"Okay, okay. Look, I have to pick up my niece from school at three-thirty. Could I come to your office before then?"

He took out a card and scribbled something on the back before handing it to me.

"Two o'clock. The office is in downtown Rochester. That's my cell phone number. Call if you're going to be late."

"I'll be there."

"Be sure you are." He turned heel and walked down the driveway without making a sound. I wondered if his cowboy boots had rubber soles.

No sooner had I closed the door than my phone rang. I ran upstairs to answer.

"Madame Blackman's house of the criminally insane."

"You won't believe what I found," said Karen.

"You won't believe what just happened."

"There's a guy, right here in the Shore who knows all about spirit messengers. And listen, he's a mage. He's an expert on the spirit lore and Senequois Indian legends."

"The FBI came to my house. The agent told me if I don't go for an interview today, he'll arrest me."

"He's a mage! Is that too cool or what?"

I had to admit, Karen had come through for me, but I wasn't sure how this information would help, exactly.

"If I get arrested, I'm out of a job."

"You're not going to lose your job. Can't you see? This is good news. You're not crazy, and you don't have teratosis. You're just discovering your psychic abilities. Remember Sonja? She got tested last year. She said it was a piece of cake. They ask you a few questions and take your picture. That's it. She said it's like getting your driver's license renewed."

"He sounded pretty serious."

"She said it took less than an hour. Two weeks later, she got a registration card in the mail. I can't believe my best friend is a psychic!"

"That guy intimidated me. He was so, I don't know, official."

"You worry too much. Sonja said it's helped her expand her business, and given her more connections in the paranormal community. She's even going to host a booth at this year's Spirit Festival."

"Now you're making fun of me." I conjured up images of wackadoo fortunetellers with their big gold earrings and crystal balls. Every year they turned my hometown into a new-age freak show. "I don't want to be psychic. It's tacky."

"I think it's sooo exotic."

"You make it sound better than it is, I'll bet."

"You're going to thank me for this when you meet the mage. His name is Rhys Warrick. He runs that Mystic Properties place in the Shore."

Another one. "I'll bet he does. You know him?"

"No, I'm looking at an article in the archives. He's got all kinds of degrees. It says he's a guest professor-emeritus, researching the local Senequois, their legends and shaman rituals. And I found a ton of stuff on animal totems."

"You sound way too happy about this whole thing. How is this going to help me get rid of them?"

"It's too much to tell over the phone, and I can't wait to show you what I found. Let's meet for lunch, and I can explain. Trust me, you are going to love this!"

"Okay, but we have to be quick, because I'm meeting with Agent Porter at two, and I need to pick up Mina after school. Lance is out of town."

"No problem." She sounded like she was ready to explode. "How about the Sand Castle?"

"Why can't you just tell me?"

She giggled. "See you at noon."

I hung up the phone and told the four spirit messengers to screw off. In response, a fifth one popped into view. I screamed like a bloody banshee and ran to the bathroom to pee.

CHAPTER 9

I WALKED INTO the Sand Castle restaurant and immediately spotted Karen waving to me from a table near the window, overlooking the lakeshore. The dining room was nearly empty. At one time, the Sand Castle was considered the swankiest place around. Karen and I came here with our dates for dinner at our senior prom, but I hadn't been inside the place since. White tablecloths, origami napkins, and wineglasses waiting to be filled decorated each table. The Tuscan garden décor featured trompe-l'oeil murals of crumbling walls and vineyards beneath a night sky; white twinkle lights entwined with plastic vines circled floor-to-ceiling plaster columns placed throughout the room.

"I can't wait to show you what I found. You'll be blown away." Karen vibrated with pent-up excitement. She had a big manila envelope sitting in front of her, which she opened as soon as I sat down.

"I hope so." Karen's smile was contagious. "I could use some good news."

"Hello Karen, so wonderful to see you again. May I offer you ladies some wine?"

I looked up and my heart skipped a beat. Standing before us in an elegant summer suit of dove-grey and a pale silver silk tie was Mr. Wonderful. His tan was accentuated by the bright white of his crisp shirt and ash-blonde hair. Light from the lake reflected aquamarine in his eyes. I kicked Karen underneath the table.

"Oh. Mattie, this is Garlan Russ. He's the owner. Garr, this is my good friend Mattie Blackman." Karen introduced us.

"Please, call me Garr, Miss Blackman. Everyone does." He gave me a half-bow, a charming old-world European touch.

Hel-lo handsome. "Call me Mattie. I think I've seen you work out at my gym. Midtown? So nice to meet you." I gave him my best smile. His eyes were hypnotic.

He smiled and snapped open our napkins and laid one on each of our laps. His muscular hand brushed my thigh, and my skin hummed. Heat rushed to my face.

"I'll send your waiter right over." He bowed again and left us.

"Karen, that's the guy." I grabbed her elbow. "The one I told you about. My potential future boyfriend."

"You said you were giving up on men altogether. As I recall, you said there were no good men left on the planet, remember?"

"You're right, I'm giving up on men. I mean it. But man-oh-Manischewitz, I may have spoken in haste." Garr greeted a couple at the door and escorted them to a nearby table.

"I admit Garr is a first-class hunk of beefcake, but he's old enough to be your father."

"Ooh, you're just being mean." I stuck my tongue out at her. "You said Russ. You mean as in Mad Otto's son?"

Mad Otto earned his nickname during prohibition, and added to his family fortune by supplying bootleg whiskey and gin to speakeasies all over the northeast. Mad Otto's reputation for ruthlessness and dangerous associates had always kept local law enforcement at a distance. These days, rumors hinted at his dementia and need for round-the-clock nursing care.

"Yes, Garr is Mad Otto's one and only. Garr took over the restaurant a few years ago. When Otto passes on, Garr is set for life." Karen raised her eyebrow. "And he is available. Not that you're interested, I'm sure."

"Of course not. I'm just curious. How do you know so much?"

"Martin and Garr are old friends and business associates. They play tennis together, and we come here for dinner all the time. Their spinach salads are the best."

"Maybe I should come here more often."

"This is probably the last time we'll eat here. Martin says the place is closing next month."

"Why? The Sand Castle has been here forever."

"It's going to be torn down to make way for the new marina."

"What a shame. I guess the restaurant business isn't what it used to be. By the way, I drove by Mystic Properties on my way over, but it was closed."

"Just call and make an appointment. Sonja says the mage is a spelunker. Is that fascinating or what?"

I rolled my eyes. "Alright, speak English. What the heck is a spelunker?"

"He explores caves."

I made a face. "Not my idea of a good time." I gazed longingly at Garr, as he chatted up a party seated at another table. "I like tennis, though. I do like a man with big hands."

Karen snorted. "Forget the hands, it's the shoe size that matters. I still can't believe you stayed with that loser Kip for as long as you did. You probably *should* stop dating."

"Are you going to make rude comments about my love life or tell me what you found?"

Karen handed me a stack of copies. "Take a look at this."

"Why can't you just tell me? The sooner I get my strange little problem taken care of, the sooner I can resume my normal um, social activities." I admired how well Garr's shoulders filled out his suit jacket; I'd bet money the suit was custom tailored.

"Okay, but pay attention." She put on her glasses and patted the pile of paper sitting in front of me.

"The top article talks about spirit guides, and says you don't need to be from an indigenous culture to encounter them, and they're always present in our sub-consciousness. You don't even have to believe in them to experience them. Sound familiar? And look, here it says clairvoyants are most likely to come in contact with them."

I nodded and finished skimming the article. "Oh, it says here they can be both animal and spirit." What a relief. I glanced over and smiled at my gaggle of spirit guides, but they did not respond. "I'll bet somewhere in that stack of copies you have information on what each animal means."

"Ta da!" She handed me several more pages, as our waiter arrived with our coffee. We both ordered the house spinach salads with dressing on the side. I waited until he was out of earshot.

"Give me the short version," I said. "What do these

things mean?"

"The lizard is about dreams and keeping an extra careful eye on the people around you. The cat means you're in a period of magic and mystery. The toad says you're going through some personal changes, and right now is a good time for solitude."

"And?"

"Don't you get it? It's perfect. You're discovering your extrasensory abilities. Wouldn't you agree that's magical and mysterious?"

"Okay, I'm with you there. How does this help me get rid of them? I can barely breathe. My food tastes like you-don't-want-to-know. Every time another one shows up, it scares me half to death. After the fifth one popped up this morning, things are getting kind of crowded in Mattie-land."

Her eyes opened wide. "Five? Are you kidding? When did this happen?"

"When I woke up this morning, there was a disgusting rat-thing sitting next to the others at the foot of my bed. The snake creature showed up right after I talked to you this morning. They have the same skin and yellow eyes as my other three, but of the five, the toad and the rat are definitely the worst." Between discreet hits off my dryer sheet and bites of spinach salad, I gave Karen the details about my morning visit from Agent Porter.

"This is getting complicated. I think the mage is our best bet to tell us what's going on."

I sighed. "I sure hope he's as good as you say."

"Listen to you. Yesterday you thought you had teratosis. Then you thought you were going nuts. Now you've gone beyond the explainable. You're psychic.

You have spirit guides. That's huge progress, if you ask me. A lot of people in this town are are paranormal."

"Name one."

"Mayor Brunson is a registered psychic. It came up during the election last year. It's perfectly respectable, practically mainstream."

I sighed. "Okay, you win. I think I need a little time to get used to the idea, but yeah, I think you may be right. The only thing is, I'm not sure Agent Porter is going to understand about these spirit messengers. Would you come with me?"

Garr returned to our table. "May I offer you ladies some dessert? We have a selection of fine seasonal fruit sorbets, or a chocolate lava cake, if you prefer." He spoke to me this time. I blushed.

"Just the check please, Garr." Karen gave me an exaggerated eyebrow wiggle. I kicked her again.

I'll send Dennis right over. A pleasure to meet you, Mattie. Enjoy your afternoon, ladies." He winked at me as he left the table.

I smothered a gasp. "Did you see that?"

"When's the last time you actually went on a date?"

My eyes followed him, helplessly. "When I didn't have to pay? I don't remember."

"Speaking of dating, my cousin Ramona ran into your brother with Zoey Nussmeyer at Wegmans a couple of months ago." She made a face.

I shook my head. "I don't understand what's gotten into him lately. He used to tell me everything, but now I get a feeling he's hiding something from me. I had no idea he was dating Zoey. "

"Well, not anymore." She reached out and touched my arm. "Zoey's dead."

"What?"

"Don't you ever listen to the news? She was one of the first Night Shark victims they found. The wounds were so horrific, they had to use DNA to identify her."

I pushed away my salad. "Oh no."

"It's been in all the papers. All the victims have been from Shore Haven."

"That can't be. They found a body over in Picston yesterday."

"Yeah. It was Joanne Reynolds."

"The Sheriff's wife? Oh my gosh, they live right down the street from Lance."

Karen nodded. "Be careful. Make sure you keep your doors locked. And you may not know this, but she had a registered demon." She checked her watch. "I've got to get going. I wrote the mage's phone number on the envelope."

"Would you come with me? I know its short notice, but couldn't you take the afternoon off?"

"Sorry, Adam has a doctor's appointment at two. Just tell Agent Porter the truth. You'll be fine."

"Okay. I guess I'm still getting used to the idea. I don't know what's worse: the fact that I'm psychic or that you were right." We both laughed.

"Don't worry, Mattie. Everything is going to work out, your luck is about to change."

"I hope so," I said. "I want my life back."

"Let me know what the mage says."

I followed her out of the parking lot, and turned my car up the street toward the Thruway. I had a date with Agent Porter.

CHAPTER 10

AFTER THE PEP talk from Karen, my mood was on the upswing, and by the time I took the downtown exit to Rochester, I was almost back to my sunny old self again. The spirit guide information Karen provided finally convinced me. So what if I'm psychic? I shrugged. As long as I can get rid of the stink, I can live with the rest. Not something to brag about, but nothing to worry about, either. No one at work need ever know. The tension eased from my shoulders.

Government scientists had been studying extrasensory perception for years. My test results would speak for themselves. The FBI were the experts; of course they would have the resources to solve my problem. The test would be the final confirmation I needed. Afterwards, I would let Agent Porter tell me how to get rid of my spirit messengers.

I skipped up the stairs of the FBI district office feeling pretty chipper, and gave my name to the receptionist. Forty-five minutes later, I sat in the soundproofed test room staring open-mouthed at Agent Porter. He wasn't smiling.

"What do you mean I don't have any psychic abilities? Of course I do." I hung onto my chair for dear life, every muscle tensed in rigid denial of Agent Porter and his stupid test results.

"That is not what your test results indicate, Ms. Blackman. Your scores fall clearly outside the parameters of what the United States government defines as psychic ability. In fact, you registered significantly less intuitive ability than average. I cannot recall any other applicants who scored this low on the evaluations."

"This is a mistake," I said. "I told you, I've got five spirit messengers following me."

The agent shook his head. "The tests don't lie." He began to put his equipment away, dismissing me.

"Give me another chance. I was probably just nervous."

"I think we're done here."

I felt like a dying goldfish circling the bowl for the last time, as the vortex of flush sucked me down into nothingness and sewage. At this point, I had nothing left to lose.

"Wait. You said you had to investigate all reports of demons. Well I have demons. They're sitting right here in this room with us. They smell so bad, I can hardly stand it. How can you just let this go?"

He froze, and for a second at least, I had his attention again.

"Are you now telling me you are in communication with evil spirits? Think very carefully before you answer, Ms. Blackman. Demons are more dangerous than loaded weapons. They are unsafe in anyone's hands, and cannot ever be made safe. The temptation to use a summoned demon is irresistible. I am required by law to enforce a standing order of execution against anyone who is identified as a demon master. Are saying you summoned five demons, and they are awaiting your command?" His blue eyes drilled into me.

The blood drained from my face and I choked on my protest. I bit my lips shut.

"I thought not." His jaw relaxed. He finished packing away the laptop and slipped my paperwork into his briefcase. The interview was over. I had been tested and found unworthy.

Hot tears stung my cheeks. "What am I supposed to do? How do I get rid of them? I could lose my job."

Porter sighed and took a clean white handkerchief out of his jacket pocket and handed it to me. I buried my face into the soft cotton and sobbed. Porter didn't say a word. After a few moments, I got a grip again, and blew my nose. I stared at the handkerchief in my hand and wished I'd thought to bring a dryer sheet.

"I don't know what to tell you, Mattie," he said. He was being gentle with me, I could tell. "Most people aren't so disappointed. Perhaps you should talk to someone."

"I'm not crazy." The forms I'd filled out before he administered the tests had asked all kinds of questions about my family history of mental illness. I could just imagine what he was thinking. "Can I ask you a question?"

"Oh-kaaay."

"What would you do if you were someone without any psychic ability, like me? I mean, if you were experiencing olfactory and visual hallucinations?"

"I'd consult with a psychiatric professional."

I closed my eyes and shrank against the thought. I wondered how long the hospital stay would be, and how I would ever be able to face anyone I knew again. I remembered my mother's drug-ravaged face and dismissed it. No. Not me, not now, not ever.

I squared my shoulders and lifted my chin. "You're wrong about me," my lips trembled.

His face softened. "Hey, for what it's worth, the tests we use focus on a narrow aspect of paranormal sensitivities. The government is looking for people that fit a unique profile. Not everyone with extra-sensory abilities is identified by these evaluations."

A spark of hope flared within me. I bit my lips.

"Let me tell you something, Mattie," he sat on the edge of the desk. "We're more alike you than you imagine. I haven't got a shred of intuition, either. My test scores were almost as low as yours."

"So how did you end up here?"

"It's a long story. This is a temporary special assignment." He couldn't keep the chagrin out of his voice, and I wondered what he'd done to earn this duty. After six years working for the City, there was nothing worse than 'special assignment'.

"This is a new program, and the bureau doesn't employ many agents with psychic abilities. I contract with a local guy to help me identify and register true paranormals. He's not always right, but he's got some kind of inner radar that can spot them. And he's not an intuitive either."

"Maybe I'm like that too." I handed Porter back his crumpled, wet handkerchief. "Who is he?"

"Rhys Warrick."

CHAPTER 11

RHYS WARRICK, RHYS Warrick, Rhys Warrick. The name echoed through my mind like a mantra. The Thruway wind blasted through the open windows, and battered against my numb face as I drove back to Shore Haven to pick up Mina. Until yesterday, I'd been certain Merle Shine held the solution to my problems. Today, I'd been absolutely confident the FBI would register me as a psychic. For Pete's sake, if the Better Business Bureau and the Federal Bureau of Investigation can't help me, what's left? Everywhere I turned, doors slammed in my face. I didn't know what to think anymore. All I ever wanted was a normal, respectable, predictable life, and now I found myself pinning my hopes on a certain prehistoric professor of ancient mysteries.

I arrived at Mina's school a few minutes early, and checked out my puffy reflection in the mirror. Like a wall of ratty stuffed animals, my mute escort of yellow-eyed demons gaped at me from the backseat.

"Oh shut up," I said. "I have had more than enough of all of you. You are totally pissing me off. This is all your fault."

I thrust my face into the box of dryer sheets and in haled deeply. Nothing. I rubbed my temples and considered my alternatives. Okay, so I'm not psychic, and I'm not schizophrenic. The only remaining answer seemed to be supernatural. If Rhys Warrick could spot people with paranormal abilities, that would have to be good enough for me. The old guy had been around; Karen said he was a Rhodes scholar, professor, archeologist, and theologian. A regular wise man. A helpful one, I hoped.

On a silent signal, kids started pouring out of school, and I honked and waved at nine-year-old Mina when she emerged. My mood lifted as she ran over to the car, her coppery-brown hair flying out behind her, grinning like an imp.

"Hey Mina, how's my favorite niece?"

"You always say that," she said, and gave me a big smoochie kiss on the cheek.

I'm always delighted by the sight of Lance's freckles and blue eyes shining out at me from her mother's heart-shaped face. Once she grew into her teeth, my niece Mina had all the makings of a real beauty.

"You up for a little adventure?"

She offered me a serious look. "Dad says homework first." In his wilder days, Lance had gotten into trouble when he owed money to the wrong people and couldn't pay. He had even been arrested once. But those days were behind him now, and every time I saw Mina, I understood why.

"Oh, it's too hot to study. What you need is a visit to Abbot's."

"With sprinkles?"

I was putty in her hands. "Double sprinkles," I promised. "I need to make one quick stop first."

We cruised past Mystic Properties, but the place

was still closed, so we picked up our frozen custard drove home.

❈

After dinner, we set up the board to play Scrabble at the kitchen table. The doorbell rang, and I opened the door to find a hulk of a man standing on the front porch. His fellow goon waited behind him on the sidewalk, leaning up against a light blue Seville. They weren't Boy Scouts, and they weren't salesmen. They looked like trouble.

"Is Lance around?"

Alarm bells clanged in my head. I motioned Mina back into the kitchen.

"Go on, I'll be there in a minute," I whispered.

I memorized the guy on Lance's front porch for future reference. He stood about six-foot-two, dark-haired, tanned, and beefy; he wore a sweaty blue polo shirt and wrinkled chinos. Way too much khaki to be one of Lance's friends, and the boxer nose didn't go well with the leather tassels on his shoes. His compadre at the street sported mirror shares, dreadlocks, and a baggy Hawaiian shirt.

My heart pounded. "Lance who?"

"McNair. We know he lives here." Chino guy leered at me from behind a mouthful of gold teeth.

Where's a cop when you need one, I wondered. I reminded myself that serial killers don't ring the doorbell. I kept my face and voice neutral.

"He isn't here."

"When do you expect him back?"

Be cool, Mattie. "I'm not sure." If he wanted to, this

guy could get by me in about half a second, and we both knew it.

The guy smirked and offered me his business card. An image of the queen of spades was printed on one side, Hector Perrone's name and number on the reverse. I didn't care what his card said, Hector was a thug, plain and simple.

"Cute." I waved the card. "What's this all about?"

"Tell him to get in touch with us. Sooner will be better for him than later." Hector gave me the onceover from tits to toes and back again, before meeting my eyes; his threat clear.

As if. I fought to keep my expression bland. "Okay, I'll give him the message."

"See you around, girlfriend." He tipped an invisible hat to me, then sauntered down the walk toward his buddy.

I slammed the door and turned the deadbolt. Stupid, but it made me feel better. I snuck a peek from behind the curtains in the front window, as they got into the Seville. They sat for a few minutes, chilling in the conditioned air, I supposed, before they drove off.

Hector's business card listed the address for the House of Cards, a gambling establishment on the greasy side of Picston. I sighed and shut my eyes against the implication. There was only one reason why someone from the House of Cards would be looking for Lance. If my brother was gambling again, he was in big trouble, in more ways than one. If he lost custody of Mina, I doubted I'd ever see her again.

Violet had no use for me; she thought I enabled Lance. When she'd set up an intervention the last time, I hadn't been willing to cut him out of my life if he continued gambling. Violet had a big family to support her, but Lance was the only family I had left. There had been a nasty scene between us, and neither of us backed down.

Mina peered up at me expectantly, the Scrabble game and dictionary all ready to go.

"Who was that man?" Little wrinkles furrowed her brow.

I smiled reassuringly. "Nobody," I said. "Just someone looking for your dad."

"Come on, let's play," she said.

I gazed into Mina's earnest face. *I can't lose you*, sweetie. I sat down at the table, but my mind wasn't on the game. As soon as Mina went to bed, I'd call him. I wanted some answers.

☾

While Mina brushed her teeth and got ready for bed, I turned down the sheets on her bed and started to close the curtains. I noticed a car idling at the curb across the street. The menacing blue Seville was back. I immediately turned off the light and peeked out, but couldn't discern the faces of the two figures in the front seat. No matter; I had no doubt the thugsy twins were watching the place, waiting for Lance to show. I debated going out there and confronting them, but nixed the idea. I had a responsibility to keep Mina safe. But knowing they were out there gave me the creeps.

"Why did you turn out the light?" Mina stood silhouetted in the doorway.

"It's nighttime, silly. Time for bed. Come on, I'll tuck you in."

"I want the light on."

"Oh, you're too old for a nightlight, sweetie. Come on, into bed."

"No." She pouted. "Turn it on."

"There is nothing to be afraid of, you're a big girl now."

"Turn it on. I don't like your monsters."

I froze. Goosebumps raced up my arms and down my back. A hysterical giggle threatened to bubble over.

"What monsters," I asked. My left eyelid began to twitch.

"Them." She pointed to the corner where Blix and Larry and the rest of the gang sat. "They don't belong here."

Well okay then. Dumfounded, I switched the light back on. "Better?"

She nodded, and crawled into bed and pulled up the covers. "They don't bother me when the lights are on." She stretched her arms wide for her goodnight kiss. Speechless, I swooped in to grant it, and snuggled her into my arms, uncertain what to say.

Relief flooded through me. A heaviness I didn't know existed eased off my chest and I took a deep breath. Her confirmation meant everything to me.

"How many do you see?" I was dying to talk about them, but didn't want to alarm her by making a big thing out of it.

"Two. What are their names?"

If Mina could see them, they were real.

My heart fluttered like a captive bird; I couldn't believe we were even talking about this. "Are you sure? What do they look like?" And why only two?

"The big one looks like that goblin from that movie

you like. The other one reminds me of an alligator with a squashed up face."

I hugged her closer. "He isn't a goblin, that's Blix. I think he looks a little like my old cat, Mister Mittens. Remember him? The other one is Larry the Lizard." Okay, Blix had been around the longest, but Larry had showed up third. Why couldn't she see the others?

She nodded, as if this was the most natural topic in the world. "Larry is cuter."

I was way out of my depth here, but didn't know what else to do, but go along with her.

"Yes, he is." And I meant it. In a pudgy, squatty-body sort of way. Floppy spines ran down his back, and he kept his prehensile tail curled around one of his stubby front legs, giving him a rather unsure expression. I could relate to that.

"Can you smell them?"

She closed her eyes and sniffed the air. She blinked slowly, and shook her head, her eyes getting heavier. "Will you stay with me until I go to sleep?"

I wanted to jump up and down and scream for joy, but since my only witness was a drowsy nine-year-old, I fought to keep myself still.

"Of course, baby."

I'm not losing my mind. I knew it, and now I had proof. Blix and Larry, at least, were real. I had to get in touch with Rhys Warrick right away. His name sang in my veins like an anthem. I could barely contain myself.

"I'm not a baby." Her eyes stayed shut, and she snuggled into me. Her breathing deepened.

Once Mina fell asleep, I tiptoed into the kitchen and called the number Karen gave me for Mystic Properties, but all I got was a recording. I left my name and cell phone number, and asked him to call me as soon as possible. He had an unexpected voice; more whisky-and-grit Bob Seger than tenured college professor. I wondered what he looked like.

I called Lance next, but he didn't answer. Where could he be? My thoughts strayed to pool halls, and bars, and card parlors. He had a daughter to care for and a business to run. He wouldn't be stupid enough to get involved in gambling again, would he? I left an urgent message to call me back. If Hector and his friend were any indication, Lance was about to be in for a world of hurt.

I peeked out the curtains and my heart gave a jump. The Seville sat parked across the street. I turned off all the lights except one in the kitchen. What did those men want from Lance? Had to be money. I thought briefly about calling the police, but they weren't breaking the law or anything. I debated going out there and confronting them, but figured that was a stupid idea. Mina was my responsibility, I needed to keep her safe.

I checked the cupboards for some sort of weapon, and put a cast-iron frying pan next to the front door. My eyes strayed to my little cluster of monsters, all too small and insubstantial to be much use if things got nasty.

Blix stamped his front feet at me.

I let out a shriek and grabbed the frying pan before I realized how stupid that was. What the hell? He had never made the slightest move before. I searched the stoic faces of the other four, but observed no change or reaction in any of them. You imagined it. They're not real.

Blix licked his lips with a pointy blue tongue.

A wave of nausea rolled over me. I choked it back down.

"What are you," I whispered.

There was no possibility of sleep now; I had a serious case of the creeping heebie-jeebies. I kneeled on the carpet, and studied Blix closely. Mina was right, Blix was bigger than the others, and his eyes now focused on mine. I moved my head toward the light, and his head swiveled to follow mine, his eyes dilated. Whenever I nodded, he nodded. I waved my arm, but he didn't respond, nor did he when I moved my leg. His eyes remained glued to my face, as if anticipating something from me. I forced myself to remain calm.

"You're freaking me out, Blix. Are you a demon or a spirit?"

What was the difference anyway? Blix looked like he was standing at attention, awaiting my order. The only thing I wanted him to do was to go away. If he was a demon, giving him a command would cause him to materialize permanently. I wasn't so sure about spirit guides.

I paced the kitchen, keeping a wary eye on the critter crowd, my anxiety growing by the minute. My mind swirled with useless thoughts of Lance and demons and Porter and my suspension. I wondered why Lance hadn't called me back, and why it was so hard to get hold of that stupid mage, and why I seemed to waste so much time waiting for calls from men who never called me back. I hated the helpless feeling of waiting for something to happen. When did I become such a wimp? Enough of this already, I had to do something.

Family comes first, I decided.

I checked on my sleeping niece. I curled around her,

burying my face into her warm hair. I couldn't lose her, but I didn't want to lose my brother, either. If Lance didn't have a decent explanation about what he was up to, I'd threaten to tell Violet about House of Cards. If he wanted to keep Mina in his life, he'd better straighten up.

And come hell or high water, I'd get hold of that elusive mage tomorrow, even if I had to pull an all-day stakeout. No more nice girl. Time for Mattie Blackman to kick a little butt.

CHAPTER 12

THE NEXT MORNING, after I dropped Mina off at school, I headed over to Mystic Properties for my mage stakeout. I called Rhys again, and listened to the phone ringing inside. Okay, nobody home. In a moment of clarity, I decided against leaving another message. The last thing I wanted to do was to make him think I was stalking him. Waiting for him to show up at work wasn't the same thing at all.

Lance hadn't called me back, so I called his partner at the shop.

"Sorry, Mattie. I don't know where he is. He said he'd be back on Monday."

"Did he tell you anything about, um, having any problems lately?" Doc and Lance had been friends for decades. When Lance got into trouble with the loan sharks the first time, he'd sold his half of the business to Doc. Once Lance got out of rehab, Doc agreed to let Lance buy back in, but only on the condition that he was done with gambling. If Lance was gambling again, he'd lose the business.

"You mean the ex-wife? No more than the usual. Hey, I gotta go, I got customers."

I settled into my seat again to wait. Doing a stakeout from the only car parked on the block, made me feel a bit obvious. At this hour on the morning, the regular businesses were just starting to open, and there were plenty of parking spaces, except in front of the bakery and Henry's Killer Burgers, which was open twenty-four hours. My stomach rumbled. I should have brought a thermos of coffee, at least. I adjusted the rearview mirror and studied the five demons in the backseat. A full day had passed since a new demon joined my little monster mouse club. Blix was definitely making independent movements now. His head and eyes followed my every move. Every time I looked in his direction, he stamped his front feet and licked his lips or eyeballs with that disturbing blue tongue.

To kill some time, I got out and strolled over to stare in the window again. I scanned the postcards advertising properties for rent. Most were commercial properties, but there were a few apartment rentals. With my landlady in the pokey. I might need a new place to live. As my eyes scrolled down the list of rentals, I spotted for the first time, gold lettering in the lower left corner of the front window: Hours by Appointment Only.

Oh crap. I fumed for a minute, debating my next move. Next door, Tacker Shoes was open. Tackers started out as a shoe repair shop, selling shoes on the side. Over the years, the business gave way to shoe sales, and now, Tacker's was the only shoe store in Shore Haven. I walked in and found Bunny Tacker dusting the men's dress shoe display. She greeted me with a glowing smile and welcoming hug. Bunny had always been a skinny thing in school, but she had gained weight since I'd seen her last.

"You look great," I said.

"I got my boobs done." She pulled up her t-shirt to

show me the new ta-tas peeking out of a low-cut C-cup. "Best thing I ever did. Check this out." She flashed a twinkle ring in front of me as well. "Ronnie and I are engaged." Happiness seemed to bubble right out of her.

I squealed and oohed appropriately and made a fuss over her augmented appearance and upcoming nuptials. Okay, maybe I was just a teensy bit jealous, but ever since seventh grade, Bunny Tacker's future with Ronnie Orozco had been a sure bet.

"Hell, maybe I need a boob job too." I noted at the 'Clearance Sale' sign in the window. "What's all this?"

She shrugged. "Oh, Dad's selling the place. None of us kids are interested in taking the place over, and the land is worth more than the business now. He's decided to retire and move down to Florida. Remember when my Mom slipped on the ice and broke her hip last winter? She's fine, but terrified of falling again. They're down in Clearwater now, looking at condos."

"I'm glad your mom is doing better." The displays of shoes and purses were sparsely populated. "Must be lots of businesses selling out to marina developers. I hear the Sand Castle is closing too."

She made a face. "Not the same thing. Garr's mismanaged the place, and Mad Otto is foreclosing out of spite. Garr may be a loser, but can you imagine foreclosing on your own family? Otto sold the restaurant out from under Garr. The place will be torn down pretty soon."

I didn't like hearing Bunny criticize my potential future boyfriend. Besides, how would she know? "I can't imagine not having the Sand Castle around anymore. Or Tacker's either, for that matter."

"A lot of the big old estates along the Strand have been sold off, too. People are hoping the marina will revive the Shore, but Dad thinks Shore Haven is losing its soul. Pretty soon, regular folks like us won't be able to afford to live here. The town will dissolve into a private seasonal getaway for the rich."

"There's still Shanghai Palace, and Dave's Killer Burgers. I can't picture Shore Haven without them. Or the bakery either."

"Yeah, they'll do fine. But a lot of the old buildings have already been torn down to make room for banks. Most of the new businesses are either real estate or investment firms."

"Hey, speaking of which, what's with that place next door, Mystic Properties? Every time I walk by, they're closed."

"Oh, that's Rhys; he's a busy guy. Are you looking to move?" She looked hopeful. "Because I'm going to be moving in with Ronnie next month, and I've still got six months on my lease."

Bunny is my friend, but also an incurable gossip, and I wasn't about to tell her anything I didn't need to.

"So what's this Rhys guy like? How do I get hold of him?"

"It's a two bedroom over in Webster." She made a face. "I know, but the rent was cheap. And it has a garage. Why are you moving? Is it because of Patty? I would never have suspected her of being a demon master. Did you--"

"Actually, it's for Lance," I lied. "He is thinking of moving to a bigger place. He's out of town; I told him I'd try to find something for him this week."

"What are you talking about? Lance isn't out of town, Ronnie and I saw him last night."

"Excuse me?"

"Yeah, a big crowd of us partied after hours at the Stick and Stein pool tournament. Lance was brilliant; I'd never seen him shoot before. Big-name players showed up from all over; Detroit, New York City, even Philadelphia. A lot of people lost money on those tables, but Lance wasn't one of them. By the time we left, he had a wad on him the size of a baseball."

I stared at her, unable to speak. He'd lied to me. No wonder he hadn't called me back. What a-- *focus Mattie*. I exhaled, and stomped all my fury back down. I couldn't do anything about that now.

"Where I can find Rhys?"

"He eats lunch at the Amble Inn every day."

"That dump? I can't believe they're still open."

She laughed. "You know, the AI was the first bar I ever went to."

When we were in high school, Karen and Bunny and I used to sneak into the place on Tuesday nights for the cheap beer and college boys. She glanced at her watch. "Say, since I'm the boss this week, how about I close up for a bit, and take you over there for a Joe's Special?"

"You're on."

The entrance to the AI was a few doors away, and as I followed Bunny into the gloom, I was assailed by the scent of hot dogs, stale peanuts, and several decades' worth of alcohol fumes.

Time had not passed the AI unnoticed. It was still a dive bar, but had been remodeled at some point. Two large skylights brightened the place up, and a few booths had been added beneath the front windows. The décor was still early rope and marine hardware, but an electric train ran around the room near the ceiling, adding a touch of whimsy. Big-screen televisions loomed over the patrons, each screen tuned to a different sports event.

"Hey Herman," Bunny called out to the bearded guy behind the bar. "Two Molsons and two specials."

I followed her to the closest empty booth. We sat, and the man came around with a basket of unshelled peanuts and our beers.

"You're early today," he smiled at Bunny. "Be a minute on the specials. The cooker is almost ready."

"Mattie this is Herman the German. Herman, this is my friend Mattie Blackman."

"Ah, a pleasure to meet you." He shook my hand. His grip, firm and strong, scored big points with me for not crunching my knuckles. His eyes twinkled, and he scampered back to the kitchen. I liked him.

"Ever since Herman took over, this place has become a gold mine."

"I can tell. We got here at the right time." The lunch crowd was already starting to arrive. We sipped our beers, and a few minutes later, the waitress came with our food, a pot of mustard and a wad of napkins.

"You need anything else?"

Bunny looked at me, and I shook my head. "Thanks Trina, we're good."

I eyed the heap of deep fried red hots, grilled onions, sauerkraut, and pickle, piled high between two slices of dark rye.

"How do I eat this?" My mouth watered; I wanted to get a bite in before another wave of stinkum showed up.

Bunny laughed, and slathered mustard on hers, then wrapped the bottom half in napkins.

"Very carefully," she said, and took a big bite.

I copied her, and groaned with surprised delight

as I bit into the juicy, greasy sandwich. I could actually taste it. Clearly, deep-fried hot dogs trumped demon-stink. I had just taken another luscious bite when Bunny pointed to two men standing at the bar. The older fellow, a clean-shaven pot-bellied professor-type, wore a tonsured wreath of grey hair around his bald pate. He spoke animatedly to a dark-haired biker dude with a Fu-Manchu moustache.

"That's him. Hey Rhys, over here."

To my surprise, biker dude turned and walked toward us. Rhys approached our table like a panther stalks prey: all muscled steel, sleek suntanned skin, and glitter-green eyes. He wore a sleeveless denim jacket over his naked torso, and scuffed, black leather chaps over black jeans. He moved casually, but I could see the shift and glide of powerful muscles with every step. Mesmerized, the only thoughts that came to my mind were animal magnetism and yum-mee.

Bunny made the introductions, and his eyes settled on my chest. I followed his eyes to a big splot of mustard on my shirt. Blushing furiously, I grabbed a napkin to wipe it off while trying to gulp down my mouthful of hot dog sandwich without choking.

"Um, hi," I said, when I could almost talk.

His metallic green eyes flicked to the corner of the booth where Blix and the gang sat, then drained his beer in a single long swallow, and shook his head at me, as if contemplating what to say. Finally, he jerked his head toward the front door.

"Let's go."

CHAPTER 13

"YOU DIDN'T SAY he was a biker." I scrambled out of the booth after the mage, hurriedly tossing Bunny a ten. Her laughter chased me out the door.

The mage appeared substantially younger than I expected, his demeanor completely at odds with his academic credentials. The temperature must have been in the upper eighties, and the humidity was stifling, yet he wore denim and leather like his own skin. Black hair curled over his collar, held back with a leather thong. I'd expected someone more bookish. Not so, um, badass. I wondered what he smelled like.

We reached Mystic Properties, and I waited as he unlocked the door. "Aren't you hot? How can you stand to wear black leather in this heat?"

"You're criticizing how I dress?" He held the door open for me. "Black is my favorite color."

I paused for a moment, wondering what I'd gotten myself into. His eyes glowed with an inner gleam, scaring the daylights out of me in an incredibly primal, sexual way. *Focus, Mattie.* This guy was supposed to get rid of my stupid demons or spirits or whatever, not complicate my love life. Besides, I'd already committed myself to a certain local restaurateur. I took a deep, cleansing breath, and exhaled slowly. I could tell, his guy wouldn't have a lot of patience. I tried to picture myself plunging into an icy pool. It helped a little, but every time I looked at him, man oh man.

I followed him into a room at the back of the building, which was furnished with second-hand furniture, a braided rug, metal file cabinets, and wall-to-wall bookshelves. I perched on a folding chair while Rhys sprawled on an old grey sofa. I told him all about my little teratosis gang, the accidents, Porter, and pretty much everything else. He listened without interrupting, his face open and accepting, as if this sort of thing came along every day. By the time I finished my story, I knew I'd come to the right place.

"Who are you," he asked.

"I told you, I'm Mattie Blackman. I'm a parking control officer for the City of Picston."

"No, I mean who are your people?"

A flush rose in my cheeks. Hadn't I already said enough? How could he ask me for information I'd barely admitted to myself, much less told a stranger? I couldn't shake the feeling that the mage was the right guy for the answers I needed. If I had to go through some additional personal discomfort to get there, so be it. I trusted him.

I shrugged, with a nonchalance I didn't feel.

"Um, I don't know. My mom grew up an orphan. Her husband divorced her when she got pregnant with me." I blushed, in spite of myself. "She never spoke a word about my father."

"Did your mother ever speak about her family, or where she came from?"

I shook my head. "She grew up in foster care. She went to Shoreline High, though. Same as me."

"Where is she now?"

I strove to keep my voice steady. "She committed suicide when I was sixteen."

He nodded, but didn't say anything. Instead, he got up and began searching through the metal file drawers for something.

I don't know what I expected as a result of sharing the most painful moments of my childhood, but some sort of acknowledgement seemed appropriate. The silence stretched between us, as he closed the first drawer and started in on the second. What's with this guy? I held my temper in check, reminding myself he was my last resort. I decided to try another tack.

"You can see these spirit things of mine, can't you?"

He stopped searching and raised his hypnotic eyes to mine. I held my breath.

"No. I get a sense of something, but no. Here it is." He selected an old photograph from a folder and handed it to me. "Do you know this woman?"

My heart ached with loss and the pain of seeing her again. I choked back the emotions that threatened to undo me in front of this apparently unfeeling stranger. She looked so much younger than I remembered. Slim and black-haired, she had a brilliant smile. Her dark eyes bore no trace of the madness that would plague her later in life. Why the heck did he have a picture of my mother locked in his files?

"Where did you get this?"

"You look like her."

"What are you doing with my mother's picture? Can you help me?"

He considered me with a thoughtful expression. "I might know someone."

I sagged and fought back tears of relief. "You believe me."

"I doesn't matter what I believe. You say you failed the FBI test?"

"Porter told me I had the lowest score of anyone he ever tested." My hand shook as I handed the picture back to him.

A genuine smile crossed his face for the first time, and changed my whole opinion of him. He had crinkles around his eyes and exceedingly white, even teeth. He reached out to me, almost as if to touch my hair and caught himself. I wondered what kissing him would be like. I imagined he was a good kisser; that is, if I was interested. Which I wasn't. And even if I was, he wasn't my type.

"That wasn't your mother, Mattie. Come on, there's someone I want you to meet."

I followed him out, thinking we were going to his car, but he kept walking.

"Well, who is she? Where are we going?"

"It's not far." He had a long stride, and I had to hustle a bit to keep up. He noticed, and slowed down, which somehow embarrassed me.

We crossed the street and turned left at Empress, a pretty street lined with turn-of-the-century painted ladies, mostly Victorian and Queen Anne architecture. Large trees shaded the uneven sidewalk, which lay broken and crumbled by the groping limbs of massive roots.

My anxiety grew with each house we passed. We stopped at the end of the block, in front of a dilapidated turquoise and lavender Queen Anne with flakes of pale yellow trim. The place needed about six more coats of paint in order to be called shabby. Stepping-stones in the overgrown lawn led to a deeply sagging front porch. I knew this place. So did everyone else in town.

I wrapped my arms around myself, and fought to keep my voice calm. "Why are we stopping here?"

A large, freshly-painted, butter-yellow wooden sign hung from the front porch overhang. Carved in the shape of a hand, the garish sign boasted in blood-red letters:

DESTINY
BY APPOINTMENT ONLY
MADAME COUMLIE

"I think this lady can help you."

I wanted to scream. "I come to you for help, and you lead me to a tourist attraction? Are you kidding me?" The sauerkraut I'd eaten earlier threatened to make an encore performance. I took a step back. Words failed me. Nothing would get me inside that house.

Bitterness itched at the back of my throat. "I can't believe you brought me here." Rhys had been my last hope.

"She's not what you think."

What an idiot I'd been. What the hell made me think a mage had any more credibility than a fortuneteller, anyway? I'd been so busy looking at his eyes, I'd forgotten my mission. At least Porter hadn't made fun of me. Bang-up job there, Mattie.

I clenched my fists in fury at my own stupidity. "I just remembered, I've got to, um, be someplace. My niece. I need to pick her up. She's waiting." I couldn't get out of there fast enough.

I tripped over a crust of broken pavement and fell sprawling, cracking my elbow and against the concrete. I winced and grabbed my funny bone, embarrassed by my own clumsiness. My own weakness. My own everything.

In a flash, Rhys was at my side, his face full of concern. I couldn't stand to have him look at me like that. He put his hand on my arm to help me up, but when his flesh touched mine, I twisted away before I could embarrass myself any further. My elbow hurt like the dickens, and I focused on the pain instead of the thrumming of my skin where he'd touched me.

My cheeks burned. "I don't believe in fortune tellers." It was the best I could come up with on short notice.

"She's not a fortune teller."

"The sign says she is." Against my will, I wanted him to touch me again, but I couldn't bring myself to take one step closer to the monstrosity of a house. I wanted to disappear. I glanced up and down the street, hoping no one was watching.

"Wait, you don't understand. When I told you she could help, what I meant to say is I think she might be related to you."

I whirled on him. "Like that's supposed to make me feel better? I don't think so."

"The picture I showed you is of Madam Coumlie's daughter, Oleanna. She got pregnant and gave up the baby for adoption. I think the child might have been your mother."

Thunderstruck, I stared at him. "No." I shook my head.

Admittedly, the resemblance to my mother was

pretty amazing. I searched my memories for the name, Oleanna. I'd never heard the name before; but I liked it. Was it possible? No. To think this ancient circus freak could be related to me made my face hurt. People called her the Oracle of Death, among other things. She was an embarrassment to the neighborhood, and like an old harlot, too colorful to ignore. *Just like my mother.* The thought of being related to yet another neighborhood joke horrified me.

"I'm sorry I ever came to you for help."

"You want help? I can't help you. You're going to have to talk to the Hand of Fate."

I sighed. *I don't need this.* I didn't want to see what was behind door number two, thank you very much. I'd rather take Blix and Larry and my other little demon consolation prizes and crawl back home with my tail tucked between my legs. Perhaps Porter was right. Certainly some sort of pharmacological solution could be found; it might not get rid of my hallucinations, but I wouldn't care anymore.

All of a sudden, Rhys was standing too close to me, looming inside my personal space. He reached for my neck. Paralyzing fear stabbed me as he deliberately drew me to him. He leaned in and kissed me hard; full on the mouth. More like a bite with tongue than anything else. I got the barest whiff of spice cake and a hint of beer. It was over in a second, leaving me out of breath, my lips bruised and throbbing.

"Welcome back." That fantastic smile was back again. In fact, he seemed rather pleased with himself. He chucked his finger under my chin and steered me up the stairs to the porch. He held open the old-fashioned front door, and motioned me inside.

All my resolve disappeared, as I savored the unexpected pleasure fading from my lips.

"We can't just walk in."

"We'll be standing out here all day, if we waited for her to answer the door. She's deaf as a fossil. You want to do this or not?"

He grinned and waited for me to make up my mind. I wanted to ask him why he'd kissed me, but this was not the time. What the heck, better not rock the boat. Maybe he would kiss me again. *Don't be such a wimp, Mattie.*

I sighed. I wanted to keep my job, I needed to get rid of these inner demons. If Madame Coumlie was the only person with the answers I needed, I was going to have to talk to her. Shit.

"Let's do it then." I set my jaw and walked past him with as much dignity as I could muster.

CHAPTER 14

I PAUSED IN a musty entry hall decorated in early bordello. Dark wood-trimmed burgundy walls surrounded the doorways and stairs. Across the foyer, a framed proclamation of some sort hung above a red velvet settee flanked by ornate sconces. To the right, an archway led into a lavender living room. An oriental carpet paved the floor, and a pink camelback sofa faced the soot-stained fireplace. The room appeared unused. I turned my attention back to Rhys.

"This way."

I licked my lips and followed him through a wide doorway to the left, which opened into a circular, high-ceilinged parlor, painted in the most garish colors imaginable. Flocked paisley wallpaper flecked with maroon, orange, and purple covered the walls. A border of hand painted gold stars and other hieroglyphs encircled the windows and baseboards. Faded photos, framed certificates, and yellowed newspaper clippings festooned the room like bonbons. A massive chandelier hung from the ceiling; dusty strings of old spider webs stretched between the prisms.

The tiny woman sat at a low table in the front window. She must have seen us come into the house, but she did not turn her head to acknowledge us. I blushed to think she had watched me kiss Rhys.

Rhys tapped her shoulder, and she swiveled in her seat to face me. Her eyes were her most arresting feature. The irises were a chalky copper color, with a fiery halo of yellow-gold around her pupils. Like a bird, she cocked her head and inspected every detail of my appearance from head to toe. I shifted uncomfortably; self-conscious in the power of her gaze. Her penciled-in eyebrows and rouged cheeks gave her the appearance of an ancient marionette. She grinned up at me through nonexistent lips. I was both repulsed and inexplicably fascinated by her.

"Madame, this is Mattie Blackman." Rhys spoke with reverence and careful diction, presumably so she could read his lips. "Mattie, this is Madame Coumlie, the Hand of Fate." He motioned me closer.

Had she been standing, she would have come only to my waist. She held both her blackened hands out to me, and I hesitated. Pale runic scars disfigured the soot-stained skin of her bony hands. An incised crescent moon had been carved into each of her palms. What kind of person does that to herself, I wondered.

"What do you think, Madame? Who does she remind you of?"

Her pale eyes washed over me, and stared back at her. I couldn't have been more intimidated if I'd been facing a cobra. She'd dressed as for a special occasion, although she couldn't have known we were coming. Beneath a quilted vest of Persian blue, she wore a crisp white blouse. Ropes of polished silver and turquoise beads wound around her spindly neck. Thin white hair wrapped her skull in a tidy French twist. She gave the impression of fragility, but her eyes were flinty sharp.

My determination wavered.

"You are not my Oleana, but there is no doubt you are of my line," she said, in thickly accented French. She motioned me to a seat, opposite her at the banquette.

"Tell me, mage. What do you think of her?"

His eyes settled on my mouth as he answered. "I find her irresistible."

I blushed at the compliment. The old woman coughed, and horked something substantial into her cupped hand. I couldn't keep the revulsion off my face, and even Rhys looked disgusted. She pulled a handkerchief out of her pocket, and wiped her hand. The spasm passed and she folded the whatever it was back into the pocket of her slacks. When she'd composed herself, I realized she'd been laughing.

"Yes, well our line always affected those such as yourself in that way. But look at her and tell me what you see."

"She's like you, only more so." Rhys put his hands out, as if he were warming himself before a bonfire. "Even in here, she is hot with it."

I wondered what he meant. Hot was good, right?

"What you are sensing, mage, are her djinn. As my powers fade, hers grow stronger." She closed her eyes and appeared to inhale my essence. "Who could imagine such strength in one like this! She is a beacon to the djinn. Several hover in her aura."

Djinn? In my aura? *What's a djinn?*

"And two named djemons." Her eyes widened, and she looked directly to Blix and Larry. "What have you done, *chere*?"

"I didn't do anything."

She snatched my sweaty left hand between her cool

bony fingers and I gasped. I attempted to pull away, but claws tightened into a vise around my wrist. Her fingernails dug painfully into the flesh of my palm. She had me in a grip of stone, as immovable as iron. Regardless of her appearance, she was stronger than me. The sensation of being trapped was overwhelming. I wondered if I would be able to get away with my dignity intact.

"Don't you know? Naming them gives them power. They cannot harm anyone if they aren't named. Even your silly FBI knows that." In spite of my resistance, she pulled me closer to her.

"You didn't tell me you'd named them." Rhys stroked his moustache, his face grim.

"Let go." I kept my voice calm. She replied with a lipless smile.

"You're hurting me." I jerked my hand as hard as I could, but the old witch didn't move a muscle. I gritted my teeth and wished I'd never come here. I should have listened to my instincts about this house when I had a chance. Alice in Wonderland would've run screaming from this place.

"I said, let go of me!"

She loosened her grip, finally, and I snatched my hand back, scared and humiliated. My palm seeped blood where her fingernail had dug into me. I wanted to leave, but for some reason, couldn't force my legs to move.

"That's not important now, mage. You found her and we don't have much time. I had all but given up hope. You have done well."

"What are you talking about?" I held my throbbing hand to my chest.

"Listen to me, *chere*. Time is short. You are unprepared for what is to come."

She'd given my wrist some sort of a burn. I flexed my fingers and stared at a shiny black crescent mark now centered on the palm of my left hand. She held up hers, and showed me she had one just like it.

I rubbed my palm against my shirt, trying to rid myself of the mark, but it didn't even smear. "What did you do to me?"

"I knew it," Rhys said. "Her resemblance to Oleana is uncanny."

Madame Coumlie merely nodded. "You should be proud of your heritage. We are the last of the Fates, you and I, descended of the gods themselves. Our ancestors were born a millennium before the dawn of Christianity. Our bloodline has survived for thousands of years. When I die, all the powers of prophesy, destiny, and death will come to you, the only surviving woman of my line. The transfer of power has already begun."

"No." I got my legs working again and stood. "I'm not listening to any more of this. I am not what you say. I came here to get rid of these things. That's the only reason I came." I glared at the mage. "You were supposed to help me."

"This has nothing to do with what you want, chere. This is your destiny. When I die, my powers will pass to you and you will become the next Hand of Fate. It has always been this way. It is a great honor and responsibility. Even now, as I sense my powers waning, they bloom in you."

"Listen, lady I'm a parking control officer for the City of Picston. You're talking crazy." I had lost complete control of the conversation.

"Hear me, mage." She waggled her finger at Rhys, ignoring me completely. "The situation is clear to me now. Someone has unleashed the djinn from their sealed cavern beneath Sentinel Hill. They must have been loose for some time. They will attach themselves to sensitives, such as young Mattie here. With every passing moment, she is attracting more djinn to her, but she is not the only one at risk. There are many unsuspecting people in Shore Haven who will be tempted to name their djinn when they appear." She turned to me and continued.

"Once named, a djinn becomes djemon, servant to their human master until released. By your laws, anyone with a named djemon becomes a demon master. Under the new anti-terrorism act, anyone proven to be a demon master may be sentenced to death. I cannot imagine what your government's actions would be if they discovered an entire community of demon masters here in Shore Haven. You understand the threat, no? The anomalous community cannot risk exposure. The djinn must be resealed inside the cavern quickly."

"How many are we talking about," Rhys asked.

I fought to keep my rising panic under control. "Hey, what exactly is a djinn, anyway?"

"A djinn is a spirit without a master." Rhys said. "It is not a creature of the flesh. It resides on the astral plane, imperceptible to most humans. They are attracted to paranormal activity, and can, on occasion, be perceived by humans with certain extrasensory gifts such as yourself. They possess no inherent qualities for good or evil. They exist to serve a master."

A missing piece clicked into place for me.

"So these things I'm seeing are djinn? How come

it didn't show up when I took the FBI test?"

Madame Coumlie convulsed into a new phlegm seizure, and I couldn't tell if she was laughing or coughing this time. The handkerchief reappeared, and she was able to get control of herself.

"The FBI doesn't know everything, Mattie." Rhys smiled, and his features softened. "And we're not about to correct them." In the back of my mind, I guessed the old lady had been laughing.

"Once a djinn is named, *chere*, it becomes a djemon. The first time a named djemon is given a command by its master, the creature materializes on the physical plane. Once a djemon attains physical form, it becomes most dangerous. The djemon gains power and strength and grows by obeying its master's commands. Over time, a djemon can become extremely powerful; even more so than the master. This is the reason your FBI wishes to regulate psychics, no?"

"How do you get rid of them?" Now we were getting somewhere. "I mean, after they manifest?"

"You die." She started to laugh, and the choking horking spasm drowned out the rest of her words.

"She means to say djinn and djemons can't be killed," Rhys said. "They're not alive. They don't eat or sleep as you would expect. They don't breathe. All they do is wait for the next command from their master. A djinn is harmless, but once manifested, a djemon made flesh can become a powerful creature."

The import of agent Porter's words came to me with a chill. "They're a loaded weapon."

Rhys nodded. "They defy the very laws of nature. Tell me, Madame, how many djinn we're talking about here?"

"In 1930, I returned four hundred and twelve into to the cavern, but thousands more never escaped. If the portal is open again," she shrugged. "Perhaps only a few have been named or made flesh."

"I've got six trapped already."

"If the seal is broken, mage, you will need to repair it. Take the girl with you. She must be the one to fix things." Madame Coumlie's face had gone ashen. Her fit had taken a lot out of her. "My time grows short."

"No way," I said. "No can do. I don't want to get involved in any of this. As a matter of fact, I'm leaving. Right now."

Rhys and the old woman looked at each other and she grinned that creepy, lipless smile at me again.

"Oneiri," she called. "I summon you." She clapped her hands.

Out of nowhere, Madame Coumlie's djemon materialized out of thin air into the middle of the room. Charcoal in color, Oneiri appeared to be about the size of a large pony. Heat radiated from its solid body like a furnace, and the floor reverberated with the echoes of its fury as it snarled at Blix and Larry.

I gaped in disbelief as adrenaline surged through every fiber of my being. "What the hell is that?" I already knew the answer. Oneiri looked like Blix on steroids. Madame Coumlie's djemon was unmistakably a sphinx.

CHAPTER 15

THE SIGHT OF Oneiri in the flesh thrilled my breath away. He turned his yellow eyes on me, and the menace of his gaze had me shaking where I stood. My cell phone rang, but I switched the darn thing to vibrate without answering. I sidled around the perimeter of the room for a better view.

"Voila; you see? Everything is so simple, *chere*. Oneiri here was a djinn once, like your petit pets. He came to me in my dreams, so long ago. Like you, I did not know about naming such a thing, and yet here he is made flesh."

Another low growl rumbled and Oneiri gave a loud snort before sitting back on his haunches to await his mistress's command. His resemblance to Blix was undeniable, but where Blix resembled a scrawny, hairless kitten, Oneiri projected raw power and predatory elegance. The difference between them defined unnatural versus supernatural. A near-human face glowered at me from behind leonine features. He vibrated with the force of barely contained energy and danger, a fantastically scary combination.

Awestruck, I could barely speak. "He's real."

His paws were the size of trike tires. I had no doubt that Oneiri would be as deadly as he appeared. Oddly, I had no fear of him, merely a healthy respect for Oneiri's size and obvious lethal capabilities.

"*Oui.*"

"He doesn't smell."

"A big bonus, non? Manifestation has many advantages."

I ached to touch him, but didn't dare. "How did he get so big?"

Oneiri shook himself, and the slithering of his ebony wing feathers sounded like the shuffling of cards. A genie on a flying carpet could not have enthralled me more.

"Where do you keep him?" I couldn't contain my amazement. "He's just so big."

"Once named, everyone uses them," Rhys said.

"The life force energy of their masters sustains them, chere, but they can also grow powerful from absorbing the life force of their victims."

My heart skipped a beat. "He's killed people?" The phone in my pocket vibrated, but I paid no attention. A million questions flooded my mind, and I desperately wanted to know more.

I edged my way around the sphinx until I stood next to my great-grandmother. Blix paced back and forth, intensely agitated. Even Larry seemed distressed, licking his eyes repeatedly with a long blue tongue. The rest of my herd remained motionless. I noticed two more fanged toads had joined the party.

Oneiri's eyes were at the same level as mine, as big as tangerines. I raised my hand to pet him. "Hey guy."

Oneiri lowered his head and laid back his pointed ears, each of which sported a single gold ring at the tip. I snatched my hand back and bit my lips. Better not.

"So this is what Blix will grow into? What about

Larry? What about the rest? Why do I have so many?"

Rhys said, "Pay attention, Mattie. This is important. Every time you speak or think their name, they grow in power."

Chastened, I realized Rhys was right. Blix had already moved away from the herd, and seated himself on my left side. Larry too, had taken a few steps closer. He stamped his stubby little feet and stared at me with new intensity.

"So how do I get rid of my djinn?"

"The unnamed ones can be compelled to return to their chamber, as I did long ago. Rhys, in the cupboard behind you, you will find a volume labeled 1930. Bring it to me."

The opened armoire revealed dozens of dark green, leather-bound books; each marked with a hand-lettered date along the spines. Rhys selected one from the shelf, and handed it to her. She appeared to know what she was looking for, and flipped right to the correct page.

"Here." Her gnarled hand smoothed the page as if to caress the words written. "Times were difficult, the summer after the stock market crashed. No visitors came to Shore Haven that summer. Old Master Russ closed the Amusement Park, and the employees struggled to fend for ourselves. I was newly married to your great-grandfather Dirk Coumlie. He worked as a carpenter, but there was no work. We took boarders into the house, to help make ends meet, but there was no money."

"The townspeople became desperate; waiting in long lines for every scrap of food, we subsisted largely on handouts, rumors, and hope. For some, suicide became the antidote to despair, as people who lost everything could not imagine a better future. Misery drove others to take what they needed, and robberies, muggings, and break-ins became commonplace. Shore Haven gained a reputation as a rough area; a place of seedy characters and illicit activity. Those of us fortunate enough to have a place to live turned our homes into armed camps. And then the killing started.

"People began to disappear. Sometimes the bodies would be found days later, with the flesh shredded from their bones, sometimes they wouldn't be found. The rumors spoke of creatures prowling the streets on the darkest nights, in the company of a hooded man. In The Sentinel, the killer became known as the Lakeside Lurker.

"Shore Haven descended into a state of siege. The police refused to accept the truth, and were too afraid to dig the killer out of hiding. Curfew laws kept all but the most foolish inside their homes between sundown and sunup. Neighbors banded together for safety and stood guard over each other after curfew. Tales of the old Senequois legends surfaced, of evil spirits imprisoned beneath Sentinel Hill. Letters to the editor begged the mayor and governor to do something. I felt I had to act, but I did not know what to do.

"Oneiri was with me even then, and Dirk and I came to suspect supernatural forces at work. We came to believe the perpetrator was using djemons to rob and murder the citizens of Shore Haven, and if we captured this demon master, perhaps we could end the madness.

"Dirk and I went into the caverns beneath Sentinel Hill. We found where a crevice had been hacked open, and I saw many, many djinn gathered within. Whoever had broken the seal had done so with purpose, and was now a demon master.

"Every night, we scoured the streets, looking for both victims and the master. With Oneiri's help, we eventually found a man hiding in the shadows. As soon as I saw him, I understood we had found the master. His vile aura revolted me. He surrounded himself with several unnamed djinn, and a large djemon."

"Who was he?"

"By the time we found him, his demon had become so powerful, he no longer controlled the demon. The demon had become the master. He had lost his humanity.

"I could not understand the mindless fervor I found burning within him. I had never seen so many djinn before, and I had never been in the presence of such so large a djemon. The Lakeside Lurker's djemon had evolved into an energy parasite, existing only to feed on the soul energies of his victims. The more it fed, the more powerful it became. By the time we cornered him, the master's mind and morality had vanished, leaving only the brutish shell of a human behind.

"We fought with hammers; the only weapons we possessed. Oneiri and I held off the djemon while my husband fought the master. We held them until the police arrived, but Dirk was wounded."

"What happened to the guy?"

"He died, but not before his djemon delivered my Dirk a mortal wound. There was nothing to be done."

"What happened to the djemon? And all the escaped djinn?"

"I compelled most back into the cavern, and resealed the breach. I documented everything here in my journal."

"You did all that?"

She shrugged. "I am the Hand of Fate."

My phone vibrated again, and this time, I figured I'd better see who it was. Lance, of course. "Sorry, I've got to take this," I explained.

"Let me talk to Mina," he said.

Oh man, I must be late picking her up. I cupped my hand in front of my mouth and hissed my frustration into the phone. "Why didn't you call me? Where are you?"

"She called me. You forgot to pick her up." He sounded pissed.

"Doh! I'm already on my way." This was not the place to be having this conversation. "Look, I absolutely must talk to you, but I can't right now. Call me tonight."

"She's waiting." He hung up.

"Wait!" I stared at the phone for a half a second, tempted to smash it to smithereens, and realized Madame Coumlie and Rhys were staring at me, expecting an explanation. "Sorry. I have to go. I'm late. Wonderful to meet you; really. This has been quite an experience. I'll catch you later." I ran.

By the time I reached the end of the block, the humidity hit me, and I felt like I was running slo-mo through jello. The black sky threatened with the boom of an imminent thunderstorm as I cursed leaving my car parked so far away. I prayed I'd outrun the lightning, and raced back to Mystic Properties.

CHAPTER 16

I ROARED UP to the school, picked up a sulky Mina, and zoomed us over to Eastview Mall as big fat drops pelted the windshield. Taking her to the mall was the least I could do to square things between us. I even let her pick out some lip gloss as penance for making her wait. Mina chose Fairy Berry, while I favored the more sophisticated Ravishing Red. Under ordinary conditions, Lance would kill me for buying her make-up, but since he wasn't around, I decided to live dangerously and take my chances. Mina pranced beside me, delightedly blowing air kisses to all the other shoppers.

She kept trying to tell me about one of the boys in her class, but my thoughts roamed elsewhere. I relived the moment when Madame had summoned her djemon right in front of me. The sight of Oneiri, combined with the old lady's story drove just about every other thought out of my head.

Oneiri dazzled me. I found his physical presence both awesome and exhilarating. I glanced around for my little entourage and noted both Blix and Larry now walked right beside me. Djinn, she'd called them, until they're named. And once commanded, they materialize into djemons. The thought of Blix growing up to be something like Oneiri was beyond my wildest imagination. I'd noticed a fine plush fuzz on his skin, and wondered what it felt like. I wished I would have touched him when I had the chance. I hoped Madame Coumlie would let me pet him.

Yeah, but the souls of their victims is what makes them grow so big. How'd you like to have that on your conscience? A sobering thought. I wondered how many people he'd killed.

Did the FBI know she was a demon master? And she could see all my djinn, where Mina couldn't. Maybe she was my great-grandmother after all. And what had she meant about Sentinel Hill? She couldn't be serious in thinking I'd be able do anything about capturing all those loose djinn, could she? Would Oneiri be helping me? I had so many unanswered questions.

Focus, Mattie. Finding my great-grandmother was all well and good, but her problems were not mine. All I really cared about was getting rid of my stinking djinn. Why hadn't I asked her to banish them when I had a chance? Bang-up job there, Mattie. Why didn't you think of that?

☾

Later that night, after I got Mina tucked in and sound asleep, my mind continued to race. I paced living room instead, waiting impatiently for Lance to call. When someone knocked at the front door, I jumped, thinking it was the guys from House of Cards. But when I peeked out the window, Rhys stood on the doorstep.

I spared myself a quick check in the mirror. Hair and lipstick okay, no stains on my shirt, and the living room picked up; okee doke. I opened the door.

He looked good enough to eat. He'd changed into black jeans and a matching tee shirt.

"Madame asked me to bring you this." He handed me the green journal. "She thought it might come in handy tomorrow. You made quite an impression."

"How did you find me?"

"Lance works on my bike. I've been here before. When you mentioned Mina, I realized you must be his sister."

I flipped through the pages of the journal, dismayed at the cramped, tiny writing. Some of the pages looked to be written in French, or for all I knew, Greek. She'd made tiny drawings in the margins as well. This would take me a while to get through. I put the book down, figuring I'd read it later, and trailed Rhys into the kitchen. He helped himself to a bottle of beer from the fridge, and even knew where Lance kept his bottle opener. The mage took a long swallow, draining half the bottle. Nice arms. The room seemed unusually warm, and sweat trickled from the back of my neck into my shirt. I had a fan on in the living room, but the kitchen was stuffy.

"Here, I brought you something." He pulled a vial out of the pocket of his jeans and unstoppered the brown glass.

I shook my head and frowned. "I don't do drugs."

"This is not a drug." He waved the open vial beneath my nose.

"I've got teratosis, remember? All I can smell is demons. What is it?"

"Essence of sweet orange oil. Completely harmless."

He covered the mouth of the vial with his thumb and gave it a shake. "You trust me?"

I tensed. "What does it do?"

"Maybe nothing. Maybe everything. Close your eyes."

My first instinct was to just say no to the mumbo-jumbo, but after my encounter with Oneiri today, all my internal compass points were out of whack. Why not?

I took a deep breath and closed my eyes. Rhys tilted my head back and anointed a spot in the middle of my forehead, just above my eyebrows.

"This is your third eye." His thumb smoothed the oil gently into my skin. "Clear your thoughts."

I cracked an eye open. "Easy for you to say."

"Relax."

Riight. I pretended I was relaxed.

"Now. Take a deep breath."

I inhaled. The heavy dredge of putrid muck that clogged my sinuses suddenly evaporated, and cool tendrils of silvery relief reached into every cavity within my brain. My eyeballs relaxed into refreshing cool sockets, and even my inner ears tickled with the clarity of sensation.

I shivered with pleasure and grabbed Rhys' hand; burying my nose into his open palm to gulp the heavenly scent of aged leather, beer and mocha spice cake.

Rhys's grin stretched from ear to ear. "You should see your face," he said. He restoppered the vial and handed it to me. "It's yours. Once a day ought to do it."

Tears of relief streamed down my cheeks. My hands trembled and I held the vial to my lips. "Oh my god, I can smell again. How does it work?" Even my eyesight seemed sharper.

"It doesn't always. I'm glad it helped." His eyes focused on my mouth.

"Thank you so much," I closed my eyes and took another deep lungful of air. "You've saved me." The muted scent of djemon still remained, but the intoxicating aroma of sexy mage dominated my senses now. This I could live with.

He licked his lips. "Come by the shop after you drop Mina off in the morning. We'll go check out the cavern."

Reality slapped my euphoria to smithereens. Not my problem. The idea of crawling around in some creepy old cave rated about the same with me as cleaning hair out of a clogged drain.

"Um, about the cave thing, you'll have to go without me. I'm more of a fresh air and sunshine kind of girl."

"You gotta be kidding. Caving is the best fun you can have with your clothes on. You'll love it. You're not afraid of the dark, are you?" He leered at me suggestively and took another long swallow of beer.

I pushed him away. "I kill my own spiders." I tried to remember the mage wasn't my type, but he smelled too damn good, and I couldn't keep the idiotic smile off my face. I felt too wonderful. And with my newly improved vision, I noticed for the first time that Rhys had dimples hiding beneath his Fu-Manchu. Not so badass after all.

"If the Sentinel Hill cavern has been compromised, I'll need to inform the authorities." He drained the rest of his beer in one long gulp and was looking at me like I was next on the menu.

My body responded with a rousing hand of inner applause. Rhys Warrick fairly oozed sex appeal, I realized. In fact, I was noticing all kinds of pleasant aspects of the mage I hadn't considered before. Funny how getting one's sniffer fixed can affect a girl's libido.

"What's so special about Sentinel Hill, anyway?"

"Good question. Four hundred years ago, the local tribes wondered the same thing." He shrugged. "Let's just say some places in the world hold an attraction for the supernatural, and Shore Haven is one of them."

The scent of Rhys' aftershave had me thinking wicked thoughts in spite of myself. I leaned closer. "You mean like New Orleans and Taos?"

He brushed a wisp of hair off my forehead. My hands automatically reached for his stomach, caressing solid muscle through the thin material of his shirt. Oh my. Rock-hard abs jittered beneath my touch, and he moved closer. I closed my eyes and breathed him into me.

"Yeah." He whisper-kissed my neck, and I yearned for more. "Something like that." He nibbled along the edge of my jaw, and breathed into my ear, sending me the shivers. I slipped my hands beneath his shirt and up his velvety chest; caressing soft hair and the hard buttons of his erect nipples. I sighed and he put his mouth on mine.

I was ready for him this time. That kiss melted me right down to my happy spot, and sent pulsations of pleasure though my body. My back arched and my toes curled in appreciation. Man oh man. It was over way too quick, and I opened my eyes to see him grinning at me. He lifted me back to my feet. Yowza.

He grinned. "Wear sturdy shoes tomorrow," he said, and left.

I stood, dazed and motionless for a minute, reliving the memory. Hands down, that had to be the best kiss ever. Whew. I touched my fingers to my still-throbbing lips. He even kissed off all my Ravishing Red lip gloss. I wandered into the living room and stood in front of the fan to cool down. No sooner had I come to my senses, when another knock sounded at the door.

I smiled. Back for more, obviously. I wondered if bedroom aerobics would be an appropriate activity tonight. Definitely not. Especially with Mina sleeping in the next room.

I steeled myself and answered the door. I caught a glimpse of chinos before Hector sucker-punched me in the gut. I crashed to the floor, curled into a fetal position, gasping for air. My only thought was Mina. Hector grabbed me by my arm, lifted me clean off my feet, and backhanded me across the face. I saw my own blood spatter across the wall and sofa.

"Where's your boyfriend?" Hector sounded so calm, he might have been asking after his mother. He hit me again.

I had no breath to answer. I couldn't have told him anyway, I didn't have a clue. He hit me again. And again. And at some point, Mina ran into the living room and started screaming. It was a high, shrill panicked, keening sound. Her eyes stretched wide with terror. I tried to tell her not to worry, but I couldn't catch my breath. I had never felt so helpless. Dimly, I hoped Mina's screaming would bring help. I told her to run, but couldn't get the words out.

Hector leaned over me and I tried to brace myself, but my lungs were too busy fighting for air. Black spots closed in on my vision, and Hector's voice came far away.

"Listen bitch. You better tell your boyfriend he's got twenty-four hours to pay up, or the next time we'll be having this conversation with the kid. Understand?"

I nodded wordlessly. Hector let go of me and I

flopped to the floor like a dead doll. Out of nowhere, the idea dawned on me that as obviously lethal as Oneiri had been, the real monster was Hector. So much for normal. In spite of myself, I started to laugh. I squirmed and rolled; coughing, gasping for air, and laughing, unable to stop myself. Hector seemed offended by this, and after delivering a few more vicious kicks to my ribs, everything went black.

❂

I came to, lying on Lance's sofa. Mina leaned over me, holding my hand and sobbing, her sweet face all red and puffy. I pulled her to me.

"S'okay baby, s'all right. I'm fine." My words came out on little puffs of breath. I attempted to sit up and immediately decided I was much more comfortable where I was. I wondered how I got to the couch.

"Hey there." I recognized the concerned face of Lance's neighbor, Hal Winslow, peering at me over his thick glasses. "You want to tell me what happened here?"

Oh boy. This would be all over the entire Shore about thirty seconds after the bakery opened tomorrow morning. I couldn't tell Hal about Hector or House of Cards. One whisper of Lance's troubles would give Violet all the ammunition she needed to regain full custody of Mina. I needed to think up a story real fast. I sat up slowly, stalling for time.

"Everything's fine," I lied. "Show's over. Nothing to get excited about." Mina clung to me as I got up. My ribs and back hurt, my left eye had swelled shut.

Hal's wife Marie came out of the kitchen wearing

her bathrobe over her nightgown, and powder blue slippers.

"Here you go, Mattie." She handed me a wet compress. "You're still bleeding."

I nodded, and held the cool cloth to my bloody nose, my mind racing to come up with a plausible explanation.

"Let me just get Mina tucked in, and I'll be right back."

Marie and Hal exchanged looks, but I retreated with Mina into her bedroom and closed the door behind us. Mina had stopped crying, but her eyes told me of her fear, and she kept a death grip on my arm. I sat her on the bed, and put my arm around her.

"I thought you were dead," she said, and started to cry again.

"Shhh," I whispered. "I'm okay, but we're not going to stay here tonight. Let me go talk to the Winslows, and then we'll go over to my house to sleep."

"Who was that man?"

"Nobody. He doesn't matter. We're safe now. I'm going to go out and talk to the Winslows and then we'll pack you a bag and we'll go over to my house. You can sleep with me tonight. Will that be okay?"

"He hurt you. I want my dad."

"He'll be home on Sunday." It was as good a guess as any, if I didn't kill him first. "You sit here for a minute." I hugged her as well as I could and went out to face the Winslows.

They both looked pale as they huddled together on the sofa, Marie holding Hal's hand, like a couple of wrinkled teenagers.

"I am sorry for all the bother, really," I said. "Someone slashed my ex-boyfriend's tires, and he thought it was me. He backhanded me and I fell. I guess it just knocked the wind out of me, that's all. I'm sure it looks worse than it is."

"That's the worst lie I ever heard," Hal said, and Marie nodded.

I sighed, knowing that nothing I said would make any difference. "Thank you for not calling the police."

"The guy was already gone when we got here, or I would have. I know Lance is having problems with the ex-wife. Maybe this guy?"

"This had nothing to do with Lance. I'm sorry if my friend alarmed you." I wiped my face and this time the cloth came away blood-free. "I don't want to make a big deal out of this. I'm okay, and I'm sure my friend feels terrible." I tried to smile like it was true.

"Some friend. You ought to think about a restraining order."

"Well, thanks again; I'm fine, and Mina is settling down. I'm grateful for all your help. I appreciate it." I eased them towards the door, and they took the hint. I waited until I saw their lights go out, then got Mina and I packed up and into the car. Five minutes later we were safe at my apartment. I called Lance again, but he still wasn't answering. By the time we got to bed, I didn't think I'd be able to sleep a wink, but Mina and I curled up like kittens and I was gone.

CHAPTER 17

I WOKE UP hurting. My back and ribs had stiffened up, and I had to pee, but not so bad that I wanted to try getting up. The sick feeling in my stomach wasn't from reliving the terror of last night's attack, it was the total lack of emotion behind Hector's promises to hurt Mina that ignited a cold fury within me. I couldn't blame Hector; clearly, the man was a sociopath. No, the true villain here was Lance. If anything happened to Mina, I'd never be able to live with myself. How could my own brother put his daughter through this? How could he?

I sighed and looked at my alarm clock with my good eye. Almost time to get Mina ready for school. I braced myself and rolled over to the edge of the bed, trying to stifle my groans. Blix and Larry lay curled up next to me on the bed, while the rest of the herd gave me a glassy-eyed stare from across the room.

"Is it time to get up?"

"Yes, sweetie. And after school, today we're going to go see your dad." I got up and headed for the bathroom, swerving toward the living room when my cell phone rang. It was Lance.

"Well it's about time. What the hell is going on," I demanded. "And why haven't you called me? Last night your buddy Hector showed up and beat the crap out of me."

Dead silence answered from the other end of the phone.

"Don't you dare hang up on me, Lance. Hector said that if you don't pay up by today, they're coming back for Mina. Now I want some answers, and I want them now."

"Is she okay?" His voice was just a whisper.

"No, she's not okay, she's traumatized. She was all alone watching me get my ass kicked last night. I'm not okay either, thanks for asking." I caught sight of myself reflected in the toaster. I had a shiner as big as Ralph Wilson Stadium. A scab crusted over my split lip, and my cheek was swollen red and purple. "And why the hell do you owe money to The House of Cards?"

"It's not what you think." He sounded bad, but I didn't care. I was too pissed off.

"Well maybe you better tell me what's going on, because I've about had it. Bunny Tacker told me she saw you shooting pool the other night. You lied to me. You're not out of town. Where the hell are you?"

"I need to stay lost for a few days. I'm out at the faire."

Of course. Lance worked weekends at the Renaissance Festival out in Sterling. He'd been out there every summer since high school and was one of the few actors that got paid to perform. I didn't remember what role he was playing this year, but he was often the sword master or the Queen's Champion or some such thing. The fair ran every weekend through the end of August. A few rustic cabins housed the paid actors.

"Mattie, are you still there?"

"Yeah."

"You sound different."

"Yeah, well I'm not the same person I was yesterday." Mina stood in the doorway and I attempted to regain some measure of composure, for her sake. "We can't stay at your place. For now, we're at my apartment. I've got to take her to school in a few minutes, but I want some answers, Lance. After last night, I'm not sure she should even go to school today."

"Is that daddy? Let me talk to him." Mina's scrubbed face looked so clean and eager, I wanted to cry.

"Just a minute. There's Lucky Charms in the cupboard. Pour some for me too, okay?" Her face scrunched up, but I held up a finger. "You can talk to him in just as soon as I'm done."

I hobbled towards the bathroom, and shut the door. Lance said, "Let me talk to her."

"In a minute. Tell me what's going on."

"I'm just helping out a friend, that's all."

"What kind of friend, Lance, a loan shark? Hector told me that if you don't pay them, they're coming back for Mina." My voiced cracked. "They're coming tonight, Lance. Doesn't that mean anything to you?"

"Look, they're not going to bother you again, I promise. Now let me talk to her," he said.

I wanted to scream. "You're not answering me. You're gambling again. I know you are, so you can stop lying right now. You have no right to put your family through this. I'm not sure Mina should even be living with you. You are not safe." I didn't like threatening him, but I didn't need to justify anything where Mina's safety was concerned. "I'd rather see her with Violet."

"I am not going to do this over the phone, Matt.

121

Bring Mina out here after school and we'll talk. Don't tell anybody where I am. Please."

"They probably already know."

"Not these guys. They're not local."

My heart ached to hear him talk like this again, and scared me even more. "What are you doing with these people Lance?" If he owed money to the mob, I didn't know what I would do. I couldn't imagine my world without him, but I had to keep Mina safe.

"Look, I'll tell you tonight, I promise. Don't worry. Let me talk to Mina."

❦

As the warm water of the shower rinsed the dried blood away, I scrubbed at the black sickle mark on my hand. In spite of my best efforts, it wouldn't come off. My whole body was black and blue. Fist-shaped purple and red bruises seeped across my ribs and back and upper arms. I got out of the shower and inspected the damage to my swollen face with my good eye. On one hand, the huge shiner overshadowed the split lip. On the other hand, the huge shiner overshadowed just about everything.

I remembered my promise to Rhys to accompany him to the bat cave after I dropped Mina off at school. That is, if a kiss and a promise were the same thing. I recalled the buttery feeling he'd left in my legs, and I was pretty sure that it was. Well, one look at my face would put an end to those ideas.

Gingerly, I dressed in jeans and boots and a tee shirt, and immediately started to sweat. Although we'd had a few sprinkles yesterday, the impending storm was holding off and the humid air wasn't going anywhere until it broke.

I looked around for my gang of followers and frowned. I now had more than a dozen djinn. Their presence weighed on me. I wanted to get rid of them in the worst way, but somehow they'd dropped lower on the priority list. Thankfully, the oil Rhys had given me made a big difference. I hardly even noticed the smell. I sighed and headed into the kitchen.

Mina and I were halfway through our bowls of soggy cereal when someone pounded on the door downstairs. We both jumped, and she started to shake. "Don't answer! Maybe they'll go away."

I forced myself to remain calm in order to reassure Mina. Poor thing hadn't asked for any of this.

"No worries." I kissed her and eased her back into her chair. "It's probably just my landlady," I lied. I went downstairs and checked the peephole before answering. Sheriff Reynolds in uniform and two suits squeezed together on my porch.

Oh great. The Winslows must have called the cops after all. I opened the door.

"Can I help you," I asked.

Sheriff Reynolds stared at my shiner like I was some kind of monster. "What the hell happened to you?"

"Nothing. Just an accident."

"The mayor said you weren't hurt."

Oh lord, give me strength. He was referring to the scooter crash. I blushed to my toes. "No, this happened yesterday. I um, did this myself. Walked into a door."

Three cop faces stared back at me and obviously not one of them believed me.

"Is this a social call?" I asked, as innocently as

I could. "I wasn't expecting visitors. I need to get my niece to school this morning."

One of the suits took his identification out of his jacket pocket and handed it to me.

"Matilda Blackman? I'm Agent Thomas, and this is Agent Duran. May we come in?" Their identification said FBI.

"What? I already talked to the other agent. He told me there's nothing more I need to do."

The three men looked at each other.

"What are you talking about?" Reynolds asked. He had dark circles under his eyes and his clothes looked like they'd been slept in. I was surprised to see him on duty so soon after losing his wife, but I supposed no one would have dared to keep him out of the investigation. "Who did you talk to?"

"Agent Porter," I said. "He already debriefed me. Don't you guys talk to each other?"

The two FBI guys smirked and I gathered that they didn't think much of Paranormal Control Officer Porter.

"We're here on official business, Miss Blackman," said Duran. "May we come in?"

"What's this about, Sheriff? I really need to get going."

"We're trying to locate Lance McNair. I understand he's your brother?"

My heart skittered and I eased to the porch, closing the door behind me. I didn't want Mina to hear anything before I knew what was going on.

"What's happened?"

"Do you know where he is," Duran said.

"Is he here?" asked Thomas.

"Um. I don't know where he is. What's happened?"

"Nothing too serious, we have a few questions for him that's all."

"We're following up on a tip," said Thomas.

"What's this about?"

"We're investigating several murders in the area. Your brother's name has come up."

The realization of why they were here finally hit me. I grabbed the porch railing, my heart beating about a million miles an hour.

"You guys are with the Night Shark taskforce."

"He hasn't been at work for several days."

Two days, and they send out the FBI? "There's some kind of mistake. He's been out of town for a couple of days. I'm babysitting his daughter. You're wrong about Lance."

"He was seen loitering near one of the dump sites. We'd like to talk to him."

"You mean at the Spanky Kleen? You've been talking to Heckle and Jeckle." How could they even think of Lance as the killer? "This is ridiculous. My car had a flat, and Lance helped me change the tire. End of story."

The men exchanged glances. Had I said the wrong thing?

"Have you seen or spoken to him since?"

"Hey, you're making a big mistake. I need to go now. Mina's going to be late."

Duran handed me his card. "Please tell him to get in touch with us as soon as possible. We'd like to talk to him."

"Of course." I nodded and took the card. "I'll have him call you." I went back inside and locked the door, trying to catch my breath. I'd told more lies in the last three days than in my entire life.

CHAPTER 18

I DROPPED MINA off at school, but couldn't shake the hunch that she was in danger. She would be safer in her classroom than with me, but the thought of leaving her bugged me anyway. I checked out my black and purple reflection again in the rear-view mirror. Ugh. Well, at least I had a good excuse to get out of this little caving adventure. Rhys didn't need me, anyway. One look at my face would be enough. Then I could hang around the school until Mina got out, a much better choice.

The memory of Rhys' kiss came back to me. Further exploration in that area was tempting, but I hadn't actually promised Rhys I would go. He had kissed an implied agreement out of me, but he wouldn't be expecting me to actually show up, would he? True, the memory of that sort-of promise was hard to forget, and gawd amighty, he smelled good. Anyway, my ribs were killing me and I still had oozy scabs all over my knees, so crawling around in some dark bat cave with the mage wouldn't be pleasant.

I zipped into the alley behind Mystic Properties and parked next to a shiny black pickup. I got out of the car just as Rhys emerged from the back door of the shop. He carried a box full of gear, and did a double take when he got a glimpse at my shiner.

I blushed, feeling self-conscious.

Rhys came closer to inspect the damage. His face darkened as he examined my bruises, but didn't ask.

"I'm not going. You don't need me anyway."

"Bullshit." He walked past me and lowered the tailgate. "I can't go without you. I can't see the djinn. If they're loose, I need you to spot them."

Oh, right. "You can sense them, though."

He threw the box into the back, slammed the gate; then came around and jerked open the passenger door for me.

"What are you mad at?" I didn't want to go, but backing out was not going to be as easy as I thought. "How did this become my problem?"

His jaw twitched. "Does Mina see your djemons?"

I gasped. "How did you know?"

"You are not the only person in Shore Haven who is attracting djinn, Mattie. If Mina can see your djemons, chances are she's also got enough juice to attract djinn of her own. These loose djinn represent a serious problem for the whole community. How long before Mina, or any other intuitive, start to name them? To use them? Anyone with a manifested demon is considered a terrorist in the eyes of the federal government. Demon masters don't get tried in the courts Mattie; they're executed. Is that what you want?"

Icy cold ran through my veins. "We have to do this, don't we?"

He gave me a curt nod. "Your chariot awaits, my lady."

I sighed, and forced myself to clamber up into the cab. Why men always seemed to drive giant trucks made no sense to me. I fastened my seatbelt.

"We need to make a quick stop; I've got something I need to take care of." He started the engine.

"No, you're right. This can't wait. We do the cave thing first."

"This stop is on the way."

"Where are we going?"

"The hospital. They've got something trapped in the basement."

"What?"

"We'll soon find out."

"Why did they call you?"

"You sure ask a lot of questions."

Interesting.

We drove down Third and headed toward the hospital. Third is the main thoroughfare running through Shore Haven's commercial district. The street veers to the east, off Seneca, and dead-ends at the Russ Meat Packing Plant in Germantown, at the north end of Shore Haven. The town founder, Helmut Russ bought much of the land in the 1700s and built a meat packing plant where Sentinel Hill meets the water.

St. Agrippa's Hospital sat on the corner of 5th and St. Julian, which served as the dividing line between Shore Haven and Germantown. The hospital sat across from St. Peter's Catholic Church, and was one of the oldest buildings still standing in the Shore. Not on a par with more modern hospitals, but the Russ family donated the land, and the family still funded maintenance for the place.

We parked in the visitor lot. Out of the back of the truck, Rhys grabbed a pole with a noose on one end, and a small cat carrier, which he handed to me.

I nodded toward the pole thingy. "What's that?"

"Snake stick."

"They have a snake?"

He didn't answer and had longer legs than me, so I had to hurry to catch up. My ribs protested.

Curiosity gnawed at me. "I'm not scared of snakes or anything, but I wasn't exactly expecting to be wrangling anything today, that's all."

I hustled through the main lobby after him and we waited for the elevator. People eyed Rhys and the snake stick, me and my black eye and crate, and kept their distance. Nobody got into the elevator with us, so our ride down to the 3rd level basement went uninterrupted.

The janitor is waiting for us," Rhys said. "All you need to do is hold the carrier for me and be ready when I drop the whatever inside."

The doors opened, and we faced an overheated forest of ductwork, pipes and furnace. Rhys seemed to know where he was going and turned to the right, heading down an aisle framed by massive plumbing and machinery. In the distance, heavy metal music screamed over the drone of generators. Dim fluorescent lighting gave the place a hellish glow.

A few turns later, we arrived at a tiny office where a guy sat with his feet up on his desk, reading a car-racing magazine. The guy did a double take when he saw my purpled face and turned down the tunes.

"Hey, that was fast." His shirt had an oval patch with the name, Terry, embroidered in red letters.

Rhys introduced me. "This is my assistant, Mattie."

"Hi," I said, and like a dope, held up the cat crate. He nodded, and led us through the warren of the engineering room to a metal stairwell, which led to a lower level.

"It's not a rat," he said to Rhys. "And something has been chewing on the electric cables. I'm worried about fire."

We followed Terry down the stairs to the sub-basement. The thrum of machines seemed quieter here; the lighting dimmer too. We walked past row after row of metal file cabinets.

"I was afraid it was going to chew its foot off and get away, so I covered him with a garbage can."

"Good thinking." Sure enough, at the end of the row, a metal garbage can sat upended on the cement floor with a big hunk of iron pipe sitting on top.

Terry slapped the side of the can, and the trapped creature inside responded with the sound of scrabbling and hissing.

Terry grinned. "Pretty pissed off, huh."

"Thanks Terry. We'll take it from here."

"Fine by me. Swing by the office on your way out. I'd like to know what it is."

Rhys nodded, and Terry didn't wait around. I began to worry about what was under the garbage can.

"So is it a snake or a rat or what?"

Rhys removed the heavy piece of pipe, holding his hand firmly on top of the can as the scrabbling inside increased. "We'll wait a few minutes for it to calm down a bit."

"What are you going to do?"

"You worried?" He grinned.

"No. Maybe. A little."

We waited for the angry sounds underneath the can to quiet down. He motioned me a few feet back, and with the snake stick in one hand, he tipped up the edge of the can just a teeny bit.

Instantly, a black nose and a pair of needle-like claws appeared and scrabbled to get out.

I gasped. "What the hell is that," I asked, but I already knew the answer.

"Get ready." He tilted the can, and the jaws and head of the thing squeezed through the gap. Rhys lowered the rim, trapping the head just behind the ears. The ugly thing hissed and wiggled, but Rhys applied enough pressure to hold it in place. He slipped the noose-end of the pole over the creature's exposed head.

I opened the plastic crate, and moved as close as I dared, holding the open cage in front of me.

"Set the carrier on the floor with the door open at the top," he instructed. "Get those gloves on, and have the towel ready. When I pull him out, he's going to be fighting mad. I want you to wrap the towel around him, and help me lower him into the crate. When I tell you, shut the door and lock it, but not until I tell you."

I nodded and did as instructed. The thing screeched like a banshee, its anger directed at the towel in my hands.

"Here we go."

Rhys pushed back the trashcan, and lifted the thing up by the noose around its neck. The creature was a dusky black in color, save for a ring of yellow around his black pupils, and a few bristly grey sprouted hairs, but the overall impression was nasty opossum road-kill. The creature thrashed furiously, whipping the air with a long naked tail, a large rattrap attached to one of its front feet. Its fury filled the basement.

"It's not going to fit," I said.

"Sure he will." He pinned the creature's head to the cement floor and its squeals escalated to an ear-splitting volume. "Throw the towel over his back and grab him. Hold him down."

Yikes. Adrenaline pounded through me. I took a deep breath and flung myself on top of the thing, trapping it mostly between the towel and my hands. Two-inch claws and serrated teeth tried to reach me. If I let go, no doubt I'd be slashed to ribbons. The tail whipped around frantically, as the body squirmed beneath the towel. With one hand, I gripped the thing across the back, just in front of the front legs, and with my other, I grabbed it just above the tail at the haunches. It was so thin, I had no problem holding it securely. The feverish heat of its rage soaked through the towel.

"I've got him."

"You ready?"

"Yeah."

He lifted the thing up by its head with the pole, and I followed his movements, holding the writhing body over the open carrier door.

"Tail first," he said.

Stiff-armed, I forced the lower half of the thing into the plastic crate. I let go, and Rhys pushed the rest of the creature inside, holding it down with the snake stick. I closed the wire door against the catch pole.

"Okay, be ready to slam it, I'm going to loosen the noose."

"I got it."

I kept the pressure on the door, and Rhys released the noose and drew the pole out of the box. I slammed the door and turned the lock mechanism. We both stepped back as the thing continued to fight and scream.

I breathed a sigh of relief. "Whew, I'm glad that's over." My arms stung where the naked tail slapped welts across my bare skin.

Rhys picked up the towel that had fallen to the floor and draped it over the opening to the carrier. The opossum-thing quieted down right away.

"Bollocks." Rhys stared at a spot over my head. An identical opossum creature glared at us from on top of one of the file cabinets, two rows away.

I flinched. "Look, there's two of them." I pointed to another one, peering out at us from end of the row. "We're going to need more, um stuff."

Rhys swore and picked up the cat carrier, being careful to keep the towel over the front. I followed, carrying the snake pole and the rest of our gear. We stopped by Terry's office on the way out, and Rhys told him that we'd be back to set more traps. Terry paled, and nodded.

"I suggest you keep people out of the records room for a while," Rhys said.

"Shouldn't be a problem. What are they?" Terry's question echoed my own.

"Rats," Rhys answered. "A non-native species from Micronesia. Don't know how they got here, but maybe somebody's pet, or escaped from the zoo."

"You're saying they're somebody's pets?"

"Oh sure. People are crazy for these exotics. Then they get tired of them, and let them loose. Don't worry, we'll get 'em taken care of for you, no problem." Rhys headed toward the elevator, and I scurried along behind, not wanting to stay a minute longer. The sounds of machinery drowned out Terry's protests.

We rode the elevator in silence, ignoring the stares

of the curious as we headed through the reception area and out to the truck. Rhys put the cat carrier on the bench seat between us. I waited until we exited the parking lot before I said anything.

"That is not a rat."

"And we have a winner," he said, grinning at me. "Care to try for double Jeopardy, where the prizes are even bigger?"

"It's a materialized djemon, right?"

"Yep."

"So this thing has a name? Could it hurt someone? Could it kill?"

Rhys didn't answer right away. "Well, they're quick and stealthy; they have unnatural strength for their size. This one and the others we saw are still pretty small, but I think a sedated person in a hospital bed wouldn't have much of a chance."

The thought gave me the shivers. "Remind me to never wind up at St. Agrippa's. Why did they call you?"

"Mystic Properties has a contract with the hospital for vermin control. You did a good job back there, Mattie. Thanks."

I basked in the compliment. "This isn't the first one you've caught."

"Nope." Rhys turned right at 6th Street, which rimmed the lower edge of Sentinel Hill. The road rose before us, the pavement eventually giving way to packed dirt. We bounced along, and the caged demon hissed with each jolt. Rhys stopped the truck in front of a locked gate stretching across the road. He got out and pulled a large ring of keys from his pocket, selected a key, and unlocked the gate. We drove through and continued our drive up the hill, after he locked the gate behind us.

"I'm asking for an explanation here, Rhys. At least two more of those things are running loose in the basement of St. Agrippa's. How did that happen? Does the FBI know? Wait a second." The hairs on my scalp prickled. "Could a djemon made flesh be the serial killer?"

"That's what I think, although the djemon would have to be much larger than the one we caught today. If the killer is a demon master, he's had that djemon a long time. It takes decades for one to get big enough to do any real damage. My guess is that the big one has gotten too powerful to control. In that case, the master may have started naming new demons."

I felt sick. "Have you told Porter?"

"Of course. He was with me when I caught the first one. Let's just say the local field office doesn't think much of Frank Porter or his theories."

I sat back in my seat, stunned. We'd stopped at another gate, this one merely a locked chain across the track. Rhys unlocked this one too, and we drove through, and again, he locked the chain back into place behind us.

"One of the first victims found was a registered demon master. So was the most recent, Joanne Reynolds. But all the most recent victims were individuals known in the AI community to have unregistered demons. All the paranormals and supernaturals want this guy caught, but they dare not expose themselves to federal scrutiny, so as far as the FBI is concerned, the two demon master deaths aren't significant. But I think the Night Shark is using a demon to kill demon masters."

"I thought the FBI kept track of all the demon masters."

Rhys smirked. "The FBI doesn't know everything Mattie, and the anomalous community here in Shore Haven wants to keep it that way. Most demon masters keep their identity, as well as their demons, a secret. Law enforcement in this town is particularly suspicious and antagonistic toward the supernatural, and the AIs cannot afford to risk exposure."

"Didn't you show them the djemons?"

"Sure. They said the same thing you did. How can something so small be dangerous? And to be honest, the first one we caught was about half the size of this one here. None of the injuries on any of the victims found so far match up with the bite radius of any known djemons. If the killer is a djemon, it's big. The FBI insists the marks on the victims are man-made, but they can't identify the tool yet, and so far, no DNA has been found. But djemons don't have DNA. They're animated, but not alive. There are no skin cells, saliva, or hairs shed."

Goosebumps rolled up my arms.

Rhys stopped the truck and turned off the engine. "From here we walk. Come on, I've got coveralls and gear in the back." He grabbed the cat carrier and I stepped out into the sultry wilderness on Sentinel Hill. The forest dripped with moisture, a mist of sweat flies surrounded us.

Rhys handed me a set of white coveralls, a pair of scuffed leather gloves, and kneepads. "These belong to a friend of mine. She's about your size."

They were clean, at least. I tried to get them on over my jeans, but they wouldn't button. I told Rhys not to look, and hid on the other side of the truck, while I took off my pants and put on the coveralls. They were still snug on the bottom, and way too big on the top. I had to roll the pant legs up four times. The giant cavewoman must be built like Barbie. Great.

Rhys passed me a miner's hardhat and showed me how to work the headlight, then slung his daypack over one shoulder, and grabbed the cat carrier.

"Come on, it's not far."

I followed him through wet woods toward the entrance of the cave, a million questions poised on the tip of my tongue.

"Do you know where you're going?"

"Been here a few times."

"Shouldn't Agent Porter be with us?"

"Frank's a big guy. He can't fit through the entrance. That's why he gave me the keys."

Sweat trickled from my hair into the collar of my coveralls. Rhys set a brisk pace, and I had to trot to keep up with him. Ten minutes later, we emerged into a rocky clearing.

"Here we are." Rhys rummaged around in his pack until he came out with a couple of small flashlights and handed one to me.

"You ready?"

I looked around, but didn't see anything. "Where is the entrance?"

Rhys pointed to our feet.

CHAPTER 19

"YOU HAVE GOT to be kidding."

The half-hidden entrance wasn't much more than a crack in the ground between two rough granite boulders. I'd imagined something grander; more along the lines of an Open Sesame kind of entrance. Anchored to the surrounding rocks, a sturdy grate covered the aperture and must have been in place for a long time. The lock looked shiny new.

Rhys grinned like an idiot as he unlocked the gate and turned on his headlamp. I did the same, my discomfort growing every second.

"Take it slow, mind your head." He sat down at the fissure opening, dangled his legs, eased the cat carrier through, then lowered his body feet first and disappeared from sight.

I took a deep breath, and exhaled slowly. What was I doing here, anyway? Crawling into a hole in the ground with a guy I barely knew? Sure, he's a great kisser and all, but what if I got lost and couldn't find my way out? What if something happened? Mina would be left at school again, and no one would even know where to look for me. Hell, I could be dead.

"Mattie?" Rhys scraped his way back to the entrance. Things sounded pretty tight inside. I bet Agent Porter wasn't the only person who couldn't fit through the entrance. I bet Cavewoman Barbie didn't fit either.

Rhys's face popped into view from beneath me. "I thought you weren't afraid of the dark?"

"I'm not."

"What's the problem?"

I didn't answer.

He hoisted himself out of the entrance with a grunt, and approached me with a small coil of blue nylon cord in his hand.

Instinctively, I backed away. For a half-minute of eternity, I wondered if Rhys could be the Night Shark.

He froze, his green eyes twinkling.

I pointed at him. "Don't you laugh at me. I just remembered, I need to make a phone call, that's all. You know, in case I'm late."

"Cell phone service doesn't work up here, Mattie. I should have said something earlier. Don't worry. We'll be back in time for you to pick up Mina."

Panic flooded through me. "What's the rope for?" I thought about running back to the truck, but Rhys had the keys. No one would ever find me.

"Come 'ere." He grabbed me by the baggy front of the coveralls, pulled me toward him, and wrapped a length of the nylon cord around my waist before I could react. He tied a fancy knot and gave a it a tug.

"There. Now you can't get lost or separated from me." He tied the other end around his own waist, using the same knot. "Better?"

Oh. Good thing I hadn't made a total fool of myself. What a ninny. "I'm not scared."

"Most people get scared the first time." He grinned that bad boy grin again. "This part of the country is riddled with caves. I wish I could take you someplace special for your first time, but as caves go, this one's not bad. Once we get inside, you'll be fine. You okay?"

I'd met Rhys less than twenty-four hours ago. I chewed the inside of my lip. "Yeah."

"Liar."

I had to do this. I took a deep breath. "No, I'm ready. Let's go."

Rhys lowered himself into the darkness. He flashed his light around to show me what it looked like.

"Any bugs in there?"

He gave an encouraging tug to the line around my waist.

"Come on, girlie. Time's a wasting. Who needs bugs? We've got monsters to find." The little-boy-chasing-pirates look on his face sold me. Plain and simple, this guy loved crawling around in the dark. I'd be as safe with him as anybody. And he was right about the monsters.

I descended into the portal.

❦

The narrow passageway led downward. Loose rocks and scree made the trail dicey, and the low ceiling made forced us to crawl or walk hunched over. Rhys showed me the best handholds, and we made good progress. The cold sank right into my bones, and I wished I'd brought a jacket. I was glad for the rope connecting me to Rhys.

Now that I was down here, the cave didn't bother me. I couldn't understand the allure, but I even turned off my headlamp. With Rhys leading the way, and Blix and Larry and the gang bringing up the rear with their eerie eye-glow, I felt like I was part of some strange underground safari. If worst came to worst and the lights went out, there was more than enough light from my weird little herd to guide me back to the entrance. A reassuring thought.

We alternated between creeping, crawling, and sidling our way through the dry tunnels. The few tight spots we encountered had been harder on Rhys than me.

"Sooo. Have you been here with Miss Cavewoman?"

"Why do you ask?" I heard the amusement in his voice.

"Just curious. Based on this custom rig of hers, I wondered if she would have the same problem as agent Porter."

"This is official business. I wouldn't bring her here."

"But if you did. Would she make it past the entrance?"

"You jealous?" He grunted his way through another narrow spot. "Careful, you'll need to step up to get through here."

"Not at all. I'm a natural girl. I don't need any artificial enhancements." I squeezed through the narrow spot without grunting.

"Okay cave girl. Turn on your headlamp and take a look."

We reached a spacious chamber, about forty feet across. The cold air sharpened here, and I shivered in the draft.

"I smell licorice," I said. "Pretty strong." I had gotten used to the muted scent of my own flock, so I hadn't noticed the stink had gradually grown stronger as we edged our way along.

A row of cat crates lined up against one wall of the cave, and each one, I assumed, contained a captured djemon made flesh. Rhys set the new crate down next to the others.

"What are they doing here?" I crouched down to get a better look. Five pair of luminous eyes stared back at me from homely faces. Two of them hissed at me.

"This is where they stay. They can't get out, and no one can get to them so they're safe."

"But you can't leave them here. How can they live?"

"They're not alive. Not like you think. They don't eat or sleep. They don't die. They exist to obey the demon master who named them. Until the government figures out what to do with them officially, they stay here."

"What if their master calls them?"

Rhys shrugged. "So far, none have escaped. Either he's forgotten about them, or they're not strong enough to get out."

I shivered. "I can't imagine a worse thing than spending my life locked up in the dark. It seems so wrong."

"You're anthropomorphizing. These creatures are eternal, Mattie, like a rock or stone. Whether they're sealed up in the cavern or in a crate doesn't matter. And they're too dangerous to be let loose. Come on, I want to show you something."

I followed him into the next cavern, and where he pointed out murals of primitive graffiti painted on the walls all around us. In the light from our headlamps, a series of silhouetted figures and creatures danced across the sooty walls of the cavern.

I stared in awe. "Oh wow, I've never seen anything like this."

"This one depicts the story of a major battle between the indigenous local spirits and the ancestors of the Senequois people. Here the tribal shamans are driving the spirits into the caves and imprisoning them beneath this hill."

I sensed the chaos and fear of the tribesmen as they battled the strange spirit figures. The energy of the conflict was palpable. "They're beautiful."

We approached the cave wall, but Rhys cautioned me from touching the mural's surface.

"The images are incredibly fragile. These two here, are the shamans of the village. Medicine men. They're chasing the djinn back under the hill. This part here depicts the ceremony of celebration, after the tribesmen seal the cave, and to the left here, are warnings not to disturb the spirits within."

"The colors are so bright."

"You're one of only a half-dozen people on the planet who has seen these images since the ancestors of the Senequois first painted them."

"So where's the sealed cave?" The temperature in the caves had to be close to freezing.

"This way," he said, and headed to the left.

"Wait a second. The djinn smell is coming from over there." I pointed into the darkness in the other direction.

"I don't smell anything." He shrugged. "There's not much over there. Let's check the seal first."

"You go. I want to check this out." I was already halfway across the cavern when the cord on my waist pulled taut. I started to untie it, but Rhys stopped me.

"Nobody goes exploring alone. That's rule number one." He retied the knot I'd undone, and checked it again.

"Yeah, but there's something over there. I can smell djinn, Rhys. I just want to look." I felt certain another entrance was close by. "Besides, this place isn't that big. I won't get lost."

"We stick together. There are a few cracks in the wall over there. They lead to the bat cave. You won't be able to get through, Mattie. The fissure is too small, even for you. Come on. We'll check the seal first, and we can check those cracks on the way back. That's what we're here for, remember?"

Focus, Mattie. "Okay, you're right. Lead on, captain."

A short time later, we reached yet another locked grate. Rhys searched his key ring again for the correct key and unlocked the grate, then slipped the lock into his pocket.

"This is the last gate, up ahead."

"Why are you taking the lock with us?"

"I wouldn't want to get locked in here by accident."

After all we'd been through to get here, the thought that we might not be alone worried me. We passed through the entrance and the path widened enough to allow us to walk side-by-side. We arrived at the seal a few minutes later. An irregular chunk of concrete and metal looked to have been poured into a crevice less than a foot wide. Rhys took off his gloves and ran his hands over the rock face, searching for cracks. Rhys grunted, apparently satisfied.

"Is the seal intact?"

"Appears to be. If the seal hasn't been breached, the influx of djinn into the Shore didn't come from here. But we are back to square one with where those djinn are coming from."

"You mean maybe they got kicked out of someplace else and moved here?"

"I don't think so. This whole area has been a magnet for spirits since before the first humans arrived. It doesn't make sense to me that a new population would move in. At least without someone noticing. Let's take a look at what you smelled in the main cavern."

After re-locking the grate, we returned to the main cavern. I followed my nose to the far wall of the cave, and stopped beneath a fissure some ten inches above my head.

"Here. This is where the odor is most intense. It's almost overwhelming, really. You can feel a draft blowing through here, too." I took my glove off, and held my hand in front of the gap. "Can't you smell it?"

"We can't get through. I explored this chimney with a scope a few years ago. The crack leads downwards for eight feet or so, and opens into to a fair-sized cavern. Other than a big colony of bats, there's nothing there. I never found any other exit."

I was itching to get into that tunnel. "Boost me up, Rhys. Let me try."

"Nobody goes anywhere alone. In case you hadn't noticed, there's no rescue crew or cell phone service down here."

"No, no, it's okay. I just want to look. I've got to, Rhys. Come on, give me a boost."

I pulled on his collar until he bent down and I stepped into his hands. I gripped the edge of the tunnel as he boosted me up, and brought me high enough to see inside.

The stench of anise, bat urine, and guano smacked me back. Rhys was right about the crevice; the rock floor slanted sharply downwards. The entrance was tight, but definitely doable. Now that I was here, I couldn't stop myself. I had to see.

"Higher," I said and he raised me up another half a foot. I leveraged my elbows over the edge of the crack and pulled myself forward far enough to squeeze my shoulders through. "Give me a push. I know I can make it."

I thought for a minute he wasn't going to, and I started to wiggle forward on my own. Then strong hands grabbed my legs and pushed my hips through. Blood rushed to my head. I was nearly vertical. I was lying on my stomach in the tunnel, Rhys's hands on my ankles.

Rhys tugged at the line around my waist. "This cord isn't strong enough to hold your weight. If you fall, I'm not sure it will hold you."

"I have to look, Rhys; there is something in here. I have to."

"I'm serious Mattie. No fooling around."

"I smell a boatload of djinn in here, Rhys. Of the two of us, I'm the only one that can fit through and see if they're in here. Isn't this why you brought me?"

After a long moment, he patted my boots. "You win. Keep three points of your body in contact with the surface at all times."

As I inched forward, the tension on the cord around my waist increased. The smell of licorice and ammonia was choking. Rhys gripped the sole of one boot, but from my vantage point, I couldn't see the cave floor. The end of the tunnel was still a foot away. My hands stretched out in front of me, and I figured I would need to get my face close to the entrance in order to see the floor of the cavern. Once I did that, my hands wouldn't be able to push me back. The light from my headlamp reflected off the cave wall opposite, some hundred feet away. I noticed a few bats flying around, but unless I inched toward the mouth of the tunnel, I wouldn't be able to see anything else.

"Let go, Rhys. I need to get closer."

Instead, his grip on my boot shifted and he began pulling me back.

"If I let go, you're going to fall. You won't be able to get back and that cord isn't going to hold you."

I had to see what I already knew was inside that cavern waiting for me. I felt an irresistible pull, which had nothing to do with gravity, and everything to do with compulsion. I had to scratch that itch.

"No!" I kicked away his hand. Immediately, the startled bats went crazy. They swarmed the cave, seeking to escape; several flew into the tunnel and banged into me. The crevice was too narrow to protect my face with my hands; the best I could do was turn my face into my shoulder until the bats settled down.

Rhys yelled at me, which only made things worse. The stench was awful, but I needed to check out the cavern floor. Without Rhys holding my boot, gravity dragged me closer to the entrance. I was so close.

I inched forward. My hands and elbows cleared the lip of the tunnel, and dangled uselessly into the thin air in front of me. It wasn't until my chin reached the edge that I could see the bottom. Satisfaction bloomed within me. I knew it. Even through the swarms of bats, the entire floor of the huge cavern was covered with thousands and thousands of djinn.

Ahhh. I knew it. I switched off my headlamp and some thirty feet below me, the glowing eyes of thousands of djinn lit up the blackness. They must have been there for centuries. Like an invisible army. In a far corner, at the very edge of my vision, I spotted two materialized djemons, seated on a small cot next to an old camp stove. I strained forward for a better look, and began to slide forward.

Panic shot through me. "Pull me back, pull me back," I called to Rhys. I braced my legs against the walls of the tunnel, but the weight of gravity was against me. The pressure from the line around my waist, increased. My useless arms waved helplessly in front of me, unable to help.

"Let go, I'll pull you up."

The line bit into me, and I feared it would snap. "I can't, I'll fall."

"I've got you. But you've got to stop bracing yourself. Make yourself small, and I'll pull you up. Do it, Matt. Trust me."

I fought to control my fear. Blood pounded in my brain, I was certain to fall headfirst and break my neck. What had I been thinking?

Get a grip Mattie. I took a deep breath, then forced myself go as small and limp as possible.

Steady pressure on the line dug into me as the thin rope took my weight. I tried to tell myself the nylon cord was strong enough to hold me, but worried that the rock could cut right through such a light line in no time.

Inch by scraping inch, Rhys pulled me up the chimney. First my shoulder, then my elbows pulled back up to where they touched inside the walls again, and I was able to help Rhys as he hoisted me back in. My view of the cavern floor disappeared. As soon as my hands were inside, I thrashed about for leverage.

"Damn it, girl, don't fight me," Rhys yelled. The bats got riled up again with all the yelling, and I had to force myself to remain limp. Each pull dragged me farther up into the tunnel, and eventually, I sort of reverse caterpillared myself to help. When Rhys grabbed my feet, I sobbed with relief. He dragged me free of the tunnel in one long pull and I fell into his arms.

He hugged me tight, breathing hard and planted a kiss on my forehead.

Shivering with cold and fear, I hugged him back, savoring the heat of his body.

"You had me going there for a minute."

I couldn't stop shaking. "I saw hundreds in there, Rhys. Thousands. And someone's been inside. There's a chair and camp stove set up. What do we do?"

In the yellow glare of the lamps, his eyes gleamed cold as he considered what I'd said. "There must be another entrance. What did the journal say?"

"What journal?"

"Madame Coumlie's. What did it say?"

Oops. "I didn't get a chance to read it. Sorry."

He gave me a look. "Well, read it. We'll talk to her tonight and figure out what to do."

Oh man. I was planning to have my showdown with Lance tonight. "Sorry, no can do. Tonight isn't good for me. I've got something I have to do."

He put me down. "More important than this?"

There was no way I was going to put off talking to Lance. "Well, no, but it's something I have to do. Someplace I have to be."

"All right." He said it like it wasn't a problem, but I knew better.

I steeled myself. I could almost feel the doors

slamming between us. Rhys picked up his pack without a word and headed back toward the entrance. I followed, and we were silent until we exited the cave and he locked the grate behind us.

After two hours on the cooler, the warmth of the July afternoon felt wonderful. Thunder rumbled around us, and the air smelled strongly of ozone. The storm was breaking right on top of us; quarter-sized splats of rain slapped the trees.

"We're going to get wet," I said.

"Looks like."

I had to run to keep up with him. By the time we made it back, were both soaked to the skin and shivering, and I was shaking with exhaustion. Everything hurt.

"I want to swing by and tell Madame Coumlie what we found," Rhys said.

My teeth chattered uncontrollably. "I'm dropping Mina off with Lance tonight. That's why I can't go with you. I need to talk to him. Why can't Porter and the FBI handle things from here?"

"Why would you do that?" Rhys kept his eyes on the road as we wound our way back down the hill, the truck in low gear. "I thought she was with you for safekeeping. From what I hear, Lance is in big trouble."

Why was it that Karen and Bunny and Rhys knew more about my brother than I did? "Why, what have you heard?"

"No more than what was in the paper this morning."

Here we go again with the paper. I swore I would start reading it every day. "What did it say?" My shivering wasn't just from the cold any more.

Rhys braked to a stop and turned to face me. "The Sentinel had a huge spread on the Night Shark serial killings this morning. The article showed pictures of the victims and the missing. Lance was identified by name as a person of interest. Everybody is looking for him."

"Oh crap."

CHAPTER 20

I REMEMBERED STARING at the slapping of the windshield wipers in the truck, and Rhys hustling me through the back door of Mystic Properties, but not how I ended up in the shower with Rhys' naked arms around me. The hot water beat against my sore back with soothing pulsations. I'd stopped shivering.   Dressed only in our underwear, I could feel how very happy Rhys was to have me there. I rejoiced my decision to wear lacy blue bra and panties this morning, and not the white cotton. I felt positively sexy.

I curled a lock of his wet hair behind his ear, and he gave me a relieved smile. "What happened?"

"You went to lunch without me. You got here under your own power, pulled my clothes off, and dragged me into the shower. Not that I'm not happy to oblige." He leered at me and grinned. "Blue is my favorite color."

He reached behind me and turned off the water, and helped me out of the tub. Rhys' dark brown briefs complimented his tan. He handed me a towel, then grabbed another for himself.

The news about Lance came flooding back to me, and I remembered Mina. "Oh crap, what's the time? I can't be late for Mina." I started rubbing my wet hair.

"Relax. You've got time. Your jeans are here, but

your shirt is soaked. I'll bring you one of mine. Be right back." He disappeared and I heard his tread on the stairs above my head. He must live upstairs. Interesting.

I stripped out of my wet undies, dried myself off, and shimmied into my hot dry jeans. Wearing jeans without underwear made me feel a little slutty, but in a good way. I wrapped the towel around my shoulders and was wringing my hair out into the sink when Rhys came back.

"You decent?" He waved a t-shirt at me from the doorway, and hooked it on the doorknob without looking in. I wrapped my lingerie into the wet towel and slipped the tee shirt on.

What on earth was I going to do about Lance? I needed to talk to him; about the murders and the gambling and everything else. But I also wanted to talk to Madame Coumlie, correction, my great-grandmother, and find out how to get those djinn back into their prison under Sentinel Hill, and figure out where they escaped from in the first place.

I emerged from the bathroom and found Rhys pouring two cups of fresh-brewed coffee. The rain had stopped, but the skies outside were still dark.

"I have a plan," Rhys said, and handed me a cup. He held my gaze, and the unspoken tension between us hummed. "A compromise."

"I'm listening." The coffee smelled wonderful. So did Rhys.

"We pick up Mina and head over to Madame Coumlie's. We need to tell her what we found. I imagine she'll get a kick out of meeting her great-great granddaughter."

"I don't think so. I'm not ready to let her meet my

niece yet, not without some ground rules first. Look what she did to me." I held out my hand and showed him the black crescent mark. Yellow bruises encircled my wrist. "Besides, I really need to talk to Lance."

"What about a sitter?"

"I'm the sitter. She's my responsibility. I don't want to leave her with anyone else. Anyway, I need to explain to her about the djinn. I don't want her to accidently name them, like I did."

"Okay, take Mina and go see Lance now. I'll get hold of Frank Porter and report what we found in the caves. Give me a few hours. Meet me here at, say seven? We'll go talk to the Hand then."

It was a good compromise. I wasn't sure about leaving Mina with Lance, although I'd have better prospects of getting him to talk to me if she came along. But with Hector out there somewhere, I couldn't take the chance. I had to think about what was safest for Mina. I decided to drop her off at her mother's house after I talked to Lance.

"Make it eight." I kissed Rhys on the cheek, which was about all I trusted myself to do, and headed out to my car. Man oh man, how did my life get so complicated?

☾

I arrived at Shoreline Elementary School just as classes got out for the day. Ten minutes later, the crowd outside the school had thinned and most of the cars had left, but I still hadn't seen any of Mina. A warning tingle came over me, and I got out of the car. Mina knew we were going to see her dad after school. She wouldn't forget about something like that.

I decided to check her classroom, in the unlikely event she had detention. Mina never had detention. Talking to the teacher, maybe. She wouldn't like it if I came up to the classroom, especially looking like I did, but too bad.

Mrs. Godfrey's fourth grade class was the last classroom on the first floor. With every step, my warning tingle got louder. I reached Mrs. Godfrey's room and peeked in, both my fingers crossed.

"Hello, Mattie." Mrs. Godfrey was putting supplies away in one of the big cabinets at the back of the classroom. She didn't look happy to see me.

"Where's Mina?"

Mrs. Godfrey frowned. "She was picked up at noon. By order of Child Protective Services. The office tried to reach her father, but couldn't get hold of him."

My gut twisted inside me. I wanted to scream. "You mean Violet, don't you. Does Lance know?"

"They went through the principal's office; all the papers were in order. I got a message to release Mina early, but didn't know anything until after. I did what I was told."

I didn't wait to hear any more. I ran out of the classroom over to the main office and demanded to know what was going on. The school administrator, Andrea Gregson was sympathetic.

"There was nothing we could do. Mina was released into her mother's custody. She had a court order, Mattie, I'm sorry. Violet brought Child Protective Services with her."

"How could she get a court order?" I already knew the answer to that one. With Lance on the short list for murder, Violet wouldn't have any trouble persuading the courts that Mina would be better off with her. She would be safe with Violet, but I hated the way this whole thing had played itself out. Lance would be furious, but had no one to blame but himself.

"Maybe it's for the best." Andrea put her hand on mine and tried to reassure me. "Lance has a lot on his plate right now."

"What are you talking about? Does he already know about this?"

"No, not yet. I'll tell him tonight."

I gave her a blank look. "Excuse me?"

"Mattie we're getting married. No ring yet, but I've got him working on it. My divorce became final yesterday."

Exasperation tore though me. "I don't believe you. Lance would never --."

She smiled like a cat with a mouthful of cream. "I found the perfect ring over in Pittsford. Two carats, emerald cut."

I shook my head in disbelief. "My brother doesn't have that kind of money."

"You're just jealous. You don't know him as well as you think you do. He's quite the pool shark. All he needs is the right encouragement from the right woman. He's making money hand over fist now, thanks to me."

I wanted to scream. "You can't be serious. You can't be marrying my brother, you're not in love with him."

She arched her neck at me. "He's not your anything anymore. He's mine now. And when I say jump, he asks me how high. We're going to make a lot of money together. You don't have anything to say about it."

☾

My fury kept Rusty's pedal to the metal as I drove out to Sterling to confront Lance. In my whole life, I couldn't recall ever being this mad at him. He'd hidden his relationship with Zoey, and now this affair with Andrea. I didn't like her one bit. If I'd stayed a minute longer, I would have slapped her. Better to save it for Lance. What was he thinking? Why didn't he tell me?

Sheesh. The thought of Lance and Andrea was just awful. She wasn't one bit interested in Lance. When it came to marriage, Andrea Gregson was a four-time loser. I could just see her draining Lance's bank account and taking off when someone better came along. She was using him. She was poison.

My cell phone rang.

"Hello, Mattie? Garr Russ here. Your friend Karen introduced us the other day at my restaurant."

My stomach fluttered. Be still my heart.

"Oh hi." I struggled to keep the car on the road. "Of course, I remember. I enjoyed meeting you."

The flicker of thrill quenched somewhat by guilt over my near-naked shower with Rhys. Don't be silly Mattie. Man oh man, here was my potential future boyfriend actually calling me.

"I'm planning a little sunset cruise out on the lake this evening. Just a few friends and a couple of bottles of wine. Would you be interested in joining us?"

I went all tingly. A real date. My thoughts returned Rhys. Handsome as he was, Rhys seemed to be pretty involved with Madame Coumlie, Cavewoman Barbie, the FBI, and a whole universe of dark things that didn't belong in my world. Garlan Russ, on the other hand, was a respected member of the community, an entrepreneur, and heir to a huge fortune. Any girl would be flattered to go out with him. Too bad it was tonight. "It sounds wonderful, but I'm afraid I've already got plans for this evening."

"I've got a thirty-eight foot Bertram. You'll love it. You don't get seasick do you?"

"Sounds great." I imagined myself sipping champagne and nibbling appetizers as the sun drifted toward the horizon. I had a short white skirt that showed off my legs. I wondered what his friends would be like. "Can I take a rain check? How about next week?"

"Let me tell you something, Mattie. When I see something I want, I go after it. I'd like to spend some time with you. What about tomorrow? Dinner?"

Wow. Determined, wasn't he? "I'm flattered, and I'd love to go out with you, Garr. Really. But I'm going to be kind of busy for the next few days." I hoped he knew just how hard it was for me to turn down his invitation.

"Ah. There's someone else?"

"Not exactly. It's a family issue. I'm not sure if dinner tomorrow will work for me. I'd hate to say yes and cancel at the last minute."

"Breakfast then. You've got to eat. Come on Mattie. Give me a break here. I'd like to get to know you better."

Why not? "Breakfast I can do. Where do you want to meet?"

We agreed to meet at Killer Dave's the following morning, and I hung up feeling more cheerful than I had in days. I had a new yellow sundress I hadn't worn yet. That would be perfect. Then I remembered the black eye. Oh, right. I checked the mirror, and it was all kinds of purple and ugly. Tomorrow wouldn't be any better. Oh man. I couldn't let him to see me like this. No way.

I started to call him back to cancel, but decided to wait until after I talked to Lance. One thing at a time, Mattie. After talking to Garr, my anger at Lance had almost evaporated, but I still had to convince my brother to square things with the FBI. He had to turn himself in. I was positive that this whole thing could go away in about a twenty-minute conversation with the authorities. Obviously, they had the wrong guy. After that, we could focus on the House of Cards fiasco, getting him the hell away from Andrea Gregson, and rehab. What a mess.

CHAPTER 21

I PARKED IN the visitor lot, and hiked through the field to the entrance of the Sterling Renaissance Festival, metaphorically putting on my armor for the confrontation with Lance. I promised myself I wasn't leaving until he agreed to come with me to talk to the FBI and then go back to rehab.

The Festival site itself is permanent, with a gift store, outbuildings and wooden amphitheaters designed and built in the style of a 16th century Elizabethan village. I'd quit coming when I'd gotten my job with the city, so I hadn't set foot on the grounds in years.

The theme for this weekend was obviously Pirate Invasion. Lots of blokes with black eye patches ran around brandishing cutlasses and shouting 'Argh'. I headed for the jousting field, as this would be the most likely place to find my brother. I followed the dirt path past the dunking pond, the village of vendors, the washerwomen, and the nut man, to the spectator grounds in front of the jousting ring. People were already starting to leave, heading out early to beat the traffic, but a decent sized crowd remained seated in the shade. The smell of dust and sweat and manure greeted me as I watched a pair of knights on horseback collide at a full gallop. The crowd groaned when the loser hit the dirt and applauded as his pages helped him to his feet.

I spotted Lance right away, surrounded by a bevy of damsels and pirate wenches. He wore his Jack of Spades costume; a form-fitting black leather outfit with thigh-high boots, a jeweled dagger, a Zorro-type mask for a disguise and a wicked dueling blade at his side. I picked up a couple of marble-sized rocks, and hefted them in my hand as I waited for a shot.

Growing up as the daughter of the town prostitute, I got bullied a lot by older boys who persistently wondered if I had the same proclivities. Lance taught me to how to protect myself, and as long as I had a rock, I always had a weapon. Before long, the boys stopped bothering me. I was still a dead shot. My first throw hit the dirt on the outside edge of his boot, kicking up a wisp of dust. Lance winced, stepped back, and caught sight of me in the crowd.

He nodded, noted my black eye, but he didn't leave his post. I waited in the shade, watching the jousting and ogling the men in tights. I had to wait another hour before the jousting finished and visitors and performers alike began to drift away. I made my way from the berm to the foot of the stage and waited for him to finish chatting up some of the other actors. He seemed to be deliberately dragging out the conversations; anything to put off facing me.

Come on, Lance, enough already. The pressure inside me began to build. Finally, after everyone else drifted away, he turned to me.

"Hey sis," he sounded tired, as he draped a sweaty arm across my shoulders. I stiffened, but allowed him to guide me through the trees out to the actors' camp.

"Where's Mina?"

"I didn't bring her." Even his Zorro-mask couldn't hide my brother's paleness.

"Where is she?"

"She's fine. Safe."

"You look like hell."

"Getting beat up will do that for you." This conversation wasn't going the way I wanted, and I couldn't seem to broach the subject.

"No, I mean something's different." He studied my face with interest.

I ignored him. "What's going on Lance? No more bullshit."

He swung around and started back up the hill toward the faire. "Why don't we get something to eat first? The food court will be closing up soon, and I'm starved."

I bit my tongue and followed behind as he bought us each a couple of big beef ribs and strawberry shortcakes. We sat on a stone bench and Lance ate while I tried to curb my impatience. I couldn't eat. I had no appetite for what was coming. I waited until he finished eating before I lit into him.

"The FBI came to my house this morning, looking for you. You're a person of interest in the Night Shark case." He swore and started to protest, but I interrupted him. "You have to go talk to them."

"Where is Mina?"

"Don't change the subject. You're gambling again. Those goons from House of Cards didn't beat the crap out of me for no reason. Your friend Hector told me he's coming after Mina next. I can't believe you'd endanger your own daughter for something so stupid." Now that

I'd started, I couldn't seem to stop myself. "And why the hell does Andrea Gregson think you two are engaged? Are you serious? When were you planning to tell me about that?"

He wouldn't meet my eyes. "This doesn't concern you."

"Like hell it doesn't."

"Tell me where Mina is."

"Not until you tell me."

"This isn't like you, Mattie," he said. The muscles in his lower jaw clenched rhythmically. I imagined the wheels turning as he tried to decide how much to say. I hadn't seen that crafty expression on his face since the last time he'd been in the grip of his addiction.

"It breaks my heart to see you like this, Lance. I thought you were all over this. You're ruining your life, and Mina's too."

"I can take care of myself."

"Fine. Just tell me what's going on. Because you're digging yourself into a deep hole, and the whole thing is about to cave in on you. You have to talk to the police, Lance, you have to clear this up. And I don't care what Andrea Gregson says, you have to go back to rehab. This has got to stop."

We fumed at each other in silence for a few minutes. I'd never spoken to him like this before. Violet had always been the bad guy, giving Lance the ultimatums and the third degree. I'd always sided with Lance, and refused to acknowledge how he'd allowed his gambling to become more important than his family. Violet never trusted me to give Lance an ultimatum. Maybe she was right, back then. But not anymore.

"It's not what you think. Something came up, and

I'm helping out a friend, is all."

"Explain it to me. Please? Why is the House of Cards looking for you? Andrea Gregson is not your friend. She thinks you're buying her a two-carat diamond ring. She thinks she's your business manager, for cripe's sake. She thinks she owns you. She's not the one with the black eye here, Lance."

He wouldn't look at me.

"Andrea's got something on you. Tell me what it is. I can help."

He shook his head. "No, no you can't. Not now, maybe never."

The raw expression on his face was a shot to my heart. It was no use. He wasn't going to tell me. I tried a different tack.

"The FBI wants to talk to you. They think you have something to do with the Night Shark murders."

He still wouldn't look at me. A sick feeling curdled my gut as the silence stretched between us. I could see the internal struggle on his face, but for the life of me, I couldn't read him.

"They've connected you to two of the victims."

"I'm not even going to answer that."

"You need to talk to them."

"Not until after I finish playing tonight." He gathered up the napkins and paper plates and dumped them into the trash. "A couple of days isn't going to make any difference."

"What is the matter with you?" Why wouldn't he listen to reason? "The Sentinel named you as a person of interest in the case today. You made the front page, Lance. You want to know where Mina is? Violet got an emergency court order rescinding custody. She came and got Mina this afternoon. Mina is gone."

Lance cursed and slumped against the bench. "Of course she is." His eyes glinted with unshed tears. "I suppose I shouldn't be surprised."

I handed him the FBI agent's card and my cell phone. "Call them now, while you're still in one piece. I'll drive you into town myself. You can get this cleared up, get yourself out of whatever mess you're in, and get yourself into rehab. The sooner you straighten this out, the sooner you can get Mina back." I crossed my fingers and silently prayed he would make the call.

Lance stared at the card, turning it over and over in his hand, but in the end, he handed me back my phone.

"Sorry, Matt, no can do. I feel bad that everything got so messed up, okay? I'm really sorry you got hurt. I got myself into a bind, and for better or worse, I've got to find my own way out. I just need twenty-four more hours to get this mess cleaned up."

I wanted to scream. "You dated Zoey Nussbaum. The yellow jag you were driving the other day belonged to Joanne Reynolds. These guys don't have any other leads. They're coming after you."

"They can't hurt me. This is all going to fall away, you'll see." He'd decided; I could see it in his face. He refused to understand. I shook my head. Nothing I said now would make any difference. He'd made up his mind.

"I wish you could hear how ridiculous your argument is. You're not making any sense. Someone is going to remember you're out here, and call the police. If they come out here, they are going to arrest you and put you in jail. Mina will end up with Violet permanently and you and I will never see her again."

At least he had enough sense to look miserable. He

put his arm around me and pulled me close. We didn't say anything, for a while, just huddled together in our misery, watching the departing crowd of festivalgoers, laughing and sunburned, head for home.

"I know what I'm doing. Don't worry about Andrea. I'll get the money and pay off House of Cards and then I'm done. I'll do the right thing, whatever you want. Okay?"

"What if you don't win?"

"You worry too much."

"You'll talk to the FBI? Promise?"

"Yeah. I'll go."

"Pinky swear." We linked pinkies and the deed was done. Not what I wanted, but close enough. Let it go.

I breathed a worried sigh of relief. Maybe things would work out after all. I could tell them Lance planned to turn himself in. One more day wouldn't make such a big difference, would it? Lance bugged the hell out of me for being so stubborn, but I had no more say here. I had plenty of my own problems to worry about too.

A new thought came to me. "Hey what do you know about Rhys Warrick?"

A wary expression crossed his face. "He's got a nice bike. Why?" I felt myself blushing and Lance rolled his eyes at me. "He's definitely not your type."

"He introduced me to our great-grandmother."

"You're kidding me, right?"

"I'm serious. Rhys showed me an old picture of her daughter, and mom looked just like her. It turns out that the daughter got pregnant and gave the baby up for adoption. Anyway, mom's mother died a long time ago, but our great-grandmother is still alive. It's that old fortuneteller, Madame Coumlie. The Hand of Fate."

His eyes widened in amazement. "Well, well. That explains a lot. Wait a second." He stared at me intently. "You say Rhys introduced you to her?"

"Yeah, why?"

He grabbed my shoulder. "You have a djemon, don't you."

The blood drained from my face.

"I knew it." He clutched me in a fierce embrace. "I should have guessed."

I pushed him away. "You have a djemon?"

He nodded, his face grim. "It showed up a few years ago. I didn't want anybody to know. I didn't want to risk losing Mina or the shop's contract with the City. By the time I asked Rhys about it, it was already a materialized demon. Madame Coumlie taught me how to keep it hidden, but not before Andrea found out."

"How did she find out?"

"I went to school with Andrea, but I never really knew her. We got to know each other at Gamblers Anonymous. She didn't attend the meetings regularly, but would call me from time to time, just to talk. She told me her problems, I told her mine. I should never have told her about my djemon."

He shook my shoulder. "Don't make the same mistake I did, Mattie. You can't trust *anyone* with this kind of secret."

"What about Madame Coumlie?"

"Okay, yeah. Not everyone in this town registers their demons. All I'm saying, is if you decide not to register yours, you're better off keeping it secret from everyone. You never know when someone will turn on you."

"So why is Andrea doing this to you?"

"You've got to understand her situation. She was married to Stan, and having a rough time of it. Stan worked at the House of Cards. He was the night shift floor manager. Last year she decided she wanted out of the marriage. She said Stan was seeing other women, and she was sick of it. But she had run up a huge credit card debt and a serious tab at House of Cards, and Stan said he wouldn't let her go until she paid off what she owed."

"So how did Andrea's problem end up being your problem? She's got a good job."

He gave me a sheepish look. "She only works at the school part time. She couldn't come up with the kind of money we're talking about. She begged me to help her out, but I told her I couldn't. I cleaned out my savings to pay off her credit cards, but she wanted more."

I shook my head. "I can't believe you let her talk you into that."

"She threatened to go to Violet unless I helped her out, and she swore she'd leave me alone after she got her divorce from Stan. I let her talk me into going down to House of Cards and taking over her chit. I figured they'd think twice about coming after me. She was already in trouble when I took it over. I had to start playing again in order to pay it off."

I felt sick to my stomach. "Jeezalou Lance. This is blackmail."

He nodded. "At the time, I figured it wasn't that big a deal. There were some big players coming into town for a nine-ball tourney, and I figured I could earn the money in a few days. The tournament winnings wouldn't cover all her debt, but with the after-hours action, I figured I could clean up and even have a little left over for myself. The big guns arrived yesterday. I won most of the money I needed last night. Tonight I'll get the rest of it. And then I'll just walk away."

"Then why are they coming after you? Hector told me you were late."

"Yeah, well, the tournament got postponed a month. Couldn't be helped."

"Why didn't you go to the police?"

"And risk losing Mina? You must be joking. Doc and I would lose our contract with the department, and I'd be arrested for an unlicensed demon. Take your pick, I'm hosed." Lance stood up to leave.

My brother is a demon master. "She's never going to leave you alone. She looks at you and sees dollar signs."

"You let me worry about that. I've got to do this my way. I'm going to pay off the House of Cards first. Then I'll talk to the FBI."

"Why bother? Now that Violet already has Mina, Andrea can't hurt you."

Lance caressed my bruised cheek. "What do you think the FBI would do to me if Andrea told them I've got an unregistered demon? No one can know about this."

For a fleeting moment, I wondered if Lance might be the Night Shark. No way. I had more questions than ever now, but they'd have to wait. "How did everything get so complicated?"

We stared at each other for a full minute. Then he put his hand on my head and ruffled my hair. "Catch you later, Sis." He gave me a half-salute and sauntered off toward the actor's camp. I watched him go, wishing things had gone differently.

I plodded back to the parking lot, each step heavier than the last. It was out of my hands now. If his luck stayed with him a little while longer, he'd be in the clear, and after he talked to the FBI, he'd be able to get into rehab and persuade Violet to share custody. At least, I hoped so.

I called Karen. I wanted to tell her everything, but didn't. I told her about Rhys and the djinn and my newly discovered kinship to the Hand of Fate. She screamed and said it was the coolest thing she'd ever heard of. She made me laugh. I told her about going into the caves below Sentinel Hill and finding the cavern full of djinn.

"Mrs. Coumlie thinks I'm her heir, and says I'm going to be developing some sort of mystical powers. She told me I need to get all the djinn back into the cave just like she did, eighty years ago. This is all happening so fast. It's a little too 'out there', don't you think?"

"What powers?"

"I forgot to ask. She gave me her journal, but I haven't had a chance to read it yet. Rhys and I are going over there tonight to tell her what we found."

"What about the police? Have you told them?"

"Well, I think the FBI should be in charge here, but they don't believe in the djinn, and Madame Coumlie seems to think Rhys and I are the only ones who can solve this thing. I have no idea what to do, and if you ask me, Madame Coumlie might not be completely rational." The yellow bruises on my wrist were fading. "She scares me, a little."

"Do you know she's the library's biggest donor? She funds all the children's section book purchases every year."

"You've got to be kidding."

"You of all people should know better than to judge a book by its cover, Mattie. What about Rhys? What's he like?""

A terrific kisser. "He's on board, I think. And hey, guess who called me?"

"I knew it! He called this morning for your phone number. Are you going out tonight?"

"I can't. I'm up to my neck with Lance and this crazy Hand of Fate stuff. I'm supposed to meet him tomorrow for breakfast."

"What's the matter? I thought you were dying to go out with him. You don't sound very excited about it."

"Just a lot on my mind. Too much weirdness, I guess."

"Well perk up, girl. A fine-lookin' man is interested in spending some quality time with you. Things are on the upswing."

"You're right." And I meant it. "I'll let you know how it goes."

She laughed. "Don't do anything I wouldn't do."

CHAPTER 22

I WALKED THROUGH the open back door of Mystic Properties; the tension in the room thick as butter. Rhys and Porter seemed to be in the middle of a disagreement, and stopped talking as soon as I entered the room.

"What did I miss?"

"The FBI declined to pursue the demon-as-the-killer theory," Rhys said. "They're convinced the correct strategy is to focus their efforts on a human suspect."

I glared at Porter. "So they're going after my brother? You're making a big mistake. And who leaked his name to the newspapers? Lance has nothing to do with any of this."

"Look, I carry no weight with the taskforce. First of all, I'm here on special assignment." Porter ticked off the points on his fingers as he spoke. "I'm an outsider. Second, no physical evidence exists which proves an animal made any of the marks found on any of the victims. The only demons in the flesh we can compare bite radii against are much too small. Third, no saliva or other DNA evidence was found that would allow us conclude the marks are bites and not some strange tool which hasn't been identified yet. And fourth, and I'm sorry to tell you this Mattie, the only people who can see these so-called djinn are a senile old woman and you. Neither one of you ever tested positive for psychic ability, and you both share a family history of mental illness. The taskforce thinks I'm a kook. Gimme a break guys, I shouldn't believe you either."

My face burned. "But you do." I wondered if Oneiri had a big enough bite radius.

Porter glanced at Rhys and then turned to face me. "Only because I trust Rhys. He's got a nose for this stuff. He tells me you're related to that crazy old woman."

"I know I'm not crazy." Maybe my Mom wasn't either; she might have been messed up, but I now believed she'd been misdiagnosed. "Rhys and I went down into those caves. I saw thousands of them, and they weren't locked up like they were supposed to be. At least two were materialized, named djemons. And I saw signs that someone had been inside."

"The FBI doesn't make arrests based on imaginary creatures. We need hard evidence."

"These things aren't alive," Rhys explained. "They don't have DNA. A demon master must be directing these djemons. It's happened before. Check the newspapers. Madame Coumlie said it happened in 1930. Find the master, and you'll have your Night Shark."

"Yeah, well we've gotten a lot of complaints about the old woman being a demon master herself. I'd be willing to believe it, based on her looks alone, but the fact is, I've tested her a half-dozen times. The old girl doesn't show up as anything special on the radar. Maybe you and your brother are related to her, but that doesn't change anything. I'm more inclined to agree with the profilers who believe the family mental history points to serial killer tendencies, not paranormal ability. From what I hear, the task force has accumulated a stack of evidence against the brother."

"You don't even know my brother."

"Mattie and I are on our way over to Madame Coumlie's now," Rhys said. "Why don't you come with us? I think if she tells us how she rounded up the djinn back then, Mattie and I can do the same thing. She might even be able to shed some light on your killer."

Rhys was all business now, and I liked being included as part of the team. Sirens sounded in the distance. A fire in the Shore would be dangerous. Streets in Shore Haven were narrow; the houses had been built very close together.

"Lance promised me he'll turn himself in on Monday. You'll see, he has nothing to do with these murders. You guys are wrong about him."

"Are you in contact with him?" Porter asked.

I hesitated. Maybe I shouldn't have said anything.

"I may not be directly involved in the investigation, but things would go better for Lance if he turned himself in sooner. Some guy with a bounty-hunter complex might decide to take justice into his own hands. Who knows what might happen."

The idea of someone hunting Lance scared me. The approaching sirens drowned out further conversation. We moved to the windows, and two fire trucks raced by. Porter got a page. He checked his phone and started for the front door.

"There's a three-alarm fire at Madame Coumlie's over on Empress."

I hopped into the truck with Rhys and we raced Porter to the scene. Barricades were already in place, preventing us from getting any closer, so Rhys parked the truck and we ran toward the house.

Fire crews had the hoses out, but I saw no sign of smoke or flames. By the time we made our way through the crowd to the perimeter barricade, the engine teams were already standing down and starting to roll the hoses. Someone said false alarm, and I felt relieved, until the paramedics brought out Madame Coumlie on a stretcher.

My great-grandmother, I reminded myself. In spite of my fear of her, my heart squeezed tight at the sight of her tiny form swathed in blankets. Her eyes were closed. Fearfully, I slipped through the barricade and reached her side as they prepared to load her into the ambulance.

"Sorry miss, only family in the ambulance."

"It's all right." I reached under the blanket, found her tiny hand, and squeezed. She squeezed me back; she was aware of everything going on. "I'm family."

"Are you Mattie?"

The voice came from behind me, and I turned to face a white-haired gentleman in a two thousand dollar suit. By the way he wore his receding hairline, Florida tan, and Botox, I guessed lawyer.

"Gerard Fontaigne." He handed me his card. Yep. A lawyer.

"If you're coming with us, you better get in." The paramedics were waiting. I still had hold of Madame Coumlie's hand.

"Sorry." I shoved the card into my pocket and climbed into the back of the ambulance. They let me sit next to her. The doors slammed behind us, and through the rear windows, Rhys and Fontaigne made identical 'I'll follow you to the hospital' gestures.

The medics kept assuring us everything would be fine. They put an oxygen mask over Madame Coumlie's nose and mouth, and adjusted the airflow.

"We'll be at the hospital in two shakes. Your Gran's lungs sound pretty congested. Is she taking any medications?"

"I don't know." When I realized we were headed to St. Agrippa's. I shuddered--I remembered the loose djemons Rhys and I had seen in the basement. The idea of one of those things coming after this tiny woman while she slept horrified me. "Can't we go someplace else? What about St Lukes?"

"Sorry, there's been an explosion at the Brewery. Their emergency room is closed. Besides, St. Agrippa's closer; we're already here."

He was right. We were less than a block away from the entrance. I decided to stay with her all night if that's what it took to keep her safe. I had to. At any rate, with the grip she had on my hand, I doubted I would be able to leave her, even if I wanted to.

"It's okay, Gran," I whispered. The word felt unfamiliar but pleasant. "I'm not going to leave you."

She coughed in acknowledgement, and I cringed at the phlegmy sound. The medics raised the back of the stretcher to make her more comfortable, and we pulled up to the emergency entrance.

"Here we go."

☾

The rest of the evening passed in a blur of admission forms as we got my great-grandmother settled. The lawyer, Fontaigne, eased me through the paperwork and surprised me with his efficiency. Gran had no immediate physical concerns, but she had several ongoing health issues, and coupled with her age, the emergency room doctor decided to keep her overnight for observation. They'd given her something to help clear up her lungs, and she was breathing better, but clearly exhausted. The lawyer had insisted on the private room, but knowing what was in the basement, I didn't want to leave her alone. The nurses told me I could stay as long as I liked.

As she slept, her grip on me loosened, but I didn't try to take back my hand. Asleep, she appeared so very frail. I wondered what she had been like in her younger days. The tattoos and scars would have been fresh then, bright and shocking; those odd eyes of hers truly frightening. She reminded me of a child's withered apple doll, awash in a sea of hospital linen. My heart opened to her vulnerability.

Gently, I opened her hand and studied her dry, leathered palm. I made a mental note to bring her some hand lotion. She had the exact same crescent mark as mine, but hers stood pale against the darkly marked skin. The stain appeared to be old scorch marks stretching halfway to her elbows. I wondered what her life had been like. She probably had amazing stories to tell.

It hit me then. The Hand of Fate was my great-grandmother. Somehow, this scary old witch had become my Gran. I guess love isn't always where you expect to find it.

"Gran," I whispered, trying out the sound. I liked the sound of it.

She'd said she had searched for us a long time.

Knowing that tugged at my heart. If she'd found us earlier, things would have been different. She would have loved all of us; Mom, Lance, and me. She was part of us, too; part of me. That made her more real to me, somehow. I wanted to connect with her, to know her, to understand her. To make her part of my life.

CHAPTER 23

DRY FINGERS BRUSHED my hair out of my face; a cherished sensory memory of my mother I'd nearly forgotten. I opened my eyes and the white cotton blanket reminded me where I was. I sat up stiffly.

"I am dying, *chere*," she said. Her strange appearance didn't bother me so much anymore. She cleared her throat. "We do not have much time." Her voice sounded dusty with the past. I offered her a glass of water from the bedside table, but she shook her head.

"The doctor said you're fine. They're just keeping you here for observation."

She shook her head. "I have found you, and nothing more keeps me here. To gaze upon you, with a fierce joy again in my heart is enough. I am at peace. I will speak of what is to come and die. I am a woman fulfilled at last."

It struck me again that this ancient woman seemed the embodiment of a banked fire, ready to flare up at any moment; her life force an eternal flame. In spite of her eccentricities, traces of my mother stared back at me; in the cheekbones, around the brow, and the set of her chin. Where my mother had always seemed to me to be made of glass, my great grandmother reminded me of an old coin, worn away around the edges, but solid at the core, in spite of her doll-like exterior.

My throat tightened. "You're not going to die; at least not today." I wondered whether she would be able to return to her home. Where would she go? Living with me wouldn't work. I lived up a long flight of stairs, and had only a studio apartment. Maybe I should think about finding a two-bedroom.

"Listen to me, Mattie. The time has come for you to accept your inheritance." She took hold of my hand again. "I am a direct descendant of one of the original three Fates of Egypt. When I die, you will become the next Hand of Fate. You are my legacy."

I bit the inside of my cheek and wondered where Rhys and the lawyer had disappeared to. Or the nurse. Shouldn't somebody be here? "Would you like me to go find Mr. Fontaigne? He should still be here."

She ignored me. "Our ancestors weren't human, we are descended of the gods. Our line served the Pharaohs, advising the royal families for generations. In time, the Romans brought the siblings to Greece, where they became famous as the Apportioners of Fate. The Three Fates."

Her fingers dug into me. "Our ancestors were born a thousand years before Christianity, Mattie. Our bloodline has survived for more than four thousand years. You are a direct descendent of that bloodline. You are my heir."

I winced. "Okay, okay. What about your other children? My brother--"

"The eldest woman in the line inherits the legacy. You accepted the mark. When I die, the gift will come to you."

I rubbed at the crescent mark on my hand. "You don't need to give me anything."

"The gift is not material, *chere*. Long ago, when the Greeks kidnapped the Moirae sisters from Egypt, they brought them to Delphi to be revered as oracles. Lachesis' line, the Hand of Time, ended during the Black Plague. Her powers passed to the Clothos line, the Hand of Life. The last Clothos heir perished during the French Revolution, and her combined powers passed to my line, the line of Atropos, also known as Morta, the Hand of Death. The powers of the gods now live within a single line. Our line. With my passing, these powers will pass to you. You will become the Hand of Fate."

"I appreciate the offer, but I've already got a job. I work for the city of Picston."

She touched my hair. "It is a heavy responsibility. One you will assume very soon, I think. It happens even now."

She wasn't listening to me. "Did my mother know about all this?"

"When Oleanna became pregnant, she ran away from home. She gave her baby up for adoption without ever telling me who the father was. She took the secret to her grave. To have found you now is the answer to all my hopes and prayers. I never stopped looking for your mother." I saw real grief in her face, and believed her.

"My mom abused alcohol and drugs, and worked the streets to support her habits. She eventually took her own life. She had a lot of problems, but now I think maybe mental illness wasn't one of them."

My gran hugged me then, and I let her. We cried for my mother; something I'd never allowed myself to do. We cried for what we'd both lost. She blew her nose using three tissues; just as my mother had.

"I've never had a grandmother; or great-grandmother, either. I want to know about you and your life."

She shook her head. "There is no time. I need to prepare you for what is coming, chere. It has been almost a century since I came into my gift, and I have forgotten much. I do remember times so dark that I too had thoughts of taking my own life. I had no one to tell me what would happen. I would spare you that, if you would listen."

I nodded. It couldn't hurt to listen.

"I was eight years old when an agent came to our village in France and offered my father an enormous sum of money to send my mother to America. Just for the summer, he said. She would work for the Russ family as the starring attraction at Heavenly Shores Amusements. I wanted to go too, but the Agent told us the contract specified only the Hand of Fate. My mother would spend twelve weeks in America, and return to our village before the fall harvest. The man offered my father more money than could earn from five years of farming.

'When the day came to leave, my mother changed her mind. She believed that if she left for America, she would never see us again. When the agent came to take her from our village, my mother barred the door, and told the agent she would not be going with him.

'I remember that day vividly. My father and brothers had already left to work in the fields. The agent and his men became enraged. They broke down the door and grabbed my mother, pulling her away from us. She fought them with everything she had; scratching and spitting. I jumped on to the men, trying to protect her, but I was nothing more than a pesky flea to them. They beat my mother to death. Then they grabbed me and dropped me into a sack and took me with them. I woke up in the dark cargo hold of a ship already at sea. I never saw my family or France again.

'I spent the entire voyage to America chained below the decks with the other prisoners. Many of them had also been conscripted and also bound for Shore Haven. The other captives told me I was lucky to have survived, saying the men had bragged of ravaging my mother and burning our house. I imagined the horrible scene over and over in my mind as my mother's gifts passed to me.

'The conditions below deck were horrible. For weeks we lived in our own filth, unable to move freely. Rats and vermin ruled the lower decks, and their constant biting added to our misery. We never received enough fresh water, and whatever food they gave us was spoiled. We all suffered; many began to sicken and die. In the darkness, no one noticed the change in my appearance.

'I found I could perceive the life forces of others as a glowing aura. Their lifelines glowed like bright strings. I predicted who would die next by the intensity of the hues. In my distraught state, I spoke of the impending deaths, and was never wrong.

'The cook's helper took a fancy to one of the contortionists, a young girl from Shanghai, who was chained next to me. He brought us scraps of rancid meat from the kitchen. On the day land was sighted, we were excited to be nearing the end of our journey. The cook's boy took the girl's excitement as an invitation, and began thrusting himself upon her. She fought him, but could not stop the rape.

'In those days, I stood no taller than the average four-year-old child. The blows from my fists meant nothing to him. No one could reach us. I joined the others in screaming for help, but no one came. Mingmei cried and begged for him to stop. He bit into her breast, drawing blood. In desperation, I took hold of the lifeline throbbing within his aura. I snapped the thread, and he collapsed on top of her; dead. I helped her push him off her and we shoved him behind some nearby barrels and crates. We all agreed to keep the events a secret.

'The ship docked later that day in New York, and we all held our breaths until Obart Russ came to claim us and loaded us into the trucks that would take us to Shore Haven.

'When they carried me out of the dark hold, people gasped at my appearance. My eyes were as my mother's had been, with the gold ring around the iris. Old Master Obart, on the other hand, was delighted and pronounced me to be his star attraction.

'True to his word, when we arrived in Shore Haven, Old Master Obart set me up as the headliner. I spoke no English, so he brought in tutors and provided me with an education, keeping me locked up whenever I was not performing. I lived like a pet, in a well-appointed trailer on the Amusement Park grounds during the summer. In the off-season, I lived at the Russ estate. I ate at their table, and even played with the Russ children, but Obart viewed me as his property, not a human being. When his son Otto began to abuse me sexually, Obart banned me from the estate, so I lived at the amusement park full-time.

'The first several years, I divulged peoples fate from the stage, but Obart wanted more of a show, so he set me up as a fortune teller and mystic. I wore gypsy costumes, and sashayed to the stage each hour, giving public demonstrations and predictions and advertising private readings, where Master Obart made his biggest money off me.

'One of the roustabouts, a carpenter named Dirk Coumlie, made the most wonderful custom furniture, which he designed and built to fit me perfectly. The first thing he made for me was a rocking chair so comfortable and perfect for my size, I declared it to be the most beautiful thing I'd ever seen. Dirk furnished my entire trailer. He made me a walnut dressing table with matching mirror, a bed, and even an elaborately carved armoire to hold my clothes. We fell in love.

'Dirk asked Obart for my hand in marriage, but the Old Master refused, saying that a carpenter could never provide a good home for me. So Dirk built me the magnificent house on Empress Street, and when it was finished, he asked Obart again for my hand. Again, Obart refused. Finally, I begged Obart to let me marry Dirk. He told me I would need to make him the richest man in Germantown. I put my hand in his big paw and promised him that I had already made him the richest man in Germantown, and if he did not let me go, I would make him the deadest man in Germantown.

'He laughed that big hearty laugh of his, and I reached into his aura and caressed his life's thread, ever so gently. His heart began to skip a beat, and then another and another. He fell to his knees and agreed to let me go, but begged me to continue working for him. Obart pocketed all my income, so I had no reason to work for him, but in the end, we settled on a contract.

'I married Dirk and we moved into the beautiful house on Empress. I worked hard at the Amusements, but Obart would not leave me alone. He kept pestering me to make him richer. 'I do not have your talent for making money,' he'd say. Obart was a very superstitious man. He believed my magic would make him rich, but he was never satisfied.

'One day, I noticed a creature sitting in a corner of my dressing room, like a little gargoyle. Too small to be fearsome, but too solid to ignore as just a trick of the imagination. I named him Oneiri. He did no harm, and seemed to appear only when I was sitting quietly, so I accepted him as part of my life.

'I began to talk to him, and discovered the more I did so, the more animated he became. He seemed to be expecting something from me. The first time I gave Oneiri a direct command, Dirk and I were hunting for a murderer that was lurking in the streets of Shore Haven. The year was 1930, the summer after the stock market crash. Imagine my astonishment when we found creatures on the streets that looked to be the same sort of being as my Oneiri. However, these things were much bigger, completely visible, and able to move and react on their own. They attacked us.

'Dirk and I were armed, but our hammers were no defense against them, the creatures did not bleed or even seem to feel the blows that we pelted upon them. They had us down on the ground, biting and tearing at us. The biggest one had Dirk by the neck. I was afraid the demon would kill my husband. In desperation I called out to Oneiri to save us.

'Oneiri instantly appeared in the flesh and even though he was smaller than our attackers, he forced them away from us, cornering them and holding them at bay. I rushed to help Dirk, but he was already gone, his life pooling on the sidewalk of the alley."

Her whole body shook. "You must stop this madness chere." Her eyes blazed into me. "You must reseal the cavern. You must stop the demon master, whoever he is, before he kills again. I have spoken to the authorities many times, but they will not believe one such as myself. There is no one else who can do this." She gasped for breath. "Promise me."

I hesitated. "Let me call the nurse." I reached for the call button and pushed it.

"Promise me!"

Sheesh. "Okay, okay, I promise." Anything to calm her down.

"Swear to it. You will do what needs to be done. Your destiny calls to you, *chere*." She had that scary look in her eye again.

The weight of the universe seemed to hang on my answer, and if I said the wrong thing, I'd fall forever. "I don't know what to do," I whispered. "You have to help me."

"You have everything you need, *chere*. You are death incarnate."

The hairs on my arms stood on end. This was the real thing. Like a blood oath. My heart raced with adrenaline, and I felt my resolve harden within me. "I'll do it." A wave of heat passed through me, and I shivered.

She looked relieved. "You are braver than you look, I think."

"Tell me what to do."

The door swung open and Rhys came in, followed by Fontaigne. I sat up straighter and smiled at Rhys, at the same time wishing they hadn't interrupted. I glanced at my great-grandmother, but she'd closed her eyes. I checked for her pulse, and found it steady.

"How is she?" Rhys came to stand next to the bed, and took her other hand.

Fontaigne got right down to business. "Do you have a few moments, Miss Blackman? I have some paperwork to discuss with you regarding Mrs. Coumlie's estate."

"Mr. Fontaigne, I don't think this is a good time."

"Please, call me Gerard, Mattie."

The nurse popped in and shooed us out of the room. "It's after visiting hours. Mrs. Coumlie needs her rest." Since we couldn't stay, we decided to head to the cafeteria on the main floor.

We found a table off in the corner, and Gerard told us what happened.

"Madam requested me to come to the house because she'd found you and wanted her will changed to reflect her wishes in regards to her heir. Knowing Madame does not have a lot of time left to her, I of course reshuffled my schedule to accommodate her. We had only just completed the changes to the will, when I realized there was someone else in the house."

"How did the fire start?" asked Rhys.

"There was no fire." We all looked up to see agent Porter approaching. He pulled up a chair and sat down, uninvited. "You have any ideas about that, Fontaigne?"

"Do you two know each other?" I asked.

"I heard a commotion in the kitchen, and of course Mrs. Coumlie is deaf, so I got up to investigate. As I approached the kitchen, a large creature came out through the swinging door and lunged at me. I called 911. I reported a fire, knowing it would bring the fastest response."

I wondered how much the lawyer knew about the Hand of Fate and her personal djemon. Did he know about Oneiri?

"What creature? What happened next?"

"The creature went after Mrs. Coumlie. She grabbed a fireplace tool and brandished it quite effectively while she shouted at the creature in French. I'm not quite sure what she said, but she held the creature off until the first fire truck arrived, at which point the creature escaped back through the kitchen. The firemen came through the front door, and Mrs. Coumlie collapsed."

"And what were you doing during all this?"

The color rose in his face. "It happened so fast, I'm ashamed to say I froze. The sight of this tiny woman holding off such a monster was incredible."

"Can you describe this creature? How big was it?"

The lawyer's eyes shifted toward Rhys and I, as if he was uncertain how to answer. Oneiri was big, but not what I would call a monster. And why would he attack her?

"I, I'm not certain. But it was big. It had to stoop to get through the kitchen doorway."

Holy crapolli. That wasn't Oneiri.

CHAPTER 24

MY CELL PHONE rang. I stepped away from the table to answer.

"Are you Mattie?"

"Yeah, who is this?"

"Lance asked me to call and tell you he's been arrested. He gave me your number and asked me tell you he needs you to find him a lawyer."

I gripped the phone. "What?"

"The FBI arrested him for the murder of all those people. He wants you to get him a lawyer and bail him out. I told him I didn't want to get involved, so that's all I got to say." The caller hung up.

My stomach lurched; I closed my eyes, my mind searching frantically for the lie, and not finding it. Oh my god, they actually arrested Lance for murder. The evidence had to be circumstantial, they couldn't possibly have enough evidence to implicate him.

On the other hand, my great grandmother had just fought off a monstrous djemon that was probably the real killer. I hoped Porter could convince the taskforce they had wrong guy, but I doubted that a hundred-and-twenty-seven year-old dwarf and her lawyer would be able to change their minds. I tried to calm down, but my mind was in overdrive.

Madame Coumlie should never have been able to defeat a monstrous djemon at her age. She must have some sort of power, or she would never have tried to face it. If a demon master was sending its djemon to kill people, Rhys and I were the only ones who would be able to find him and prove it. No one but me could see the djinn. If she told me what to do, I was certain I could force all those demons back into the Hill cavern. I would need Rhys's help to get into the caves again. A plan began to take shape in my mind.

The men got up from the table and I caught Fontaigne's eye as we drifted toward the elevator. Lance wouldn't be going anywhere for several hours, even if he made bail, but he needed a lawyer right now. I hoped Fontaigne would help us. He wasn't a criminal attorney, but surely he could recommend someone. I hurried to catch up to the departing group.

"What's going on?" I asked Fontaigne.

"Ah. I'm going to go with agent Porter and give a statement about the demon attack, after he speaks with Mrs. Coumlie. He believes this new information on the size of the attacker will refocus the FBI's investigation toward a demon master."

I breathed a sigh of relief. "That's good to hear."

"I'll need you to come back to the caves with me." Rhys clenched the keys in his hand. "We need to find that other entrance and seal it off."

"Absolutely." I nodded. "The FBI just arrested Lance for the murders."

All three men stared at me.

"But in light of the attack on Mr. Fontaigne and my great-grandmother, they'll have to cut him loose, right? I mean, obviously they've got the wrong guy."

I appealed to Fontaigne. "My brother needs a good attorney. Can you help us?"

The lawyer nodded. "We have a fine attorney in my firm who specializes in criminal cases. Let me give him a call." He turned aside to make the call as we waited for the elevator.

"Your brother isn't going anywhere." Porter said. "I need to collect these witness statements first. Without evidence of a larger demon running loose, I'll have no pull with the taskforce."

"If we bring back the two djemons I saw running loose in the caves, couldn't we persuade the task force that someone has breached the caverns?"

"Not if they're the same puny size as the others you've showed me." Porter checked his watch. "Eyewitness testimony is the only thing I have to convince the task force of the bigger threat. The sooner I take those statements, the sooner we can get the task force looking in the right direction."

Rhys disagreed. "No one is going to believe Madame Coumlie, Frank. On looks alone, she isn't credible. We must show them the breach in the cavern. Even the FBI accepts those caverns serve as containment for paranormal entities. We need to find that breach and fix it."

Porter looked fit to be tied. "You know I can't help you in those caves, Warrick. I agree the old lady isn't credible, but with Fontaigne here as a witness, I've got a much better shot at convincing them."

I had an idea. "What about Oneiri?" Rhys shook his head and gave me an exceedingly intense expression that said shut up, but I ignored him. "Why don't we show them Oneiri?"

"What are you talking about? Who's Oneiri?"

"It's nothing." Rhys started to dismiss my suggestion, but I interrupted.

"Oneiri is Madame Coumlie's djemon. He's big enough." Rhys put his hand on the back of my neck and squeezed a warning. I couldn't understand why he was so agitated.

Porter's jaw clenched as he processed the information. "That soulless bitch," he swore a string of oaths.

"Hey, that's my great-grandmother you're talking about."

"Consorting with an unregistered demon is an act of treason. I always had a bad feeling about her anyway. She's condemned herself to hell, as far as I'm concerned. If I'd known she was such an abomination, I would have arrested her immediately."

Heaven help Lance if they discovered he had a demon. "Show a little respect. She is a human being, not a monster. Besides, Oneiri is all the proof you need." I fought to control my temper.

"You knew about this, Warrick?"

"She's the Hand of Fate, Frank. Just because your tests didn't find anything doesn't mean there's nothing there."

Porter's face reddened, his jaw clenched in anger. "You say this Oneiri thing is big enough to kill. Why didn't either of you think to tell me earlier? Seems to me she and her demon are at the center of this whole case. The woman is a menace to society. I could have you all brought up on conspiracy charges."

"Take it easy, Frank. The old lady is no killer."

"And she'd never let Oneiri hurt anyone." I shook my head. "She's not the one you're looking for."

The elevator dinged, and the doors opened. Porter went in first, radiating silent fury, and we all eased to the opposite side of the car. A sensation of hot wind whooshed across my skin, and I staggered against Fontaigne. I grabbed his arm to steady myself. A sense of foreboding came over me.

"Are you okay" Fontaigne asked.

I nodded, unable to speak, as a dreadful pressure began to build inside me.

Fontaigne whispered to me, saying he'd gotten his colleague to agree to represent Lance, at least for now. I gave him a thumbs-up and kept my trap shut, my anxiety growing by the minute. Something bad was happening. I began to sweat.

A moment later the doors opened on the fourth floor, and I took off running down the hall. A flurry of activity greeted me at the nurse's station and a group of medical personnel gathered soberly at the door of my great-grandmother's room. I raced toward them as my premonition became reality.

The women in the doorway stepped back, and two nurses switched off the monitors. The mood was subdued and respectful.

"Are you the family?"

I nodded, my eyes filling as I stared at the still form on the bed. "I'm so sorry. She passed just a few moments ago. We checked her and she was gone." She took my hand and gave it a sympathetic squeeze. "It was very peaceful, I assure you."

I bit my lips and stood in silent shock. The nurse excused herself, saying she would send the doctor by in a few minutes if we had any questions.

Porter came up behind me. "What happened? I

thought she was fine."

Fontaigne answered forestalled him. "She was one hundred and twenty-seven years old. What do you think?"

Porter glared angrily at me. "Well there goes my corroborating witness. How do we get hold of that djemon?"

Rhys answered him. "Once the demon master is gone, so is the djemon."

"Shit." Porter stomped off.

Tears prickled as I moved toward the bed. Rhys and Fontaigne stood in the doorway; the men as alone with their thoughts as I. Tears rolled down my cheeks, but I refused to cry. I glanced at them, startled to see their eyes misting as well.

Fontaigne stared at me curiously. "What's the matter with your eyes?"

I wiped my tears, not understanding. Rhys and Fontaigne came closer, shock registering in their faces.

Rhys stroked his chin. "Son of a bitch."

Fontaigne pulled me into the little bathroom and showed me my reflection in the mirror.

"All hail Mattie Blackman. The new Hand of Fate."

I gasped as I stared at my reflection in the mirror, and the color washed from my eyes, fading the iris until the brown paled to the unnatural color of new pennies. I gripped the sink to steady myself. I now had the same yellow halo around my pupils as my great-grandmother.

I blinked my eyes and turned my head, inspecting myself at different angles, but I couldn't recognize the image of me reflected in the mirror. Subtle changes to the bone structure of my face made my cheekbones appear more prominent, my jaw stronger. I ran my hands up and down my arms. Something was happening to me; inside me. My black eye and bruises faded away before my eyes. The pressure, which had built up in the elevator evaporated; replaced with a sensation of disorientation and loss.

Nausea crept up in my throat. "What's happening to me?" To the core of my being, I understood this change would be permanent. I would never be confused with 'normal' again.

CHAPTER 25

IN MY WORST nightmares, I sometimes dreamed I'd inherited my mother's schizophrenia, but never once did I imagine I would become an everlasting member of the bizarre brigade or a poster girl for the Finger Lakes Spirit Festival.

Rhys squeezed into the tiny bathroom beside us. He put his arm around me and tried to make me feel better.

"You'll be okay, Mattie. All you need are a pair of colored contact lenses. Nobody even needs to know."

Our faces in the mirror wore the same dazed expression. Today had been a long one for everybody. I felt safe here in the crowded bathroom, standing next to two men I barely knew. My great-grandmother trusted these men. She trusted me. She trusted me to find a way to stop the demon master and return the djinn back into the sealed cavern. No one but me.

I remembered what agent Porter had said about the demons. Loaded weapons, he'd called them. I simply couldn't think of Blix and Larry as dangerous. I thought about the phantom demon master and his monstrous djemon running loose in my hometown. The killer djemon started out just like me and Blix. Someone had let these things loose and planned to use them to kill. This had to stop.

"What exactly is the Hand of Fate?" My voice sounded distant and disconnected.

"Perhaps not what you think." Rhys leaned against the doorway. "The original Egyptian legends of the three fates spoke of Amun, the ram-headed god, who impregnated a priestess of one of the snake goddesses of the waters of Chaos. The three sisters borne as a result served the poor, the wretched, and distressed mortal citizens of ancient Egypt. Not until the Greeks kidnapped them and brought them to Greece did they became famous as the oracle daughters of Zeus and Chaos. The women eventually took human husbands, gave birth to children, and over the millennia the lineage faded, as generation after generation diluted the sacred family origins. Madame Coumlie was the last of her kind; a wild card, like a roll of the dice, or a meteorite. She dedicated herself to helping people in need, and supported the paranormal and supernatural community here in town."

"She wasn't just a fortune teller. I get that now." Somehow, I had inherited my great-grandmother's power, so now it was up to me.

"No. Most of her clients were anomalous."

"What?"

Rhys took my hand. "You call them paranormals, but the correct term is anomalous individuals."

"I promised her, Rhys. I promised I would stop him. With Lance in custody, the FBI is going to stop looking for the Night Shark. But the real killer must be a demon master; we've gotta find this guy."

Rhys agreed. "We find the djemon, we'll find the demon master."

Fontaigne paled, and sat down on the toilet.

"We've got to go back to the cavern. Everything starts in the caves." All of a sudden I remembered. "Oh no, I never got a chance to ask her about her powers or what to do."

"You still have the journal?"

Of course. I'd forgotten all about it. "Good point. What are we waiting for? Let's go."

Thus energized, we poured out of the bathroom and Rhys and Fontaigne headed out to the hallway.

"Hey guys, Give me a minute, will you?"

Rhys' eyes flicked to the bed behind me. He nodded and gave my hand a brief squeeze; then followed the lawyer out to the hall to wait with Porter.

I moved to stand beside the hospital bed, gazing down at her. I never even got a chance to know her; she was already gone. On to a higher plane, I hoped. Her face in repose seemed so serene.

Fontaigne told me the funeral arrangements were already in place, and she had already changed her will to make me her heir. I studied the new crescent mark on my left hand. My great-grandmother was one of a kind and proud. I'd spent my whole life apologizing for my mother and trying to be like everyone else. I wasn't some freak, I was unique. Just like her. I am the Hand of Fate. The time had come for me to own it.

The nurse came in, took one look at my eyes and gave a little shriek. She excused herself and couldn't get out of the room fast enough. Her problem, not mine.

I sighed. I rubbed my face, feeling dead on my feet with fatigue. I needed sleep more than anything.

"I won't let you down." I planted a brief kiss on her small brow. "I promise." I said a final good-bye to my great-grandmother and went out to the hall to find Rhys.

Rhys and I rode down the elevator and walked through the parking lot in silence. The weight of the humid night sky above and the events of the day had me feeling small and insignificant.

"You all right?"

"I just wish I'd known her sooner. I mean, I'm sad she's gone, but I'm afraid I might have made her a promise I can't keep."

"You want to talk about it?"

"Rhys, how did Oneiri get so big? She told me djemons live off the life energy of the people they kill. Is that true? Are they soul-eaters?"

"Whoa there, lady. Djemons are dependent on the life force of their masters to survive. They grow by serving their master. A djemon unused by its master cannot grow."

"How many people did Madame Coumlie order Oneiri to kill?"

"I can't answer that."

"I wish I'd had more time with her. There were so many questions I wanted to ask."

Rhys unlocked the truck and held the passenger door open for me, but I didn't get in.

I sighed. "Do you think she's going to hell for what she's done?"

"I'm probably not the best person to ask."

"She told me I was death incarnate."

Rhys looked away.

"She said I was descended from Morta, the Hand of Death."

"People are born and die every day, Mattie. It's the nature of the wheel."

"I don't want to kill anybody, Rhys. I don't want to go to hell."

"This is a discussion you should have with your pastor."

"Have you ever killed anyone?"

His green eyes held mine. "Yes."

I stepped back and broke into a sweat. I believed him. All I could see right now was the face of a stone-cold sociopath, completely devoid of humanity. I don't know how I hadn't seen it in him before. The world shifted dangerously beneath my feet, like the deepest desert sand.

"How many?" I whispered.

He looked away and the spell was broken. "Are you getting in or not?"

Good question. I had no doubts anymore that he was a killer, but did that make him a bad person? Could Rhys be the Night Shark? Could it have been there all along, and I missed it?

No.

He had been the first to think the killer was a large djemon. He'd gone to inspect the seal in the caves to make sure. I flashed on the image of his little-boy face gazing up at me from the caves. Nah. Rhys might be a murderer, but he wasn't the Night Shark.

"Earth to Mattie. Hell-ooo." The impatient smirk on his face decided me. Why do I find myself so attracted to men who are so irritated by me?

I blushed and climbed in.

CHAPTER 26

RHYS FOLLOWED ME from room to room, as I tore the my apartment apart, searching for the journal. I hunted everywhere, but all I found only a gleam in Rhys' eyes as he considered my unmade bed.

"The journal isn't here. I must have left it at Lance's."

"No problem."

We arrived at Lance's house in minutes. I unlocked the front door to discover the place had been ransacked. All the cushions had been pulled off the couch, the furniture had been moved around, and drawers and cupboards had been left open.

At first I thought Hector had come back. My heart pounded as I raced from room to room, to no avail. The journal wasn't in the living room, the kitchen, or Mina's bedroom either.

"It's not here." Rhys handed me a search warrant. "The FBI took the journal with them. It's listed right here on the receipt."

I stamped my foot in frustration at my own stupidity. "Oh man, I can't believe I left it here. We've got to get that journal back."

Rhys pulled out his cell phone. "Maybe Frank can help us out." He dialed, and put the phone on speaker so I could hear.

"You're out of luck." Porter was adamant. "That journal is the smoking gun the taskforce needed to get the arrest warrant for Lance McNair. That diary is hot property. Nobody is going to get their hands on it anytime soon."

"What are you talking about? She wrote the journal decades before Lance was even born. It doesn't have anything to do with him." I looked to Rhys.

"I can't say anything specific, other than the journal talks about a series of murders back in the thirties. We checked, and the journal entries coincide with the newspaper accounts of the time."

"They should, we're the ones that told you about it."

"Well, the new theory is that the journal gave McNair the idea for using a demon as a murder weapon. When you start looking at the body count, the feds are now talking about a weapon of mass destruction. The paranormal branch of the counter-terrorism task force has been asked to step in. I am now officially assigned to the case."

Rhys grimaced. "They think Lance is the demon master."

❦

"He knew several of the victims."

"Oh come on, Frank. This is a small town. Everybody knows somebody dead here."

"He was hiding from law enforcement."

"No he wasn't. Not really." I ran my hands through my hair. "This is all my fault."

Porter wasn't finished. "There's nothing more I can tell you, other than to say your brother is in deep shit.

They are even talking about bringing in the National Guard to quarantine the town. I want you both down here in less than an hour for a formal interview."

Rhys hung up. "If the taskforce is going after Lance, they're coming after us, too. At the very least, they're going to want to lock us up in a room somewhere for hours of interrogation. We can't spare the time. We've got to get out of here."

I hesitated. Never in my life had I disobeyed a law officer, but Rhys had the right idea. The only way to take suspicion off my brother was to find the demon master ourselves, even if we had to ignore a direct order from Porter. This was definitely crossing the line.

"Okay, let's go." I already knew where. There were a lot more journals at my great-grandmother's house, and no one would think to look for us there.

Rhys parked the truck around the corner from the big Queen Anne, and I followed him through the alley toward the back of the house. To my surprise, he had a key. He opened the door and we went in. I followed him through the darkened kitchen, sniffing the air for licorice, but smelled nothing more than my own little posse; the big djemon was long gone. Rhys turned on the lights in the front parlor while I closed the curtains. We immediately turned to the journals, and Rhys started flipping through one of my great-grandmother's green diaries. After a moment he put it down and started flipping through another.

"A lot of these are written in French. You don't read French, do you?"

"No." I gazed around the cluttered parlor. The room such a strong reflection of my great-grandmother's personality, I could almost feel her presence. I wanted to stop and examine every photo and read each framed certificate, but the journals were waiting.

I sank down to my knees and began paging through the closest leather-bound volume. Sure enough, most of the cramped entries were written in miniscule French script. The woman had been a prolific writer. Just looking at the pages made me sleepy. I flipped the book closed and checked the date on the spine, which said 1922.

"There is no way we can get through all this tonight, Rhys. I'm so tired I can't see straight. What if that big djemon comes back?" Rhys ignored me, totally engrossed with the journal in his hands. I threw a pillow at him.

"What?" He glanced at me, then back to the journals. "Oh, sorry. Until the other day, I didn't know about these. If they are what I think they are, they document the entire oral history of her family tree, going back generations. This is an incredible find." He began to page through another volume.

"Earth to Professor Warrick. We need to focus here, remember?" Being a mage, I imagined these old dusty journals appealed to Rhys as much as Lucky Charms appealed to me. I picked up a later volume, dated 1940. "Hey, this one's in English. Where's 1931? We should start there."

"I've got it right here. A good bit is written in French, but most is English. I think I've got someone who can do this translation for us." His voice was distant. He was already deep into reading the entries.

I found 1932 and turned to the first page. Sure enough, the entry had been written in English. The room was stuffy, my eyes heavy, and the penmanship tiny and perfect. All the lines jumbled together, and I closed my eyes for just a moment, but that was all it took.

CHAPTER 27

I WOKE UP in the morning on the floor of Madame Coumlie's parlor, surrounded by stacks of journals, Blix and Larry, and at least two dozen djinn. I groaned and shut my eyes and wondered about the time. A tantalizing aroma wafted in from the kitchen; something pungent and familiar, which overpowered the newly-tamed stench of djinn. Aah, coffee. Rhys had to be around here somewhere. I got up and followed the smell of fresh coffee into the kitchen.

The note next to the coffee maker said:

Back soon – R

Hmm. I checked the refrigerator and found some cheese, a half-empty bottle of red wine, and a half-full carton of whipping cream. Vive la France. I poured two fingers of cream into a clean coffee cup and filled it to the brim with the fresh brew. Oh yeah. I gave my silent appreciation to my great-grandmother for having such excellent coffee on hand.

Bit by bit, the events of the day before caught up with me. Lance must be going bonkers, I thought. Would he ever forgive me? No doubt he blamed me for his arrest. How I would I ever be able explain that I hadn't ratted him out to the FBI? First thing I had to do was get hold of Fontaigne for the name of the lawyer.

I turned my cell phone on. I needed to make a list, I decided. I wandered into the parlor, looking for paper, and noticed Rhys had taken about half of the journals with him. Even if we split up the reading, it would take us weeks to get through them all.

Maybe we should just go the cavern and, I don't know, wing it. If my great-grandmother and her husband were able to dispatch a horde of djemons with a couple of hammers, how complicated could it be to herd a bunch of djinn back into the cave? I contemplated my growing crew of djinn, but decided against considering them as helpers. I didn't want to accidently turn one into a djemon.

Still looking for paper to start a list, I picked up the 1932 journal. We might get lucky and find something right away. I was still scrambling around for paper and a pencil when my cell phone rang.

"Did you forget our date, or did I get the time wrong?" Garlan's voice was warm and teasing.

"Oh no, I am sorry, Garr. There was a death in the family last night. It completely slipped my mind."

After a long pause on the other end of the line, I thought the call had been dropped.

"Hello?"

"Of course. Allow me to express my condolences. Was this someone you were close to?" His voice sounded odd. Stilted.

I hesitated telling him. The Russ family had victimized my great-grandmother a long time ago; who knew what their relationship had been like recently. I decided not to mention her name.

"I only recently discovered we were related."

The back door opened, and I turned to see Rhys

come in with a big white bakery bag. He'd showered and changed. His sexy grin was back, and I beamed right back at him.

"Is there anything I can do?" Something about Garr's voice sounded forced.

Rhys started pulling chocolate croissants out of the bakery bag, wafting them in front of my face, making it impossible for me to concentrate.

"Um, can we do this another time?" I needed to get off the phone.

"How about that sunset cruise out on the lake? Just the two of us."

I blushed. He had a rich baritone voice. Persuasive; almost on the edge of pushy. Tempting as Garr's invitation sounded, I found my loyalties wavering. Of course, the coffee and chocolate croissants Rhys had just brought weren't helping, but I didn't feel right talking to Garr with Rhys' wafting pastry under my nose. I slapped his hand away. The delicious scent of chocolate was making me crazy, and I couldn't remember the last time I'd eaten.

"I'm afraid I'm going to be pretty busy for the next few days."

"Of course." Garr was not a man who liked to be disappointed, I could tell. "Perhaps another time."

I hung up, sensing something off-kilter about the whole conversation. Karen might be right; maybe he was too old for me. My thoughts were interrupted by Rhys, who swooped in and pulled me to him, inhaling deeply as he kissed my neck.

"You are absolutely irresistible." He whispered into my neck. "I could just eat you up."

I slipped away from him and grabbed a pastry.

"That's the chocolate talking. Don't come any closer. We've got work to do." I took a huge bite, and oomphed in ecstasy as the warm dark chocolate filled my mouth. I held up the croissant to Rhys and he took a monstrous bite. He devoured it, his emerald eyes glittering at me with unfiltered hunger. Oh my.

"And I need to get cleaned up. I mean, you're all clean, and I'm not, that's all." Without a word, Rhys stepped into me, and pinned me against the kitchen sink.

"I don't care." He put his hands on me, and I closed my eyes and leaned into him; feeling quite the femme fatale for this hour of the morning. His hands slid down my back and pulled me towards him, hips first. He smelled of clean man, and coffee and chocolate. Mighty good. I lifted my head and he kissed me.

All thoughts of responsibility fled as his tongue explored my mouth. I let him, giving back as good as I got, with interest. His lips were a novel experience. Firm and incredibly soft, his mouth pulled sensations from me I hadn't experienced before. My body tightened and I savored the feelings his hands aroused as he stroked my nipples and kissed my neck.

Madame Coumlie's wall phone rang, and Rhys answered.

"For you." He handed me the receiver. He mouthed the words 'Funeral Home' to me and wrapped his arms around me; putting his head on my shoulder to listen in.

"Ah, well, Miss Blackman, so glad to be able to track you down. Gerard Fontaigne suggested you might be staying at the house. Norm Saunders here. I'm just calling to assure you that all the arrangements for Madame's service are in order. Visiting hours will be held the day after tomorrow, beginning at three o'clock.

Would that be satisfactory?"

"Sure, I guess."

"Madame selected one of our high-end packages. She requested cremation, of course, but also understood the needs of the community to say farewell, and agreed to an evening viewing. Lillies, white gladiolas, and orange blossoms, a lovely combination, I must say."

"Um, nice. Do I need to do anything??"

"Traditionally, we prefer to have a family member host the viewing. I have not been able to reach any other family members yet."

I wondered who the other family members might be. "How long does this thing last?" I'd never been to a funeral before; not even my own mother's. I wasn't sure if attending would be such a good idea. What if Porter showed up?

"A few hours. Your presence is all that is necessary; and to accept the kind wishes and condolences of her friends and the community. Your great-grandmother was one of a kind. If you like, you may bring a few mementos of her life. Perhaps a photo?"

"For what?"

"She was an amazing woman. A legend, if you will. We've already received a tremendous number of calls regarding the viewing. Based on the number of queries, I decided to move her into the Founder's Room. I tell you, we haven't needed the Founder's Room for years," he bragged. "Normally, it's more expensive, but I am certain your great-grandmother would be pleased to know how many people wish to attend and pay their respects."

This was getting morbid. "Wait a minute. I don't want her funeral to be some sort of pay-per-view circus event. My great-grandmother is not an exhibition." What if they wanted to touch her, or tried to take a lock of hair or something as a souvenir? I shuddered. That would be too horrible. "I've changed my mind. Ix-nay on the viewing."

"Pardon me?"

"You heard me, no viewing."

"But it was Madam's wish. Her obituary and visiting hours are already published in this morning's paper. This was all arranged months ago, by Madam herself."

Rhys nodded, giving me a supportive squeeze.

"Not to worry." Saunders sounded confident. "Everything will be lovely and tasteful, I assure you. I will be right with you, every moment."

"Um."

"If you would be so good as to arrive a few minutes early, that would be best." He hung up.

I handed the phone back to Rhys and he replaced the receiver. Almost immediately, it rang again. This time I answered.

The caller identified himself as Marcus Galvin, the criminal attorney Fontaigne had spoken of. He told me he'd agreed to represent Lance. On the phone at least, he sounded competent and easy to talk to. I liked him right away.

"What about bail, Marcus? How soon can we get him out?"

"This is a serial murder case. We'll be going before the judge on Monday, but don't get your hopes up about bail."

"But Lance had nothing to do with those murders. There can't possibly be enough evidence to arrest him."

"I agree, the evidence at this point is all circumstantial. He was observed driving one of the victim's cars, and when they searched his house, they found some old newspaper clippings and a diary. The diary talks about demons terrorizing Shore Haven."

"That car was a customer car, and the journal was mine. I left it at Lance's house accidently. I'll just tell them--."

Marcus cut me off. "Because of the possible demonic implication, the FBI's counter-terrorism task force may claim jurisdiction. In a terrorism case, standard law and civil rights might not apply."

My lips trembled, as fear for my brother surged through me. "I can't believe it. Are you telling me they could torture him?"

"I doubt things would go that far. But if this is determined to be a case of psychic terrorism, Lance might never stand trial. He could spend the rest of his life in a prison cell on some remote island."

"How can this be happening? My brother had nothing to do with any of this! I have to talk to them."

"It's going to be several days before we know anything," Marcus assured me. "I don't want you talking to anyone just yet, but there is another way to help your brother."

"What do you mean?"

"Lance spoke of an obligation. A delivery which must be made today. To a special House in Rochester, if you get my drift. I believe he's spoken to you of it. He seems to think the residents are all cards."

The image of Hector's cruel smile flashed through my mind. "Of all the stupid things he would ask me, this is the worst." I already knew what was coming. "Isn't he in enough trouble already?"

"My client tells me you are aware of the implications of this obligation and the consequences to his family if the conditions are not met. My client has given me a package, which will release him from any further entanglements with the establishment in question. I have no knowledge of the contents of this package, but my client tells me you do. Do you understand what I'm talking about?"

Man oh man. "Yes. I mean, I don't think so. I don't want to do this. I've got too much going on already."

"I've been assured that the recipients will be happy to receive the package from you as long as delivery is completed by four o'clock this afternoon. My client asked me to tell you to be sure and get a signed receipt. And to please remember other people are depending on you to do this. You understand that I do not have any idea what your brother is asking you to do, but I do have his assurance that this action is not illegal. Regardless, I suggest you maintain a low profile for the next few days, until we determine jurisdiction of the case. If the authorities bring you in for questioning prematurely, things could get complicated. You could be detained for an extended period."

"We already figured that one out."

"I'm just asking you to deliver this package for my client and remain inconspicuous for the next few days. Can you do that?"

What other choice did I have? Let Lance be water-boarded because I was too scared to face Hector again? It was my fault he'd gotten arrested in the first place. "Of course."

"He's worried you might not follow through on this. He told me you disapprove of the other party. However, clearing this issue up for your brother will mitigate a motive for the situation he's in at the moment, and do a lot to help appearances. Do you understand what I'm saying?"

I sighed. "I said I'd do it. Please tell him how sorry I am about getting him arrested. About everything."

"You will deliver by the deadline?"

I glanced at Rhys and he nodded.

"Yes. Where's the package?"

"Over at my office in Brighton. I'll be in court all day, but I'll leave the package with our receptionist. You'll need to show identification."

"Okay. I'll be there." I rinsed the cold coffee out my cup, as I told Rhys about Hector and the situation at the House of Cards.

"Will you come with me? I don't want to get beat up again."

"No problem."

CHAPTER 28

SNEAKING INTO MY apartment wasn't as easy as it had been the night before, but Rhys parked his motorcycle a block away and we crept through the neighbor's yard, bypassing the street completely. I showered and changed in a flash, but every time I caught my reflection in a mirror, I couldn't help myself from staring. I so didn't recognize me anymore. My eyes were downright creepy. Adding eyeliner made things worse, not better. I washed off the make-up and decided to go with the dark sunglasses until I got some contact lenses. No way I'd ever pass for normal again.

I rode behind Rhys on the custom pillion of his roaring 1952 Indian Chief motorcycle. I wrapped my hair around my hand and crouched down behind his solid back. The sun and wind and throb between my legs had me grinning by the time we arrived. Rhys parked on the street in front of the Tudor bungalow that housed the Law Offices of Fort, Fontaigne, and Galvin. I told Rhys I'd be right back, and ran up the steps to the entrance.

I opened the front door and smacked right into Mayor Brunson. I grabbed my sunglasses hoping he hadn't recognized me, but of course he had.

"Hey Mattie, watch it willya? What are you doing

here?" He eyed my clothes and glanced uneasily toward Rhys waiting on his bike.

Words failed me as soon as I got a good look at Jim Brunson. A haze of midnight blue, green, and smoky black, with a glowing golden center surrounded his body. I knew instinctively I was seeing his aura. I'd never seen anything like it. A thread-like filament of glowing red neon encircled his torso, pulsing with his life force. I stood dazed, as the realization dawned on me. I could actually see his lifeline.

Brunson edged away from me, and I snapped back to myself.

"Sorry. I'm just here to pick up a package." I ignored the mayor and moved past him to address the receptionist with my best smile. "You have a package here for Mattie Blackman?"

The woman must have been in her fifties, and like the mayor, her aura and lifeline were also visible. I noted some interesting differences in the colors and qualities of the older woman's aura. Her lifeline was shorter than Mayor Brunson's, and in some places, the brightness grew pinched and disconcertingly fragile-looking.

"I'll need some identification."

After presenting my driver's license, she handed me a padded manila envelope with my name written across the front in bold letters. I took the envelope, thanked her and wished her a happy day.

Fifteen minutes later, Rhys and I pulled into the parking lot of House of Cards and parked the bike in one of the empty spots. The nondescript building had no windows, only a set of double glass doors. He asked me if I've ever been here before. I shook my head.

We strolled inside like we owned the place. I debated

removing my sunglasses in the darkened game parlor, but decided against it. I carried the envelope full of money clasped against my chest. Rhys took up a bodyguard stance behind my left shoulder and gave me a fierce grin.

"Well well, look who's here." Hector appeared out of nowhere and leered into my personal space. His clammy aura washed over me; his lifeline pulsed with good health. I didn't want him to touch me, but I stood my ground. Rhys stepped up beside me.

My heart hammered. "I want to talk to the manager."

"She's busy. You can talk to me, girlfriend." Two other bouncer types approached, but he waved them off. They drifted away, keeping their eyes on us. They all wore shoes with leather tassels. Must be company dress code or something.

"I'm here to make the payoff for Lance McNair."

Surprise flashed across his face for a moment, replaced by a sneer of total scorn.

"What, is the big man too scared to come in person? Give it here little girl, I'll be happy to take whatever you've got. You must be tougher than you look, princess. I don't see a mark on you. I must be losing my touch."

He glanced at Rhys as if to size him up.

Rhys tensed up beside me. I took a deep, calming breath. This guy meant nothing to me. The only thing I needed to do was to get Lance's debt paid off. This guy was merely a distraction, nothing more. The casino area was full of people; Hector wouldn't dare make a scene in front of the customers.

"Just tell the manager I'm here, please. I believe I'm expected."

Hector spoke a few words of Italian into a walkie-talkie. After a moment, he got an acknowledgement. He flashed a sign at one of the other bouncers and the big man came over to man the door.

"All right Miss Priss, follow me."

He led us across the main room, past blackjack tables, craps, and a carved, ornate bar. We passed through swinging doors into a well-lit kitchen, then down a dark hallway that dead-ended in an unmarked door. Hector gave a soft knock and Rhys and I followed him into a posh, well-lit office.

The oriental carpet glowed red beneath a matching cream-colored suede sofa and chairs. Along one wall stood a massive aquarium, filled with a dozen google-eyed fantail goldfish. An attractive Asian woman faced us, seated behind a carved black desk. She wore an expensive-looking black suit that must have been custom tailored to fit her toothpick figure. Two beefy men patted us down for weapons while Hector made the introductions.

"This is Miriam Wu, the manager of the House of Cards. This here is McNair's girlfriend. She says she's here to pay off his tab."

She ignored me; instead giving Rhys her attention over little half-moon glasses.

"What are you doing here, Rhys? Miss me?" I glanced at Rhys but his face said nothing. I wondered how he knew her. This was no cavewoman Barbie. Her lipstick was bright crimson, and she sported a dragon-lady manicure.

"Play nice, Mimsy. I'm just here for moral support."

I gave Rhys a look. Mimsy Wu?

She closed the red leather book in front of her and addressed me without actually making eye contact. "I'm a busy woman, miss. Are you here to pay me the money

Lance McNair owes me?"

"Lance is my brother, and I want a signed receipt."
I was glad for the sense of assumed cool the shades
gave me. I felt my bitch hormones kick in. "Mimsy.
And your word that you'll leave my brother and our
family alone."

She nodded and pulled a book of receipts out of the
drawer next to her. "Give me the money." She held out
her hand without looking at me.

I don't like you either. If there had been any other
way to do this, I would have walked out.

I started to hand over the envelope when the fresh
reek of licorice hit me, and I froze. It took me less than
half a second to find the named djemon squatting
invisibly on the oriental behind her chair.

"Well hello." I leaned over for a closer inspection.

The creature was like Blix and Larry; named, but
not yet commanded, and thus not visible on the physical
plane. The smell of this djemon, although still of anise,
had a different quality than my guys. This one wasn't
mine. It wasn't looking at me; its attention was focused
exclusively on its master. She knew it was there, all
right, but nobody else did. Except me.

"Looks like you've got a named djemon here,
Mimsy." I walked around the side of the desk to get a
better look and the two bodyguards started toward me.
I pointed at her. "Unless you want trouble, lose the
palookas." I squatted next to the demon, demonstrating
to her I knew exactly what and where it was.

She paled and dropped the receipt book. "I don't
know what you're talking about. Give me the money."

I leaned over and put my face close to hers, lowered
my sunglasses and gave her the full benefit of my

new look. She backed up a little and dismissed the bodyguards. They left without a word.

She waited until the door closed behind them before she snapped at Rhys. "Who the hell is this?"

Rhys grinned hugely; I could tell he was enjoying himself. "This is Lance McNair's sister, Mattie Blackman. You might know her better as the new Hand of Fate."

Mimsy squealed and did a double take. "Oh my god. I can't believe it." She jumped up and hugged me. "You're Madame Coumlie's heir?"

I stared at Rhys, hoping for an explanation but he shrugged me off, grinning.

"Why didn't you say so? Why are you paying off this note?"

"I'm not. I'm just delivering it." I handed her the cash. "This is Lance's money. I'd appreciate it if you wouldn't let him in here anymore." I forced myself to say it aloud. "He's a compulsive gambler."

"Yes, I know. He's got himself mixed up that skank Andrea Gregson. I don't know how she managed it, but she's got her claws in deep." She scribbled out a receipt and signed it and held it out to me. "Here, take it. I don't want your money. Lance's debt is paid in full."

Don't look a gift horse in the mouth. I took the receipt before she changed her mind. It acknowledged receipt of sixty-three thousand dollars. It was signed by one Miriam Mingmei Wu. I wondered if she was related to the same Mingmei my great-grandmother had told me about. Had to be.

"Thanks." I tried to explain. "He's my brother. He raised me."

She sighed. "I know what it's like to have a brother

in trouble. You want to help them, but they have to fight their own battles." She reached out and took my hand with her manicured fingers. She had bones like a bird. "I truly am so sorry for your loss. Madame Coumlie has always been a true friend to my family; she was a wonderful woman."

I accepted her condolences and answered her questions about the funeral. She assured me she would be attending the visitation and gave me her card with her personal contact information.

"What about that guy?" I nodded to the creature squatting at her feet. A miniature pterodactyl, if I had to guess.

"I talked to Madame last week, and she told me she would take care of it." Mimsy was closer to my age than I'd first guessed. "I do apologize for my poor manners earlier. Will you be taking over for her?"

In spite of everything, I sort of liked her. I mumbled something about taking care of her little djemon problem as soon as things settled down, although I didn't have a clue what I had just promised. I also made a mental note to stop making promises like that in the future. She escorted us out to the parking lot, assuring me that everything between Lance and the House of Cards was now copacetic. She even promised to permanently eighty-six Lance from the premises.

I climbed back on the bike behind Rhys and waited for him to start the engine, but he didn't.

"What?"

"Mimsy is the biggest gossip in town. By tomorrow, everyone is going to know you're the new Hand."

"Do I need to be concerned?"

"Madame Coumlie had a lot of clients, Mattie. Shore

Haven is a well-known sanctuary for the supernatural community, and you've just been elected president of the club. Your life is about to change."

"Don't you worry about me; I can handle myself just fine. How do you know Mimsy?"

He laughed and kick-started the engine. Any further conversation on that topic was going to be impossible. We cruised up the street and I put my head down and held on tight. I wondered what kind of club he meant. When Mimsy had escorted us outside, I'd noticed every single person in the card room, including Hector and the doormen had an aura and lifeline. Everyone, that is, except Mimsy, Rhys, and me.

CHAPTER 29

RHYS DROPPED ME off at Madame Coumlie's house to search through the journals one last time before we headed out to the cave again. He'd arranged for the French translator to come over to his place that afternoon anyway, so I told Rhys I would meet him at Mystic Properties in two hours. Besides, I had an idea I wanted to try. He took off on the bike and I let myself in with the key he gave me.

For all its gaudy emptiness, the old Queen Anne house welcomed me. I stashed the envelope full of Lance's money under the sink and brewed a pot of coffee. I would probably need that money to pay the lawyer. I heard an old clock ticking somewhere upstairs. With the curtains closed all day, the house was a peaceful oasis, but I had work to do. I took my coffee and a few journals into the living room. I settled myself in against a needlepoint pillow on the faded pink couch.

I wondered how Mimsy and Rhys knew each other. She'd been all over herself to make it up to me when she realized I was Madame Coumlie's heir. She was the only other person I'd met with an invisible djemon. I sort of liked her, except for the fact that she might have slept with Rhys, who seemed to be well acquainted with quite a lot of women.

I still had questions about her aura, though. Or lack of it; and Rhys and I didn't have auras either. I doubted the lack of an aura and lifeline meant the same thing for each of us. I mean, there could only be one Hand of Fate, right?

When Mimsy talked about Madame Coumlie banishing her djemon, it started me thinking. Banishing a djinn or djemon had to be something simple. I considered my little congregation of djinn and named djemons.

"Scat." I waved my hand at them. Nothing happened. They didn't even blink.

I sighed and opened the journal on my lap, staring at pages and pages of tight, tiny, even script. The penmanship was neat, but convoluted, and hard to make out unless I gave it my full attention and concentrated. This would take forever.

I put the book aside and slid off the couch to the floor. Blix and Larry crept closer, but the others remained huddled in a group about six feet away. I thought about how Madame Coumlie commanded Oneiri to appear. I wondered if, with my new abilities, I could do something similar. What if I gave them a direct order? It would have to be something formal, I decided. What should I say?

"I command you to disappear." I simultaneously clapped my hands, receiving a small electric shock. One of the djinn vanished, only to reappear a moment later as a fully materialized djemon in the flesh. It was real. I got goosebumps. What had I done?

The new guy surveyed the room, clearly proud of its new status. He stamped his tiny feet and stepped in front of Larry and Blix as if to say, 'I'm da man'.

This bony little fellow looked just like Mimsy's baby pterodactyl. I reached out to caress its leathery body, which was hot to the touch. Blix and Larry hissed at the new creature, and Blix appeared especially furious at the newcomer. It ignored them, and sidled closer to me, seeming to enjoy the touch of my hand. I stroked his leathery winglets and couldn't help thinking this is so cool.

Then it hit me. I had just inadvertently named the pterodactyl djinn-thing You, and given it a direct command. I'd just become a demon master. Oh crap. A shudder washed though me. I had no idea it would be this easy.

My eyelid began to twitch. What a can of worms. I'd have to register him, of course. I would be tracked and monitored by the FBI for the rest of my life. Everyone would know, and if he grew, I could be arrested. I remembered the look of warning Rhys had given me when I mentioned Oneiri's name to Porter. Obviously, the Hand of Fate had never registered her djemon; and now I understood why. Blix and Larry, at least, were still invisible.

What would Porter do to me if he found out? I thought about what he'd said about damning my soul to hell, and tried to figure out if I felt any different. Nope. Not a bit. Maybe accidents didn't count. That argument probably wouldn't wash with the feds.

I was getting the hang of this, though. Obviously, if I wanted to get rid of these guys, I would need to be specific. I gathered my thoughts and intention and focused on the exact words I wanted to say.

"I command You and the unnamed djinn in my presence to disappear from this place and go to the cave beneath Sentinel Hill, where you shall await my command." I clapped my hands.

With a zing and a flash, they all winked out, leaving me alone with Blix and Larry. I sat still for a minute, scarcely believing they'd gone. It worked! For the first time in days, I was without an entourage. I breathed a huge sigh of relief. Even the air smelled better.

I jumped up and danced around the room. Yes! It was so simple. This whole Hand of Fate thing was going to work out just fine, after all. I've got it! Rounding up the rest of the djinn and getting them back into the cave would be a piece of cake. We'd seal up the break and be done with it. I'd get myself some contact lenses, and be back to normal no time. No more teratosis. I'd be able to resume my social life again.

My next thought was for Rhys. I had to tell him about this. We could go to the caves right away; we didn't need to translate the journals. I called him, but there was no answer. I knew he had to be there, so I grabbed my pocketbook and keys, and slipped out the back door, locking it behind me. Mystic Properties was just a few blocks away. I couldn't wait to tell him.

CHAPTER 30

THE BACK DOOR of Mystic Properties stood wide open when I arrived, and Rhys' truck sat parked in the lot, so I walked right in. The stench of blood and licorice hit me like a blow. I froze. The place had been trashed; broken furniture, papers, and books lay strewn across the room. A large pool of blood stretched across the floor near the bathroom, and more spattered in an arc across the shredded couch and walls of the back office.

Oh my god. Nausea choked me. I squatted down and tested the edge of the pool with my fingers. Sticky, it hadn't been there long. A bloody partial footprint from a three-toed creature led out the back door. The print dwarfed my shoe.

"Rhys?"

I cautiously made my way toward the stairs leading up to his apartment. I peered up the darkened stairwell, and sensed movement.

My heart leapt into my throat. I shouted up the stairs. "Who's there?" I took a step back. "Show yourself. Um, I've got a gun. The police are on their way."

"Don't shoot," a voice with a trace of an accent whispered down to me. I backed away as he descended. Out of the gloom stepped a wiry man in his late thirties, wearing baggy jeans and a faded blue t-shirt. He wore his hair cropped short, almost to his skull, and a gold ring pierced the top of each ear. His eyes, an unnatural shade of pale blue, showed a brilliant yellow halo round the pupil. He had no aura or lifeline. I'd never seen him before, yet something about him seemed familiar.

"Do I know you?"

"You are Mattie." He looked scared to death. "I am the translator."

I nodded. "What happened?"

"I must go. I cannot allow the police to find me here." He tried to move past me, but I blocked his way. He stood only a couple inches taller than me.

"Wait. What happened here? Where's Rhys?"

He stared at the chaos in the room; the blood on the floor. "I, I don't know. I arrived just before you and found the door open. I heard you come in, and I hid. I thought whoever had done this might be coming back. I have to go." Before I could grab him, he took off running and was gone.

A strange sense of calm settled over me. No doubt the big djemon Fontaigne had seen at Madame Coumlie's place had gotten to Rhys. But why would he want to kidnap the mage? I started to call 911, but decided to call Porter instead. He didn't answer. I left a message asking him to call me immediately.

If the big bad demon had Rhys, the obvious place to start looking was in the cavern. Everything started from there. I grabbed the keys off the hook by the door and had the truck heading down Third before I even thought about it. I still had an hour or two before dark.

With Madame Coumlie gone, we'd been sitting ducks. Of course she had been the one keeping the demons in line; she must have the power to overrule a demon master. How could I have been so stupid? Without her to keep a lid on things, the master and his demons would be free to act. The way Fontaigne described the old woman's encounter with the big djemon, I had assumed that she had banished it, like I'd done with my little djinn. Apparently, that wasn't the case. I'd been asking all the wrong questions.

We bounced along the dirt track, and I glanced over to the passenger seat to where Larry and Blix sat staring at me. I'd use Blix to lead me to Rhys. The order would make him a djemon in the flesh, but I didn't have any choice. Porter couldn't fit through the cave entrance, and calling the police was out. They'd just haul me in for questioning. Rhys needed my help now.

I arrived at the trailhead, parked the truck, grabbed a helmet and flashlight, and slung Rhys' coil of nylon rope over my shoulder. All set. This time, turning Blix into a fully materialized djemon would be no accident. I would have to keep him a secret for the rest of my life. If a psychic penalty had to be paid for summoning a djemon on purpose, I was about to be double damned. Would it condemn me to hell as well as to prison? No time to think about that now. Time was wasting, I had no other choice.

"Blix, I command you to show me the way to where Rhys is. Find Rhys." I clapped my hands.

With a little sting, Blix popped into being. He squeaked at me, and then took off running like a cottontail Chihuahua. Every few steps, he paused to look back at me with those luminous yellow eyes. I started after him, but changed my mind and went back to the truck. I might be the new Hand of Fate, but that sure didn't make me a superhero. I didn't want to go after a giant djemon without some sort of weapon. I searched the truck, and came up with a crowbar. I hefted the reassuring weight. That'll work. I gave it a test swing and followed Blix into the woods, as clouds of mosquitoes surrounded me like a vampiric fog. I hoped we weren't too late.

CHAPTER 31

DUSK HAD DESCENDED by the time we reached the cave entrance. It took me a long time to find the right key to get the grate open in the near-dark. Blix squeaked at me impatiently the whole time. I got the gate open, and lowered myself into the tunnel. The cold hit me, and I regretted not wearing warmer clothes.

I followed Blix straight to the slanted tunnel entrance leading down into the bat cave. I spent more precious time trying to figure out how to tie off the rope. In the end, I used the crowbar as a wedge across the opening, and tied the rope to the middle. Using the crowbar as a brace, I'd be able to lower myself down without breaking my neck. This way, I'd still have a chance of getting back out again. At least, that was the plan. Of course, that left me without a weapon. Oh well.

I stood on top of one of the cat cages and boosted myself up into the tunnel. The stench of bat guano, urine, and anise made breathing difficult. As I cleared the tunnel, my headlamp showed the cavern filled with djinn. 'You' flew up to greet me; the other members of my little horde waited on the cavern floor with a few thousand of their friends.

Now came the dicey part. In spite of the cold, I was sweating as I lowered myself face first and began to pull my legs out of the tunnel entrance above me. I'd intended to somersault around and drop feet first, but I hadn't anticipated that my sweaty hands wouldn't be able to maintain my grip on the rope. As I twisted my body around to vertical, I lost my grip and fell.

I landed hard. I lay for a few minutes, gasping and clenching everything clenchable, until I could breathe again. Other than a few bruises I was basically uninjured; with a couple of nasty rope burns and the taste of blood in my mouth. The djinn crowded around me, all giving me glassy luminous stares which completely creeped me out.

"Get back." I slapped my hand across my mouth, but nothing happened. I hadn't issued the command in the proper form, I guess. Sort of like Jeopardy. I smothered a hysterical giggle. Focus Mattie.

"Blix. Where are you? Find Rhys."

Immediately, my little demon popped up in front of me, and I straightened my helmet and pulled the flashlight out of my pocket. Without the crowbar, my hands needed something to do. I switched it on, but nothing happened. Great. I shook it and heard the broken bits of bulb rattling around behind the lens. Good thing the helmet lamp still worked. I decided to hang on to the flashlight anyway, and followed Blix. There would be no going back now, we didn't have any more time to waste.

We crossed the cavern, and with each step my feet sank into several inches of fresh and petrified bat guano. I followed Blix to a doorway carved right into the rock, barred by a plain wooden door, maybe five feet high. I tried the doorknob, and it opened.

Rough steps had been hacked into the bedrock,

which led down into pitch darkness. The ceiling and walls were rough, but a few places looked as if they had been smoothed by tools. I smelled fresher air, so I closed the door behind us and followed Blix. The trail ended at a junction with what I imagined was a mineshaft. Without hesitation, Blix turned to the left, and I followed.

This main tunnel appeared larger, with smoother floors and a low ceiling, probably six feet high and about twelve feet wide. A small-gage railroad track ran down the middle, but I saw no other signs of civilization. The smell of licorice had faded behind us, and the only things I smelled now were Blix, Larry, and dirt.

I trotted behind my demon, my sense of urgency rising with every step. Rhys had been taken alive for a reason, otherwise his body would have been left behind. Hold that thought, Mattie.

We made good progress. The speed kept me warm, but I wished I'd remembered to bring water. I had no idea where we were going. I guessed we were headed back toward Shore Haven. The other end of this tunnel must open somewhere near the lake. I'd heard stories of bootleggers using tunnels under Shore Haven to smuggle whiskey across from Canada during Prohibition, but I'd never imagined them to be true.

After an hour, I was panting heavily and had to slow down. Blix peeped at me in irritation. As I ran-walked to keep up, I began to worry we wouldn't find a way out. With each step, the weight of the unrelenting blackness added to my anxiety, but I forced myself to keep moving forward. I began seeing piles of trash and rags, and old crates stacked along the sides of the tunnel. We passed alcoves stocked with bits of broken machinery and lanterns. I looked for something I could use as a weapon, but didn't find anything.

The first time I saw a door, I ran to open it. A brand new padlock prevented access. I tried knocking while Blix squeaked at me to catch up. Rhys wasn't behind that door. We passed more doorways that opened into the tunnel; all with new padlocks installed. Sub-basement doors, I guessed.

The tunnel began to curve to the right. The walls and floors smoothed out. The walls seeped moisture and the humidity increased. I noticed fixtures and pipes running along the ceiling above us. We had to be underneath the Shore by now. Hell, we should have started our search from Mystic Properties. It would have been a lot faster than driving all the way out to Sentinel Hill. I hoped we wouldn't be too late to help Rhys.

I started running again. Blix kept twenty feet ahead of me, stopping every few feet to stare and urge me on. My headlamp was dimming, but the quality of darkness seemed to be changing. The tunnel curved again to the right, and I smelled the lakeshore ahead of us.

The tunnel widened into a low cavern. Large boulders blocked the view ahead, but a warm breeze beckoned to me. The sandy ground gave way to a well-used path. My spirits rose, as the night air freshened across my face, and through a grated entrance ahead of me, I saw the night sky and the twinkling reflection of the surface of the lake. I sprinted to the opening.

An iron grate spanned across a gap in the boulders clustered along the shoreline. Although the grate appeared to be old and rusted, it was embedded in solid rock, and had been secured with yet another shiny new padlock. I tried every key on Rhys' key ring. This was not the way out.

Blix's squeaking caught my attention, and I trotted back to the cavern. This had to be where the rail line ended; or started, I guessed. Nearby, wooden worktables stood covered in layers of dust. Blix bounced up and down like a manic rabbit, as if to tell me to hurry up. The light from my headlamp had grown dimmer with every passing minute, so it wasn't until I approached the door that I noticed the skeleton.

The bones were arranged in a neat pile, with the skull placed on top so the eye sockets glared directly up at anyone who would dare to turn the doorknob. A not-so-subtle warning. A sick mind.

Blix was now banging himself against the solid door, insisting that Rhys was here, just behind the door, if only I would open it. The handle showed no sign of dirt or dust, and no external padlock barred the entrance. The only way out the tunnels would be through this door.

I took a deep breath and turned off the headlamp. If we were going to be sneaking into someone's basement, I didn't want them to see me first. I hushed Blix; and cautiously opened the door.

CHAPTER 32

I FOLLOWED BLIX up a steep narrow stairway to another closed door. The knob turned easily, and I eased myself into a darkened room. Several green power lights pinpointed the room with an eerie glow. Somewhere in the distance the comforting sound of a compressor hummed. Probably a dehumidifier. Blix dashed through the door first, and waited for me as I crept inside, closing the door quietly behind me. I paused for a few minutes straining to listen if anyone was coming, but I couldn't hear a thing over the sound of my pounding heart and the whirr of the compressor.

We were standing inside a commercial kitchen; paved with black and white floor tiles, appointed with professional grade stainless steel equipment. To the right stood a combination sink and industrial dishwasher unit; on the left, a bank of refrigerators droned. A steel butcher's table dominated the center of the room; the drain running from the cutting surface into the floor. Overhead, an assortment of sharp-looking kitchen utensils and cleavers hung from a rack suspended from the ceiling. Opposite me was the wooden door of a large walk-in freezer. Through the small window in the door, I could see frost-covered shelving just inside.

Blix slammed himself continuously against the wooden door to the walk-in. I moved closer, and he scrabbled his claws at the base of door. I pulled on the chrome handle, but it took two hands to get it open.

A dim red light flicked on and I gasped when I saw Rhys lying motionless on the floor. I sobbed; grabbed him by his shirt and dragged him through the doorway back into the kitchen. I couldn't tell if he was alive or dead. With shaking fingers, I felt for his pulse. His skin was so cold. I couldn't feel a thing.

"Come on, Rhys, work with me."

I put my lips to his neck and felt a faint throb of life. Yes! A hysterical giggle escaped my lips, and I smothered it as I heard the clatter of a pan fall to the floor in another room. I froze, feeling exposed by the red light of the walk-in. I looked up, searching for the switch.

I gazed into the frozen scream of Andrea Gregson. I stifled a yell, slapping both my hands over my mouth. The walk-in freezer was full of bodies. They were stacked on top of one another like TV dinners. Even their clothes were covered in hoarfrost. I reached into my pocket for my cell phone, but something massive big hit me from behind, throwing me off Rhys, pinning me to the floor beneath a heavy, kerosene-soaked rug. I couldn't breathe. I tried to call for help, but couldn't. As I struggled to get clear, the beating began in earnest.

CHAPTER 33

I AWOKE TO the sound of metal scraping against stone and found myself lying spread-eagled on the metal butcher's table, my wrists and ankles duct-taped to the edges. Accompanying the sound came the off-key whistling of someone approaching. The familiar melody grated on my memory, but I couldn't place the tune. Overhead fluorescent lights exposed me to the pale yellow room, exploiting my solitary fear and vulnerable position. I strained against the tape without success.

I saw no sign of Rhys. I called to Blix, and he appeared right away, staring at me with a worried expression.

"Hey Blix. Come here and get me loose."

Blix crawled up on my chest and stared down at me. He licked his eyes and gave me a mournful squeak. I took a deep breath and tried again.

"Blix. I command you to chew the tape on my arm loose. No, not my arm, the tape. Yeah, good boy. Chew through the tape, Blix. Ow, try not to bite me, ow. Okay, never mind." The needle sharp teeth bit to my wrist, but I didn't care. "Keep chewing, that's right." Hurry.

The sound of boots reverberated on stone floors, getting closer, along with sounds of metal being scraped against the walls. Fingers on a blackboard. He'd be here any minute.

Fear welled up inside me. "Hurry up." I wriggled my left hand, trying to loosen the tape, as Blix's teeth weren't a good match for the job. The tape began to give a little. If I could get my cell phone out of my pocket, I'd be able to call for help.

The whistling became louder as the demon master approached. A sharp clatter of metal sounded on the distant stone floor, as he dropped whatever he was coming to kill me with.

"Come on, Blix. You can do it." I twisted my wrist again, sweating and straining against my bondage. I felt a definite give this time. Duct tape didn't stick so good over bloody, sweaty skin. Blix was making progress. My left wrist swiveled a scooch.

Trapped like a rat in a sack, the approaching whistle made me want to scream. I tried to think about what to do. I wondered if Rhys could still be alive. I wished I'd told Porter about Rhys being kidnapped when I left that message. Man oh man, this guy was coming to kill me. No one would be looking for me.

A shriek of laughter escaped me as I remembered what tune the demon master was whistling. The one we sang as kids. About the worms crawling around in your brains and playing pinochle in your snout. Panicking now, I squirmed against the tape around my wrist. I twisted and pulled with all my strength and my bloody hand came free.

Adrenaline surged. I jammed my hand into my pocket, pulled out my cell phone and turned it on. I told Blix to work on my left ankle, and scrabbled at the tape on my right hand. As soon as the phone powered up, I saw

I had a signal and dialed Porter's number. He answered on the second ring, just as Blix got my left ankle free.

"What the hell is going on," was all I heard before Garlan Russ came at me with a machete. I grunted and kicked out hard with my foot. I nailed him right in the center of his chest and knocked him back. The phone flew out my hand, and Garr kept coming.

The machete bit into my arm with a sickening thunk. I marveled that I didn't feel a thing even as the blade lodged itself into the bone. He wrenched the weapon free and hit me again. My blood flew, splattering against the walls. Another chop bit deeply into my shin. Hit by hit, Garr was hacking me to pieces. I thrashed and kicked, trying to keep him off me.

"Blix! Larry! Stop him!" Stupid, but the only thing that came to me. Larry popped into view and the two of them jumped at Garr. Two guinea pigs against a grown man in his physical prime with a machete. He batted them away like flies, but they kept coming back, distracting him from chopping at me. In a lucky grab, Larry jumped up and bit Garr right in the crotch and held on.

Garr roared and dropped the machete and clutched at Larry while I worked frantically to free my other hand.

"Rex, get in here."

The huge head pushed through the door.

I shrieked and struggled to pull free, but the duct tape on my right wrist and ankle held. The creature's head alone had to be big as a Lay-z-boy recliner, and a great white would have envied that mouthful of teeth, each as long as a pencil. Rex targeted me with predatory glare and bellowed.

His bloody breath blasted over me and I screamed bloody murder. Fontaigne was right; the massive djemon looked like a dinosaur, but the unmistakable intelligence in his amber eyes made him all the more terrifying. The monster had to be four or five times bigger than Oneiri, maybe half a ton of heavy bones and slabs of muscle.

Larry let go of Garr and slithered across the floor to attack Rex.

"How did you find me," Garr demanded, raising the machete.

"Where's Rhys?" I screamed, my mind racing to think of something, anything to keep him off me. "Why did you release the djinn?"

He laughed and lowered the machete a little. "You think I did that? My father showed me that cavern when I was in junior high. Rex here has been with me ever since."

"You're a demon master." I had to keep him talking. I cocked my left leg in front of me and kept working at the tape on my right hand. I couldn't find the edge of the tape with my numb fingers, but knew I couldn't break eye contact with Garr.

"Look who's talking. Although yours aren't much more than fish food." His face was stone and I wondered how I'd ever thought him attractive. "Rex is as strong as I am, now." He glanced at the monstrous demon beside him. "He has his own reasons for doing what he does. I can't control him anymore. So yes, I've resorted to using the small ones."

He hefted the machete in his hand and took a stance like a pitcher at bat.

I sobbed. "Please. I'm begging you. Don't do this.

Please let me go, I won't tell anyone." We had to be somewhere inside the Sand Castle.

"Tell me who you tried to call or I'm going to have Rex here bite you. Believe me, you do not want him to bite you. He likes it entirely too much."

"You're the Night Shark. You and him together. That's it, isn't it? Djemons don't leave DNA behind."

"Rex, I command you to bite her." The thing snaked its head around Garr and made a grab for me.

"Rex, NO!" I held up my free hand in a futile attempt to fend the monster off. Its intelligent eyes focused on the now glowing crescent mark in the palm of my hand. The djemon hesitated; I knew I was on the right track.

"You're so stupid. They only obey their master. I said bite--."

In an instant, Rex chomped Garr's shoulder with a ghastly crunch. Garr screamed and the demon turned and fled through the doorway. The bite was quick, but the wound no less devastating for it.

Garr dropped the machete and fell to the floor, clutching the remains of his arm. The bite had gone all the way through the shoulder, and his shredded limb dangled as useless as spaghetti. Blood pumped in thick spurts across the tile floor. I heard myself screaming and forced myself to calm down. I didn't know if Rex was coming back or not. I had to get out now.

I had Blix work on my ankle while I struggled with the tape around my wrist. Larry's teeth weren't made for gnawing, but they'd done a great job on Garr's nuts, so who was I to complain? I scraped futilely at the tape, scratching for an edge; my numb hand too sweaty and bloody to be useful.

Garr began to moan. "Not my fault," he said, over and

over. There was something wrong with his aura. Clotted and gray, it appeared to be eroding in some areas, the gaps held together by only a transparent film of slime. He looked as if he were rotting from the inside out.

"Help!" I desperately hoped someone heard me. The duct tape at my wrist wasn't cooperating. Nothing was working. To my horror, Garr scooted himself across the bloody floor toward the machete.

"You don't know what it's like," he grunted. A sea of blood pooled across the floor and spatter dripped down the walls. I couldn't believe he still had the strength to move. He inched closer to the machete. "My father is crazy. Richer than Midas." Garr grabbed for the weapon, which skittered just out of his reach.

Blix finally gnawed through the silver tape wrapped around my ankle. I yelled and kicked my foot free. Sirens sounded in the distance and my emotions soared, but I couldn't be sure they were heading this way. I twisted myself around and landed on my feet, my right wrist still taped to the table. I began to bite at it.

Garr reached the machete. He held it with his good hand as he struggled to his knees.

"When I turned thirteen, my old man gave me a deadline. If I made a million on my own by my thirtieth birthday, I'd inherit everything." He grunted as he got one foot beneath him, and rested, panting. "Otherwise, he would give everything to charity. Can you believe that," he panted. "That's my money." He put the point of the machete on the floor and steadied himself as he attempted to stand.

"He told me his father had made him the same deal. But my crazy old man used his demon to help him." He coughed, and fell to his knees.

I couldn't make any progress biting through the tape. I scratched at the edge in desperation until I got a corner unstuck. My hands shook as I feverishly began to unwind my constraint.

Garr was just babbling now. "Rex and I started in Germantown. It was so easy. We took jewelry, coins, and cash, anything I could sell. There's a lot of money in Germantown, you know." Garr slumped over, and was quiet.

I wrenched myself free from the last of the tape and tried to run but slipped in the blood and sprawled flat on the slick tile floor. I struggled to my feet and looked around for my cell phone, but couldn't find it. I slipped over to check the walk-in, but Rhys wasn't inside. I slammed the door shut and frantically looked for a way out, but Garr lay between me and the doorway.

I edged my way around Garr. He reached out with surprising quickness and grabbed me by my ankle. I slipped and fell. I fought and bit and squirmed, but somehow, he managed to pull himself on top of me and use his bloody weight to hold me down. My right arm was trapped beneath him, but my other hand was free. I fought to get him off me.

The pounding of footsteps rumbled above us. Lots of footsteps.

"Down here!" I pounded at Garr's mangled shoulder, but he didn't seem to feel a thing. It was like pounding clay. He wrapped his powerful hand around my throat and tightened his grip.

I froze, not daring to move a muscle. My heart pounded in a panic.

"My own father lied to me. He lied to me. Every time I did what he asked. Every time, he told me I had to do more. To prove myself." Garr gazed into my eyes as if noticing me for the first time. His expression changed.

"I would never lie to my kids. I would never lie to you." He was strong and heavy as granite. With each word, his grip on my throat squeezed tighter.

"You have to understand. Building the new marina was my father's idea. A couple of key property owners didn't share my father's vision. They didn't want to sell. I used Rex to persuade them differently. I thought my father would respect me. Thank me. My father is crazy. I got nothing."

My hand fluttered uselessly at his face, my strength nearly gone.

"Rex liked the killing part. I never told him to kill. I made him bring the bodies here, but after a while he wouldn't listen to me anymore. He started killing on his own. What could I do? I couldn't stop him. I couldn't go to the cops. When I ran out of freezer space, he started leaving them for the police to find." Garr coughed and closed his eyes. "No respect." His voice only a whisper now, as his life ebbed away.

"No." His eyes opened. His sweat and drool dripped on my face. "Listen." I heard bangs overhead, as if someone was battering down a door. Garr squeezed my neck tighter. Everything sounded so far away.

"Rex has his own reasons for killing now. I can't stop him, it's not my fault. I have nothing to do with it."

I scrabbled to peel his fingers off my throat, but he was unyielding as stone. The floor felt cool and comforting. "They're coming," I gasped.

"Listen to me, you little freak, nobody's going to believe a word you say. My father owns this town. You are nothing. Less than nothing. Your mother was nothing but a psycho whore."

In the fading distance, I heard a door shatter. Shouting.

"Here." My voice would not rise above a whisper. Black spots swirled before me. I felt myself slipping away. *I'm going to die.*

"Oh yeah, I knew her. She was my first. I bet you didn't know that." He grunted, shifting his position. "You look a lot like her."

To my horror, his erection grew rigid between us. He grunted and paused to shift his grip on my throat.

"You know, you're about the right age. You could even be my daughter." He began to squeeze in earnest.

I floated. The darkness threatened to overwhelm me, as my range of vision narrowed to a glowing pinpoint. Something broke open inside me and flooded my veins with cool soothing blackness. Death. Chilled fingers caressed my inner eye and called my name. Madame Coumlie was right. A thrill rushed through me, as I accepted the truth of her words. *I am death incarnate.*

I shivered and smiled as I opened my eyes and focused on the glowing thread before me. With my free hand, I slipped my index finger around Garr's lifeline. His pulse skittered, an irregular thrum across the strand.

"What are you doing," he said. "Stop it." The pressure on my neck increased. There was no choice.

"Time to die," I whispered, and snapped the brittle thread between my fingers.

CHAPTER 34

GARR'S EYES CLOSED and he collapsed on top of me. I gasped and sobbed as I inhaled my first ragged breath of air. I fought to shove his bloody corpse off of me.

The thunder of boots sounded on stairs, accompanied by shouts and another crash. I sent Blix and Larry to hide as Frank Porter called out my name and the cavalry crossed the outer basement. They couldn't hear my hoarsely whispered answers. I finally managed to roll Garr off me, just as they boiled into the room, in full SWAT regalia. Frank pulled me free and helped me up. I got blood all over his suit.

"Mattie!" He motioned the paramedic over. "Where are you hurt?" I stared at the body on the floor. The guy checking Garr's pulse shook his head.

"Where is Rhys?" Porter pointed me back toward the stairs. I tottered over to where the paramedics hovered over Rhys and collapsed beside him.

"Here Mattie, I'm here." Rhys reached out to me. I grabbed his icy cold hand and held on tight. "Okay, we're fine, I'm fine, and you're fine."

I slobbered and blubbered over him and made a big fuss, not giving a lick what anyone thought. By the time the paramedics finished checking us, both of us had recovered enough to convince everyone we did not need or want medical assistance. Thanks to my new recuperative powers, my arm had already stopped bleeding, and neither Rhys nor I would agree to go with the paramedics, so Frank let us sit in the back of his car until they got the mess in the Sand Castle straightened out.

The night air was balmy, but Rhys and I lay huddled in blankets with the heater running full blast. We wrapped ourselves around each other, taking comfort in the gradual build up of heat between us.

I felt safe, but I didn't want to be alone. I didn't want to close my eyes and relive finding the pool of blood on the floor of Mystic Properties, or the sensation of Garr's sweat dripping into my eyes, or the bite of the machete into my bones. Or worst of all, the memory of those cool fingers of joy and death as they called my name and the eager voice in my blood as I answered the call.

Rhys had a nasty bruise to his temple, but the bloody cut over his eyebrow had already closed.

"Tell me what happened, Rhys. I thought you were dead."

"I waited upstairs for the translator, and thought I heard him at the back door. I went down to let him in, and a huge demon attacked me. I woke up to see Garlan Russ stomping the hell out of someone. I didn't know it was you."

"Why did Rex come for you? Is he dead now?"

"You're tensing up again." Rhys pulled me closer and shifted himself on the cramped bench seat so that I sprawled on top of him. "Relax." His strong hands massaged my back, kneading away knots of tension.

"That's not an answer. And you're not exactly relaxed either." I said. Some parts of Rhys were much less relaxed than others, I noticed.

"Sure I am. I am completely present and in the moment. Quiet your mind. Focus on your breath, and you won't have room to think of anything else."

"Is this some kind of Zen thing or a mage thing?" I cracked an eye and he smiled. Outside, car doors slammed and engines started up, and vehicles departed the lot. Things were wrapping up.

A few minutes later, a grim Agent Porter returned to the car.

"Hey you two sure you're all right?"

"No worries, Frank. We're fine."

"How did you find us," I asked.

"When you guys ran out on me, I tried to track you through your cell phone, but you didn't have it turned on. When I got your message, I realized you'd probably gone to the caves. We found Rhys' truck at the trailhead, and had a couple guys ready to go in and bring you out, but then I got your call. This time we were able to triangulate a signal on the Sand Castle. Without that signal, we never would have found you, or the Night Shark either, for that matter. I owe you one, Mattie."

"You saved our lives." I wondered if it was true. "Does this mean my brother is off the hook?"

"I don't make the decisions, but yeah, probably. The bodies we found in his freezer showed the same injuries as the known victims. The crime scene guys will be processing the place for days, but we found more than enough evidence to show Russ was the Night Shark and a demon master to boot. He used that room we found you in to butcher meat. We're guessing he ground up the bodies into meal and rinsed them directly into the lake. The problem was, he hadn't kept up with the backlog. We found at least a dozen victims in that walk-in, including some who hadn't even been reported missing yet. This will take weeks to sort out."

I shuddered as I thought how close Rhys had come to being another victim.

"Do you need us to make a formal statement tonight? I'm sorry about ditching you the last time."

Porter smirked, but he wasn't mad. "Yeah, you'll both need to make a statement, but not tonight. You kids want a ride somewhere?"

I didn't think I could face seeing the bloody office at Mystic Properties, so we had Porter drop us off at Madame Coumlie's house. All I could think of was sleep. Rhys held my hand as he led me up the driveway to the back door.

CHAPTER 35

HOLDING RHYS'S HAND all night seemed like a wonderful idea until the porch light came on and the translator came out brandishing a broom. Rhys called out to him, and he appeared both relieved and embarrassed. He noticed our bloody clothes and blanched.

"What happened to you?" He ushered us into the kitchen.

"What are you doing here?" I asked.

He shrugged. "I had no place to go, so I came here."

So much for my plan for quiet time with Rhys. Rats. We should have gone to my place. I heard Rhys sigh, and wondered if he shared the same thought.

"No problem. Have you two met?" He turned to me.

"Briefly." I nodded. "How did you get in? I'm sorry, I didn't get your name?"

"Henri at your service, Madame."

It wasn't until he said Madame that I realized why he seemed so familiar. "Oh my god. You're him; aren't you? You're Oneiri."

Rhys and Henri exchanged concerned looks. "Not exactly," Rhys said.

"Well why don't you explain exactly," I demanded. Henri bore no resemblance to Oneiri, but something about Henri nagged at me. The tops of Oneiri's ears had held the same gold rings, I remembered. I sniffed, but detected no telltale scent of licorice. "You said djemons died when their masters did, Rhys. Why did you lie to me? Why is he here?"

Oneiri-Henri began to yammer something unintelligible in French, and Rhys held up his hands. "Take it easy, both of you. Henri here is no longer Oneiri. Remember when Madame Coumlie told you she referred to the unnamed djemons as djinn?"

"What does that have to do with anything?"

"Djinn were, are the helpmates of the gods; able to assume two forms. In their original form, before they're named, they are small creatures. They keep this form until they are blessed to become a servant. Becoming a servant is a big deal; to serve is everything. Most wait for an eternity until they are recognized by a master."

"And then they become a demon. I get it."

"Demon is human term which connotes evil. The djinn are not inherently evil, Mattie. Who do you think built the pyramids, anyway? They're merely servants; they exist to serve. Once they become attached to a master, they assume the same prevailing characteristics and traits as their masters. Everything they learn thenceforth is based on the personalities and proclivities of those they serve. Do you understand?"

"So how does Oneiri become Henri?"

"When Madame Coumlie died, Oneiri was released from his servitude. He had grown large enough as a djemon to assume a human form. We call ourselves anomalous individuals. You call us djenie. In the djenie form, he can blend in and live undetected as human. A practical choice made by many freed djemon, if they've grown big enough. Smaller djemon must choose a smaller, non-human form."

A growing sense of unease came over me. "What's to prevent a djinn from killing its master?"

"Many years of active service are necessary before a djemon grows large enough to survive its master's passing. Oneiri had been with Madame some forty or fifty years, right?"

"I proudly served the Madame for more than a century. Please allow me to say that at no time was I tempted to shorten my service to the Hand of Fate. To the contrary, I would have laid down my life to save her, and did on several occasions." Henri's eyes brimmed, his emotions close to the surface.

"A djemon which destroys its master is immediately banished."

"Banished where," I asked. I couldn't shake the belief there was something more they weren't telling me.

"Who knows?" Both Rhys and Henri shrugged.

My eyelid began to twitch. "So what happens to you now," I asked Henri. "What do you do?"

Henri smiled for the first time. He had an appealing boyish expression women were going to love.

"Madame thoughtfully remembered to provide for me after her death, so I will not need to worry about employment for quite some time. Rhys is helping me to get on my feet, for which I am extremely grateful. He has arranged for my identity papers, birth certificate, citizenship papers, my identification, and is teaching me to use the computer. With his help, I will be able to blend into human society and hide in safety. Tomorrow, I will be fitted for the contact lenses. Soon, I will look like everyone else."

The truth hit me like a bucket of ice water. "So that's what Mystic Properties is? A halfway house for djenies and other anomalous individuals? And you create identities for them. Falsify documentation. That is what we're talking about, right?"

Rhys reached for me, but I backed away.

"No, there's more. Something else you're not telling me."

Henri frowned. "Non, Mattie, you do not understand. Once we lose our immortality, we are helpless. We must learn to adapt and hide, or we die. Many die before they ever learn to live. The mage helps us. This is one of the few places in the world where we can come and live in safety. Madame spent many, many years trying to persuade the mage before he agreed to come here."

"Is this true?"

Rhys fidgeted uncomfortably, as if trying to decide what to say, and in a trick of the light, the last piece of the puzzle finally clicked into place.

My heart sank and I blinked back the tears. I fought to keep my voice calm. "Oh, now I get it. You're wearing contact lenses too, aren't you, Rhys? You weren't even going to tell me. You're not even human."

I'd nearly made love to a demon. Or djemon. Or former djemon. Djenie. Whatever. What the hell was I thinking? Here I thought he was well, something. Maybe even someone special. The expression of guilt on his face confirmed the real story. I turned to leave, but he took my hand, folding it between his two. I didn't want to go, but I couldn't stay. I couldn't even think.

"Wait." He lifted an eyebrow towards Henri, who took the hint and had the good grace to leave us. Rhys lifted my filthy bloodstained hand to his mouth and kissed my palm, pressing it to his lips. I just stood there, unable to move.

"I thought you knew. I honestly believed you knew when you first met me. I don't have a walk-in business, Mattie. Anomalous clients come to me strictly through referrals."

"I didn't come to you through a referral. I got your number from Karen."

"Your great-grandmother hired me to find you four years ago. If you hadn't resembled Oleanna so much, I would have never given you a second thought. I never would have answered your phone calls. I never would have kissed you." He released my hand, and I felt a sense of loss.

"Yes. I was a djemon. A very long time ago, I served a well-educated master who lived a long and prosperous life. Fortunately for me, my master chose to educate me and in doing so fostered in me a passion for learning. When my master died, I was released from servitude. Even so, I barely survived my transition to mortal life. Once I found my way, I decided to help others who faced the same challenges. Over time, other anomalous individuals came to me for assistance and when I could, I tried to help them. Is that such a crime?"

This was not what I'd expected to hear. It made me feel petty to think I had judged him without knowing him. I remembered what Henri had said. "Why did you come here?"

"I was living in Scotland when Madame Coumlie contacted me. She asked me about coming here and assuming guardianship of Shore Haven. She pestered me for years, trying to persuade me to at least consider coming for a visit. I admit the Hand of Fate is a legendary figure, and I was curious, but I did not want to come to America just yet."

"Why?"

He shrugged. "I had my studies and still so much to learn where I was. North America is truly the New World. We corresponded regularly and after several years she sent me a formal invitation, signed by dozens of anomalous individuals. Residents of Shore Haven, some of whom had lived here for centuries. I was intrigued. I agreed to come for a visit. When I arrived, I sensed the same thing that attracted so many other refugees. A sense of place, a rightness. It's hard to explain, but there are places on this planet that attract our kind. These places become lodestones for us."

"You mean you have to stay here?"

"No. We just like living here. The air feels clearer, the water cleaner. Who knows? For us, these places feel like home. Of course, with all the government regulations, it is much riskier to live in the US than Europe or the Middle East, but as soon as I met the Hand, I decided to stay. Shore Haven is my home now."

"For how long?" I didn't want him to leave, but things were moving a little fast for me. I needed time to think.

"That's up to you." He hooked a finger through my belt loop and tugged. I came closer, and he threw his arm around my shoulder. "The first time I saw you, I knew you would be trouble, but I had no idea. My only thought from that moment was that I wanted to know you. I mean it, I ache to touch you. But I make no apologies for who or what I am."

If Kip, or a cop, or even a stockbroker had just given me this speech, I'd be over the moon. But Rhys Warrick wasn't any of those things. He wasn't normal; hell, he wasn't even human. I had to admit I wanted him too, I wanted him bad. But wanting Rhys meant accepting all those scary unknowns along with him. No way to tell what kind of worms I'd find in that basket. It was enough to give a girl pause. He studied my face, waiting for an answer, and I owed him one.

But not today.

I let out a deep breath. "Look, I'm wiped out. We both are. Could we talk about this tomorrow? When we're both a little more coherent?"

He nodded, and I thought I saw something shut down in his expression, but at that point, I was just trying to be honest.

I squeezed his hand. "I don't want to say anything I might regret."

"Sure. We can talk after the funeral."

Oh man, I'd forgotten all about it.

CHAPTER 36

FEELING FRAGILE AND heartsick, I turned on the shower, and stepped inside to take off my clothes. The deep gashes on my left forearm and shin had closed, but the edges were still angry. Dried blood and guano clotted my hair, and angry purple bruises mottled my ribs, back, and butt.

The physical pain faded as steaming water poured over me, and I savored the heat. I scrubbed myself until every last bit of me squeaked pruney clean. By the time I finished, the morning sky was beginning to show itself as a grey haze above the horizon. I tossed my filthy clothes into a big garbage bag. I remembered to call Blix and Larry from their hiding places, and set them up in a casserole dish lined with an old dishtowel. Not much of a bed, but would have to do for now. I set my alarm for noon and crawled under the covers, wet hair and all. I was asleep before I hit the pillow.

The alarm woke me a few hours later. The heaviness I'd felt earlier had vanished. Funny what a good cry and a few hours of sleep can do. I got up and checked myself in the bathroom mirror. Not a mark on me, not even a bruise. Only a thin pink line remained along my arm where the machete had bit me. I looked good.

Seeing my strange reflection in the mirror, I tried

to convince myself I hadn't actually killed Garr. I would never forget the sound his lifeline made as it popped between my fingers. But the fierce thrill of joy I experienced when he collapsed on top of me must have been dream. The loss of oxygen must've caused me to hallucinate. That part couldn't be real; that would be wrong.

Blix lay snuggled up in the casserole dish, and I found Larry curled up in the kitchen sink. He seemed to like the water. Both sat up, alert as soon as I came into the room. Cute. They were starting to grow on me. I didn't need to banish them with the others. I couldn't imagine sending these two little guys to some dark cavern for the rest of eternity. My mother had died after spending two years in a locked ward. These little ones had never done anything wrong, they didn't even smell anymore.

"Relax, guys, you've got the day off."

I went into the bedroom to find something to wear to the funeral. I didn't want to wear pants, but the only black dress I owned happened to be a sleeveless linen cocktail number with black beading around the neckline. A little dressy for the afternoon, but I decided to wear it. Black was Rhys' favorite color. Besides, it looked good on me. I paired it with a peacock blue pashmina. The viewing would be inside, and I would need the scarf. If Rhys and I went out for dinner afterwards, I could carry it. Perfect.

I realized I'd made my decision. I wanted Rhys. I didn't care what he was. Nobody's perfect. Who was I to talk, anyway? I wasn't exactly Webbers bread anymore, either.

I checked my cell phone messages. Karen had

left a message saying she'd see me at the visitation, and Fontaigne left a message saying Lance had been released, and they'd both be there. Nothing from Rhys. I wondered if Oneiri would be at the funeral. Henri, I corrected myself.

A sudden thought made me shiver. If I did kill Garr, what happened to Rex?

CHAPTER 37

I PULLED INTO the parking lot of Saunders Funeral Home at ten minutes to three, Rex still on my mind. I wanted to talk to Rhys before everyone showed up. A few cars had already arrived, but I didn't see his truck. Then I remembered it was still parked on Sentinel Hill. Oops. I bet he wondered about that.

I stepped into the air-conditioned reception area, and an elderly man greeted me, introducing himself as Norm Saunders, the Funeral Director. I gave him my name and kept my dark glasses on as he led me to the Founder's Suite. Saunders escorted me to a seat at the front of the room, near the casket and flowers.

"We have everything in readiness." He pointed out the flowers, and the quality of the materials appointing the child-sized casket. The dark woods and brass handles shone beneath white flower sprays, giving the setting a somber, mature theme.

My great-grandmother wore a lavender suit, with her hair neat and styled in a French chignon. Tiny as a doll, her olive skin and firm chin spoke to the strength of her character.

"My Gran would be pleased," I told him. People began to trickle in, and I sat where he told me.

"I'll be right over there." He pointed to a spot near

the door. "If you need anything, give me a signal." He handed me a program and scooted back to the entrance. Karen arrived with her family. She'd brought her mother as well, and they filled the row behind me.

Violet came in a few minutes later, with Mina in tow. She was polite, and less stiff than I'd expected. She offered her condolences and agreed when Mina took my hand and asked to sit next to me. A surprise, since we hadn't spoken in years.

"Thank you for coming Violet. Thanks for bringing Mina, too."

"I do realize you want the best for Mina. I'm sorry things had to work out this way, but Mina's well-being is the only thing I care about." She put her arm around her daughter and pulled her closer. "I'm going to ask the courts to award me permanent custody. This time, I think the judge will agree."

I nodded. "I understand, and for what it's worth, I think you're doing the right thing. I want Mina to be safe, too."

Violet turned to face me. "I never thought I'd hear you talk this way."

"I love my brother, but I can't ignore his problems any more. He's put Mina at risk. I don't want to lose her, but I want her to be safe." My lips trembled, and I fought to keep my composure. "She is better off living with you, Violet."

"This doesn't mean you won't be able to visit her, Mattie. I want you to know that. We can work something out."

I nodded, too full of emotion to answer, glad I'd worn sunglasses.

Mina pulled on my arm to whisper in my ear. "Are

you going to make the monsters go away?" She had dark circles under her eyes.

I remembered Lance's admonition. "They're gone. They won't bother you anymore."

She cupped her hand to my ear and whispered. "No, the other one. He's following me." Her brow wrinkled with worry. She pointed to a spot just past the casket. Sure enough, the faint outline of her unnamed djinn sat not three feet away. "He keeps staring at me."

My great-grandmother had been right. Shore Haven was experiencing an epidemic of loose djinn running around town.

"We can fix this right now. Come on."

I told Violet I was taking Mina to the ladies room, and we scooted down the hall to the conveniently empty restroom. I locked the door, and as soon as the monkey-like djinn appeared I clapped my hands and sent the creature to the cave.

"Is he really gone?"

"He's really gone, and he's never going to bother you again. Ever. And I don't want you to tell anyone about this, or we'll be in trouble. This is our secret."

"Is he dead?"

"No, honey, I sent him back to his home. I want you to forget all about this. Can you do that?"

She nodded.

"That's my girl. Come on, let's go back, your mom is waiting for us."

She heaved a big sigh, and we rejoined her mother. Gerard Fontaigne had arrived, and taken the empty seat I'd been saving for Lance.

"Where's Lance?" I asked. "I thought he was coming with you."

"I dropped him at his house to change, but he told me he had some things to attend to."

Worry gnawed at me. "Is he mad at me?"

"I don't think so, Mattie. He seemed preoccupied by something. Distant. I drove by on my way over here to offer him a ride, but he wasn't home."

"Maybe he went to pick up his car at the impound." Maybe he'd heard about Andrea's death.

"Perhaps."

Soothing music came over the speakers, and I settled into the padded chair. Every few minutes, more people arrived. I looked for Rhys, but couldn't find him. I studied the picture on the front of the program. A sepia-toned print showed Madame Celeste Coumlie standing proud beneath the palm-shaped sign in front of her home. She must have been in her early thirties. Her dark hair trailed to her waist, and her unnatural eyes stood out in the photograph, but her bare arms showed no markings. Other photos inside the program included a picture of the wedding party and even a photo taken with President Herbert Hoover. Several testimonials written by people who knew her best, memorialized her wonderful qualities. I recognized a few names and even a couple of famous actors. The room filled up, almost every seat was taken, and more people continued to arrive. Most had auras and lifelines, but I spotted more than a dozen who didn't. I wondered if they were all djenie. Several guests arrived with invisible djinn in tow.

Over the next two hours, a steady stream of people filed by the open casket to pay their respects. Herman the German, Frau Deckhardt, the owner of the Shanghai Palace, Bunny Tacker and her fiancé Ronnie all stopped by. Mimsy Wu even introduced me to her mother.

I finally caught sight of Rhys and Henri, but they stayed at the back of the room, deep in conversation with an older man I didn't recognize. I watched him for a few minutes as they stood in the doorway, and then Rhys followed the man outside. I stood to follow him, but Mayor Jim Brunson intercepted me.

"I am so sorry, Mattie. I admired your great-grandmother and knew her for many years. She encouraged me to go into politics. I had no idea you two were related."

I blushed. "Thank you for coming." I was getting pretty good at this funeral-speak, but not so good at making chit-chat with the Mayor after nearly running him down with my scooter. "I'm sorry about the other day. I mean, I got a little distracted, I'm glad you're okay."

"No apology necessary, I may have over-reacted. Mrs. Coumlie had been ill for a long time. I know how difficult it can be to concentrate on work when you're so worried about your family. Caring for the elderly can be an enormous strain. You should have said something. I'm revoking your suspension. Your job is waiting for you. Come back to work whenever you're ready."

I started to protest, but my common sense kicked in. "Thank you, sir," was all I could manage.

"Call me Jim, Mattie." He shook my hand and I beamed at him in return.

Well slap me with a feather and call me stupid. I felt like I'd just won a new car.

Norm Sunders chose that moment to pop up and congratulate me on the overflow attendance. He complimented my new buddy Mayor Jim on the large turnout of local politicos and asked if Senator

Barnes would be attending. As the men drifted away in conversation, I realized who was missing from the throng. Other than my brother, the only obvious no-shows were from law enforcement. In fact, not one of my friends from the police department or Parking Control had come. The message was clear, the realization stung. A lot.

Karen tapped me on the shoulder. "Congratulations. I told you everything would work out."

I shrugged. "So why didn't anyone from the department come? Not even Mike."

She looked around the room. "You're right. Oh, you understand where those guys are coming from, they're just like you. They aren't comfortable with um, this kind of stuff."

"You mean the paranormal community. Anomalous individuals. The Hand of Fate."

She waved her hand. "All of that. Like it or not, you're one of them now."

"They're never going to accept me." I lowered my sunglasses. "Not like this. They'll shun me when I go back to work, too."

"So get contact lenses. In a few weeks this will blow over. They're still your friends, Mattie." She gave me a worried look.

"What?"

"Maybe this isn't the best time to tell you, but Martin got a huge promotion a couple of weeks ago. The bank is relocating us to San Francisco. I wanted to tell you earlier, but you were so upset, I couldn't."

I was stunned. "Wow, um. Congratulations. You're moving?"

She nodded and squeezed my hands. "At the end of

the month. Martin's already found a couple of houses for me to look at. We're flying out next week to decide which one to make an offer on. I'm going to miss you, Mattie. I can't imagine living so far away from you. You've been like family to me."

My throat felt dry. I tried not to show how upset I was. "We'll still talk all the time. I'll come out and visit. Abbot's won't be the same without you." I'd just lost my brother, great-grandmother and best friend, all in one day.

"I'll call you as soon as we get back, if not before." We hugged. Martin came up to us and put his arm around her.

"Don't worry, Mattie. The boys and I will take good care of her. As soon as we get settled, you come out for a good long visit."

"Thanks Martin, I can't wait. Congrats on the promotion." I followed them out to their car and watched as they drove away. My old life was slipping away from me, and I could do nothing to stop it. I walked back into the funeral home to search for Rhys. The place was thinning out, but I didn't see him anywhere. I hoped he hadn't left already.

"You look real pretty today." The warm voice of my brother sounded like music to me.

I wrapped my arms around him and hugged him tight. "I'm glad you came. I'm so sorry, it's my fault you got arrested."

He appeared pale, but good humor crinkled at the corners of his eyes. My brother was back. "No shit. They must have followed you out to the faire. They had me in custody less than an hour later."

I choked back my emotions. "Oh, that. Um, sorry. I

was talking about, oh never mind. You're out." I gripped his gnarled hand in mine. "I talked to Violet."

"Yeah, I ran into her in the parking lot."

"And?"

He looked away and shrugged. "And nothing. No promises."

I blurted it out without thinking. "Andrea's dead. The Night Shark got her."

"I heard about that." He raised an eyebrow at me. "Can't' say as I'm real broken up about it."

"I've got your money." I held up my hand at Lance's reaction. "Wait. I have to tell you something." I pulled off my sunglasses.

Lance let out a low whistle. "What have you been up to?"

I took a deep breath. "Um, Madame Coumlie is our great-gran."

"So you said."

"Well, I'm her heir. The oldest woman of the line. I'm not sure what it all means yet, but this happened right after she died. And there's some other stuff too. Stuff that's still happening. What I mean to say is, when I went to pay off your IOU, Mimsy Wu refused to take my money. She gave me a receipt and everything, but when she found out I'm the new Hand of Fate, she said your money was no good."

My brother cocked his head as he studied my appearance. "Yeah, well that Mimsy's a piece of work, all right. By the way, where'd you find that lawyer? He's a helluva guy."

I met his eyes. "You have to go back to rehab, Lance."

He stroked his chin. "I've got to clear up a few things, and Violet wants me to meet with a counselor later in the week."

"At least you're talking. That's good."

"Look sis, I'll see you around. I'm going to pay my respects to Celeste and take off."

"Celeste?"

"She was a good friend of mine long before she became our gran."

I frowned at him, incredulous.

"You don't know me nearly as well as you think you do." He kissed my forehead. "Go on. Your boyfriend is outside waiting for you."

"Are we okay?"

He smiled. "See you around, brat."

"Later, grease monkey."

I took a deep breath and pushed back out through the double glass doors into the parking lot. I spotted Rhys standing amid an assemblage of two dozen people. Something about the crowd jarred my senses, something that couldn't solely be attributed to the loose cluster of unattached djinn hovering around the edges. None of these people had been inside, I realized. They loitered in the parking lot, skulking like feral cats. Several were accompanied by named djinn. They appeared dressed for a wedding instead of a funeral, in soft pastels and bright summer whites with seersucker instead of the somber funereal colors of the midsummer mourners inside. Two women in the group wore gaudy feathered hats that would have been more appropriate in an Easter parade. But something else seemed incongruous with this occasion of death.

I slid up behind Rhys, feeling my way forward, like a cat in a roomful of rocking chairs. It was their auras. Not all of them had one. Most did not even have lifelines. These were the paranormals, I realized. The supernaturals. Anomalous individuals. A dozen or more strays from the hidden underbelly of the town. These were the refugees; the real residents of Shore Haven. Hiding in plain sight, drawn here like moths to the flame, they belonged here more than any of us.

I felt a whisper, the first promise of belonging. Would they embrace me, or would they brand me an outsider, and crush me with their rejection? I choked down a sob and stood shoulder to shoulder with Rhys. These were my people too, now. I could help them, I know I could. Rhys and I could keep the intensity of the FBI and law enforcement gaze away from them. Allow them to maintain their cloak of invisibility, keep them safe from prying eyes and restore their sense of safety in their secret sanctuary. I slipped my hand into the crook of Rhys' elbow. Without turning, he drew me to him, and curled my arm protectively within his own.

I rested my head against his shoulder, and tried to concentrate on the conversation, but my emotions were too chaotic. With each breath, my chest unclenched a little. Calm joy filled me. A sense of renewed purpose bubbled up inside me.

As I listened to the conversation, it began to dawn on me that these people were all complaining to Rhys about something. They were all being plagued by djinn.

"What am I supposed to do, Warrick? They're everywhere. The feds are going to start a witch hunt any day."

"If the FBI finds out I've got one of these, you know what will happen. I'm already on their watch list."

"I hear you, Dave," Rhys answered. "I promise we're working on it. Give me a few days to get this taken care of."

A wave of heat washed over me, and I remembered my promise. What was I waiting for?

"How are you going to do that? Now that the Hand is gone, how can you expect to control these things? Who knows what's going to happen next?"

Rhys hesitated, and I answered for him. "I promise you, the djinn will be gone from your lives tonight. Give us just a few more hours." Rhys gave me that great smile of his. The one that was just for me.

"Who are you?" This from the skeptic on the FBI watch list.

"The torch has been passed." Rhys pulled me forward. "This is Madame Coumlie's heir, Mattie Blackman." He winked at me, and my heart fluttered happily. For an uncomfortable moment the group stared at me. Then, without warning, they alerted to something coming up behind me, and without a word slunk away into the shadows.

I turned to see the FBI's paranormal control agent, Frank Porter approaching at a brisk walk.

"Hey you two, I'm glad I caught you." I experienced a moment of panic before I remembered I'd ordered Blix and Larry to stay at home.

"Shoot," Rhys said.

"I wanted let you know that in addition to the bodies in the walk-in, we found body parts of three more in the main kitchen freezer upstairs. We'll need to run DNA to identify some of them. Looks like some of the missing go back years."

"He was a demon master. His djemon killed them." I hoped it was true.

"Well, not all of them. More than half the victims had been strangled. You were lucky you weren't one of them."

"Lucky for me he bled to death."

"Actually no. He died of a massive brain hemorrhage. In spite of all that blood, the doc thought he would have survived."

Guilt and confusion flooded through me. On one hand, I know I'd done the right thing. One the other hand, I couldn't forget the sound that his life's thread had made when I snapped it, or the surge of savage glee I'd experienced at the moment of his death. Morta. I shivered in spite of the heat.

"We found five more skeletons down in the tunnel below the sub-basement. Coroner is guessing that they've been there for decades, maybe since prohibition. He thinks they might have been rival bootleggers or inconvenient witnesses. We followed the same rail line you told us about, and guess where it led us?"

"The basement of Mad Otto's estate," I answered.

"Bingo. When we asked to search the premises, the old coot refused us and threatened us with his demon. Can you believe that?"

Rhys and I looked at each other, neither of us surprised. "What happened?"

"He's got a smart lawyer. Because of his age and health, he's under house arrest. With all his money, I doubt he'll ever serve a day in jail. The Bureau has never run into a situation like this before, so we're not quite sure how to proceed. Probably be in all the papers tomorrow."

"This must put you back in good graces again," Rhys said.

Porter beamed and blushed ear-to-ear. "I'm not disappointed." He glanced around to make sure no one was listening in. "The Bureau is going to be looking for a replacement for me. The paranormal task force needs people with special talents. Either of you interested? What about it?"

"You said neither of us had psychic abilities."

"Obviously those tests don't tell us everything." He nodded at Rhys, and I realized some unsaid message had passed between them. "What do you think of my offer?"

"You're barking up the wrong tree, Frank. I'm an academic, remember?"

"What about you, Mattie?"

I chewed my lip. I'd wanted to work in law enforcement, real law enforcement, not just Parking Control, all my life. But today's snub by Mike and the department's rigid stance against the anomalous community bothered me. Porter's antagonistic attitude toward the Hand of Fate and demons shocked me. In spite of what Karen said, I wasn't so sure things could ever go back to the way they used to be. And to be honest, I wasn't sure I wanted it to. I didn't picture myself as a hypocrite.

"Thanks, I'll think about it."

Porter took off and Rhys and I drifted over to my car. We leaned against Trusty Rusty, waving to people as they left, not looking at each other. After ten minutes, I couldn't stand it anymore.

"I'm sorry I freaked out last night."

"Don't beat yourself up over it."

"Can we start over?"

Rhys turned to face me, his expression serious. "What did you have in mind, Mattie? Other than sealing up that cavern, what do you want from me?"

What exactly did I want? Now that we'd come to the

moment, I didn't seem able to string the right words together. When in doubt, chicken out.

I smoothed my hair. "I have a plan."

"What's your plan?"

"Well, two things. First of all, we don't need the journals, we have Oneiri-- I mean Henri. We can just ask him, but I'm pretty sure I already figured it out. That's what I came over to tell you yesterday. I found a way to banish the djinn. I sent all mine to the cavern. It was so easy, Rhys. I think Madame Coumlie did the same thing. I think she used Oneiri to herd all the djinn back into the original cavern and she commanded them to stay there. Then they sealed it. We can use Blix and Larry to do the same thing."

His sharp eyes drilled into me. "Blix and Larry?"

I blushed. Oops. "It's a secret. Don't tell anybody." How did I forget Lance's warning so quickly?

"So you have two djemons now? When did this happen?"

I winced. "Um, three. The first one was by accident, but I sent him to the caves with all the other djinn that had been following me. Blix and Larry have been with me from the beginning."

Rhys gaped at me. "You surprise me."

"After I sent the other djinn to the cavern, I ran to your office to tell you. When I found blood all over the floor and Henri hiding in the stairwell, I figured the Night Shark's djemon had taken you. The only place I could think it would go was the caves. I called on Blix to lead me to you. And if it weren't for Larry, I'd have been chopped into little pieces by Garr and his machete."

Henri came up to us at that moment, and confirmed

my suspicions about what had been done in 1930. He had indeed rounded up the unnamed djinn that had attached themselves to the unsuspecting citizens of the Shore.

"I was able to assist Madame in finding the djinn, and once they were in her presence, she ordered them into the cavern, which was then sealed. People believed the entrance was sealed to keep the djinn inside, but that wasn't true. The command of the Hand of Fate alone kept the djinn in their cave. The seal was nothing but a safety measure to keep people out. However, as Madame's powers began to fade, so did her compulsion and power over the djinn. They began to drift beyond the confines of the cave and into the town."

"Henri, tell me about the others. What happened to the named djinn?"

He shrugged. "As long as they had not yet been made flesh, they obeyed the Hand of Fate, and were banished. The fully materialized djemon could not be compelled, except by their master. Most answered to a single man, and once he died, they were too small to survive."

"So what happened to all the new djemons that Garr named?"

"Any djemon made flesh which kills its master is banished, along with all the other djemon who served him."

Frank said Garr died of a brain hemorrhage. "What if the djemon didn't cause its master's death?"

"If they are large enough to transform into human shape, they become djenie, just as I did. It is unusual for a djemon to serve long enough to do so. Those who have not served so long remain small. They live the life of vermin, and soon die. Why do you ask?"

"Can you help us round up the stray djinn, like you did before?"

"Non. Once we transform, we can no longer see djinn. Only your djemon can help you.

CHAPTER 38

RHYS AND I agreed to meet up first thing in the morning, after Blix and Larry rounded up all the loose djinn and I sent them in to the cavern to wait for us. The FBI would be sealing the doorway entrance from the bootleggers' tunnel, but the entrance I'd used needed to be sealed as well. Once we finished, no more stray djinn would be able to attach themselves to unsuspecting citizens.

The dismissive goodnight peck from Rhys disappointed me. I wished I'd had the nerve to ask him to come home with me, but with Henri standing there I couldn't bring myself to say anything. I got back to my apartment and curled up on the couch to read, but couldn't concentrate. I recalled the panic I'd felt as I sought to find Rhys's thready pulse, cold against my lips. I felt a connection to Rhys, as if he was already a part of me; like Lance and Mina. People trusted him. I trusted him. I wanted to be with him.

There were people out there I could help because of who I was becoming. I'd given my word to help these people. My people. Being the Hand of Fate didn't mean I had to help them, but I wanted to. Rhys had the right idea. He didn't make excuses for who he was, and neither should I. Not anymore.

☾

The morning sun peeked over the horizon as we pulled Trusty Rusty up behind Rhys's truck on Sentinel Hill. This time, I'd remembered to wear my winter long johns underneath my jeans. Rhys had brought clean coveralls, a portable acetylene torch, welding mask, tools and other equipment we'd need to seal up the access tunnel I'd used last time. I'd protested when I'd realized I'd have to wear the Cavewoman Barbie getup again, but Rhys told me wearing dirty clothes into the caves violated caver protocol. Sheesh. Bit late for that.

"So who is she, anyway," I asked as we changed. "I'm not jealous, just curious."

"You've got nothing to worry about." He replaced the batteries in the Mag-lites and miners lamps, and handed me one of each.

We didn't want to tell Porter about banishing all the djinn until we were certain they were gone. As far as anyone knew, we were sealing off a previously undiscovered access for safety reasons. Rhys hefted up his pack and started down the trail. I followed, carrying the grate we were going to use to seal off the tunnel access I'd used. Thirty minutes later we stood in front of the entrance; the crowbar I'd used was right where I'd left it.

"Pretty clever," Rhys said, examining the knot.

"Are we ready?" The smell of licorice and bat guano coming from the cavern tunnel was almost overwhelming. Blix and Larry and You greeted me with excited squeaks. I'd brought along a scarf to wrap around my nose and mouth. I wanted to get this over with as soon as possible.

We planned to install the grate first. Once Rhys finished the welding, I'd crawl down to the mouth of the tunnel and perform the banishment. Then we'd lock the whole thing up behind us and be done.

Rhys put on his gloves and safety mask, fired up the torch, and adjusted the flame.

"Don't look at the flame. You'll ruin your eyes."

Oh, right. I looked away. "How long do you think this will take?"

"An hour or so. If you want, you can wait outside. It'll be warmer."

"I'm good." I was glad that this time I'd remembered to wear my thermal underwear. I was positively toasty.

An hour later, Rhys turned off the torch and stood back to inspect his work. He installed the grate and experimentally swung it open and closed.

"Finished?" I asked.

"Yup. You're up next. How are you planning to phrase it?"

"I plan to address myself to all the named and unnamed entities within the sound of my voice. That way I won't have to name them."

"Makes sense. Then what? Where are you sending them?"

"I don't want to imprison them in an earthy prison, like the early tribal shamans did, and Madame Coumlie did the same thing. I hate the idea of imprisoning them in a dark cave for eternity. I think it's got to be something metaphysical, but a real place. You're the expert on theology. What do you think?"

Rhys thought for a few moments before answering. "How about just banishing them from all physical and metaphysical earthly planes? Make sure you include something about never to return. That should do it."

"Sounds good to me." I repeated the phrase several times. "Banished from all physical and metaphysical earthly planes, never to return." This was turning out to be trickier than I'd thought it would be, but after naming You by accident, I didn't want to mess things up again.

"So how do you want to do this?"

"Let's use the rope again. I don't need to go all the way to the end. I just want to make sure that they can hear me."

Rhys tied the rope around my waist, and gave me a boost into the narrow tunnel. I felt more confident this time, knowing Rhys was on the other end of the rope. As I crawled my way through the tunnel, I heard the banging of the FBI work crew sealing up the access door Garr Russ had used. All that racket would drown out my voice. The noise had also disrupted the bats, and they swarmed frantically about the cavern. I'd need to yell at the top of my lungs to be heard above the pounding.

I reached the overhang and looked down. I was struck again by the sheer number of djinn gathered there. From what I could tell, the only demons made flesh were Blix, Larry, and You. All three stamped their little feet at me in impatient unison, awaiting my next command.

"Blix and Larry. I command you to go out to my car and wait for me." They vanished instantly. I could always banish them later, I reasoned. Anyway, it wasn't like I was going to become another Night Shark or anything. I'm a very responsible person.

The rope went slack, and I braced myself, using my shoulders and knees against the walls of the tunnel.

I yelled. "Hey! Rhys, it's too loose, pull up the slack."

There was another hard jerk on the line, then nothing. Maybe he was trying to tell me to hurry up. What did he think, I was enjoying myself here? Focus, Mattie, No telling when that pounding was going to stop. It was now or never. I cleared my throat and began to shout as loud as I could.

"I am the Hand of Fate! I command all the non-human entities within the sound of my voice. Hear me and obey."

The pounding stopped, and in the sudden silence, I heard the unmistakable sounds of a fight coming from behind me. Holy crap. What in hell was going on?

I tried to twist myself around, but the passage was too narrow. My shoulders hadn't cleared the tunnel, so by using a sort of a reverse caterpillar move, I was able to hump my way uphill back to the entrance. My feet cleared the entrance and dangled into thin air behind me. I gave myself a huge shove, got my hips clear, and wiggled backwards until I dropped to the floor.

Rhys stood toe-to-toe, exchanging blows with a gaunt man dressed in rags. He must have been a head taller than Rhys, nearly seven feet tall. In the eerie light of my headlamp, I watched Rhys take a blow that sent his shoe flying.

Adrenaline flooded through me. I grabbed the crowbar and threw myself at them, but the big guy tossed me aside like I was nothing. With a roundhouse kick, Rhys struck his opponent's knee, knocking the man's leg out from under him. He fell to his hands and knees. Rhys began furiously kicking the larger man in the ribs. The tall man grunted, but he didn't go down. Instead, he came up with a backhanded blow to Rhys's jaw that sent him reeling. Rhys tripped over one of the lanterns and went down.

The man was back on his feet. I had to do something. I grabbed the crowbar and jumped in front of him.

"Stop! Rex, I command you to stop!"

Rex eyed me with a baleful stare. "You have no hold over me," he growled, "I answer to no one now." He twisted the crowbar out of my hand like I was a child, and turned back toward Rhys, who having gained his feet, was trying to relight the torch. I had to stop Rex.

"Why are you doing this," I yelled. "What have we ever done to you?"

Rex hesitated. "I must escape the cave before the entrance is sealed. I asked the mage for help. He refused me."

"You killed your master. You killed Garlan Russ."

Rex turned to face me, panting from the exertion. In spite of the cold temperatures, he dripped with sweat.

"Only a fool lies to himself." He pointed at me. "You killed him. I am indebted to you. It was by your hand that my master's life ended and I have been freed. I have no quarrel with you."

"Why did you kill all those people?"

Righteous anger rolled off Rex in waves. "I killed only those with enslaved djemons. I did it to free their servants from bondage. I hoped in return, a freed djenie would repay the favor by destroying my disgraceful master, a shameful human mortal unworthy of any respect."

He had a point. "You're every bit as bad as Garr." Behind him, I could see Rhys trying to re-light the torch without success.

A rumble of low laughter echoed in his chest. "You are a killer, no better than me. Yet I can see that the mage loves you. I need documentation and citizenship papers to pass undetected among the humans."

My eyes met Rhys's in a moment of absolute understanding. The psychotic djenie could not be allowed to leave the cave.

Rex strode toward me, hefting the iron bar in his hand. "Perhaps you will persuade him to provide me with an identity."

I had to think fast. I scrabbled at my feet and came up with handful of rocks and started throwing. At this range, his head was huge. I couldn't miss. The first got him right in the eye. He turned his face came at me blindly, swinging the crowbar. I dodged him and nailed him with an egger to the temple. I danced out of his reach and hit him with another that took a big chunk out of his ear. He screamed and threw the crowbar at my head.

I twisted out of the way, and almost made it, but the crowbar struck my elbow with enough force to knock me down. I skittered away, yelping, and nailed him again right between the eyes. The rock wasn't big enough to stop him, but it slowed him down.

My mind raced. I was nearly backed up against the wall with no place else to go. I saw movement behind Rhys and noticed my djemon 'You' had followed me up the tunnel shaft. Behind him were a few thousand of his closest friends. The little demon stamped his feet at me, impatient for my next command.

At that point, everything happened at once. Rhys got the torch lit, and I yelled at You and the gang, "Grab that djenie!"

The army of djinn swarmed out of the tunnel like a mob of angry killer bees. Rhys stepped up behind Rex and touched the flame to the big man's ragged clothes. Immediately a towering pillar of flames engulfed Rex and the djinn.

"I hereby banish all djinn within the sound of my voice from all physical and metaphysical earthly planes, never to return," I yelled. "And take that flaming djenie with you!

I clapped my hands. There was a brilliant flash of neon blue, followed by a massive explosion, and I was hurled backwards against the cave wall behind me.

☾

I found myself floating out of my body, in a murky darkness, accompanied only by the fresh scent of an unseen sea. A deep booming resonance echoed in my head, and an unearthly voice spoke to me. I couldn't make out the words, but the speaker grew insistent. Demanding. I didn't understand the question.

My body began to accelerate through the nothingness, and I was bombarded with colorful images that flashed by me, too briefly to see. The voice kept demanding an answer, but I shook my head, not understanding. The images blinked by, faster and faster. I rocketed through space and time, my hair streaming out behind me.

I saw explosions and implosions of light replayed over and over again in the darkness. I realized I was seeing the creation of solar systems; stars, suns, and planets. Finally, I recognized a turquoise planet approaching, and my speed decreased. I saw earth glow and bloom and die over and over as countless civilizations grew and waned, and still the pounding in my head grew louder.

I was screaming now, flying over oceans, mountains, forests, and deserts. I saw the pyramids take shape and grow out of a rich green plain, and still the pounding in my head demanded an answer. I flew across fertile fields of the Nile delta toward a simple hut made of mud and reeds. Inside, I hovered near the low ceiling and watched a beautiful woman writhe in ecstasy. A moment later I felt myself suffused within her, feeling her joy, now able to hear the question being put to me.

"Which do you choose mortal? Would you serve the gods and live forever, or die in the service of mortals?"

Intuitively, I recognized the moment; this was the rapture at the creation of my bloodline. This unknown woman was to become the mother of the fates. It was the very moment of destiny. I had no answer.

I felt the flesh peel away from my bones and flames engulfed me. I screamed but felt no pain, and knew that somehow the question had been answered. I am the Hand of Fate. I knew it now, as I knew my own name.

Serve well, the voice echoed in my head.

I opened my eyes.

I was sitting upright against the wall of the cave with a flashlight in my hand. My headlamp wasn't working. I turned the flashlight on, and found Rhys crawling toward me on hands and knees. He was speaking, but sounded as if from under water. I struggled to my feet, and my ears popped. Warm liquid trickled down my neck into my collar.

I stumbled over to Rhys and helped him up.

"Are you okay?" We both said it at the same time.

Rhys started to laugh, as he reached out to touch my cheek. "I love what you've done with your hair."

Tentatively, I patted my hair, which seemed to have some kind of Medusa thing going on. I grinned in spite of myself.

"Don't make fun of my hair, and I won't laugh at your moustache. I think you're going to have to shave the whole thing off and start over." Half of it seemed to have been singed off, along with one of his eyebrows.

"What happened?"

"Um, I think I might have gone a little over the top on the banishing thing. Next time, I think I'll do it in smaller batches." I started to laugh as Rhys felt around for his moustache, and couldn't find it.

He smirked. "Ya think?" He shook his head. "I should have known you'd be trouble." He wiped his face and grimaced at the residue in his hand. He gave me another dirty look, and I busted up.

"Man that was fun. Can we do it again?"

He grabbed me by the front of my scorched coveralls and pulled me close. I stopped laughing.

"Are they really gone?" Even the smell of bat guano had faded.

"Looks like." Rhys lifted my hand to his lips and kissed the crescent shape on my palm.

I took a shaky breath and met his steady gaze. "I killed Garlan Russ last night. It was me. I had his lifeline in my hand. I felt it snap." The horrible memory washed over me again. "I would have told you." Hot tears splashed down my cheeks. "I'm a murderer."

Rhys froze, his warm lips pressing against the

crescent mark of my left palm.

"And I'm a demon."

"Djenie," I corrected.

"I can't undo what I am, Mattie. Any more than you can. All I can do is make the best choices I can when the moment arises. Would it have been better if Garr had killed you?" He pulled me close and kissed my forehead. "You had no other choice."

I thought about that for a bit. "I'm afraid to tell Porter that I'm a demon master. That I killed Garr."

"You heard Frank, an aneurysm killed him. It's in the medical report." He nuzzled my neck and I closed my eyes and leaned into him. I wasn't ready to let this go, though.

"You still want me, knowing I'm a murderer?"

He pulled back to look at me. "You've got a lot to learn. I'm willing to teach you, but I'm never going to fit into your idea of what is normal. You have a choice. You go back to your old life. Or you can embrace your destiny. It's up to you. What are you going to do?"

A week ago, I would have had my answer ready, but now, I wasn't so sure. I was a different person now, and I felt different. More alive. My life had purpose. And now that I finally gotten my old life back, I didn't want it anymore. Rhys was right. I'd joined a brand new club; one that was eager to embrace me as a charter member.

"I just accepted an offer to be the next Hand of Fate. I hear the hours are lousy, the pay sucks, and the clients are all anomalous."

"Yeah, but the benefits are mighty satisfying." He came to me then, and folded me into the shelter of his arm, and kissed me good. Then he took my hand and we walked together toward the entrance, back into the light.

"What color panties are you wearing?"

I was pretty sure he didn't want to hear about the long johns. "I'm not wearing any."

"That's my favorite color."

END

ABOUT THE AUTHOR

Award-winning author Sharon Joss writes science fiction, fantasy and horror. She is the author of six novels, including the alternate history thriller, STEAM DOGS, AURUM, and BROTHERS OF THE FANG.

In 2015 , she won the Writers of the Future Golden Pen award for speculative fiction with her novella, *Stars That Make Dark Heaven Light*.

She lives amid a thicket of blackberry vines in Oregon and writes full-time.

If you want to be notified when Sharon Joss's next novel or collection is released, please sign up for the mailing list by going to *http://www.sharonjoss.com* Your email address will never be shared and you can unsubscribe at any time

Word of mouth and reviews are vital for any author to succeed. If you enjoyed the book, please tell your friends and consider leaving a review wherever you purchased it.

1

Twenty-seven minutes late, the number eleven bus to Shore Haven roared up to the stop in front of me, in a scream of air brakes and great rolling gout of black diesel. Even without the smoky bus belch, my eyes felt like they were on fire; I'd just gotten new contact lenses, and hadn't gotten used to them yet. I muttered a silent oath and climbed aboard; my mood having already been poisoned by the unexpected and sudden demise of Trusty Rusty, my nine-year-old Honda earlier in the day. My bulky helmet banged against my leg as I made my way through the tightly-packed bus, looking for a seat, but of course at 5:45 on a Friday afternoon in mid-August, all the seats were taken.

Pressed tightly on all sides by a sweaty mass of humanity, I gritted my teeth and held on to the overhead bar as the bus swung out into traffic again. Five stops to go.

I called my half-brother Lance for a ride and a tow, but he wasn't answering his cell. His auto body shop services all the city vehicles, and if I didn't get Rusty out of the lot by midnight, the City of Picston would give me a ticket and impound it. Pretty ironic, since I'm a Picston parking control officer.

Three stops later, the number of people getting off far exceeded the number of people getting on, and the bus began to empty out. Gratefully, I slid into an empty seat for the three-mile ride to Shore Haven.

I smelled the djinn as soon as I sat down.

Djinn are unnamed djemons, or demons, as they're more commonly known. In the djinn stage, they're stinky little apparitions that are imperceptible to everyone but the person they're trying to attach themselves to.

And me.

The reek of licorice tinged with a hint of sulfur is unmistakable. Once djinn attach themselves to a master and are given a name, the scent disappears, and they're able to materialize in the physical world as real demons. But by that time, they're yours for the rest of your life.

And I should know. I've got two baby djemons of my own.

I scanned the half-empty bus; looking for the source of the stink, but no dice. When the bus stopped at the corner of Third and St. Joseph's, I stepped out into the humid afternoon, only to be hailed by a woman behind me.

"Excuse me, are you Miss Blackman?" The roar of the departing bus drowned out the rest of what she said.

As soon as I spotted the demon coiled around her neck I knew what she wanted.

As she spoke, a gust of soot whipped her frizz of reddish hair into a wild halo. "I'm looking for the Hand of Fate."

She said I could call her Jane. Jane Jones.

Yeah, right.

She was desperate for help; the demon was ruining her life. She was terrified of snakes. She was a teacher, she explained—third grade. She'd lose her teaching credential if anyone found out she had a demon. She couldn't sleep; couldn't eat. The other two demon exterminators in town had recently shut their doors, and she'd heard I could get rid of it.

Yes.

The word was getting out. A few weeks ago, someone had cracked open a cave full of djinn and they'd been running loose in Shore Haven, attaching themselves to unsuspecting people just like Jane.

We trudged up the sidewalk toward my apartment, the smell of hot asphalt and diesel fumes adding to the grime of my already sweat-dampened hair and clothes. All I wanted now was a shower and a beer, but banishing her little guy would only take a minute.

She followed me up the driveway of my landlord's house; a forgettable 1940's detached avocado green split-level ranch with white trim and a big oak tree in the front yard. Up a narrow driveway leading around and behind the garage to the very back of the property to where I lived in a one-bedroom apartment above a 150-year-old stone stable. As we passed the garage, I stopped dead in my tracks.

More than a dozen people clustered in the paved area in front of my apartment. The only person I recognized was Miriam, "Mimsy" Wu, the manager of the House of Cards; a restaurant and gaming establishment in Rochester, which until recently, catered to my step-brother Lance's gambling addiction.

"What's going on?" I asked.

"It's about time you showed up. Some of us have been waiting here for hours." Chopstick-thin Mimsy wears tiny, expensive-looking clothes that I've never seen at any of the places I shop, and if those eyelashes are real, I'll eat a bug. "Where have you been?"

"My car died. I had to take the bus."

She gave me a cat-eyed smile. Probably never been on a bus in her life. Her great-grandmother and mine were best friends, so I feel like I have some sort of screwy obligation to be nice to her. On the other hand, she probably slept with my boyfriend in the not too distant past; something I haven't had a chance to do yet.

"Mimsy says you're the new Hand of Fate," a middle-aged woman in lavender seersucker capris appeared to be the self-appointed spokesperson. "Are you taking over Madame Coumlie's appointments?"

Madame Coumlie was my great-grandmother. She died a few weeks ago and her abilities and legacy as the Hand of Fate passed to me. The whole Hand of Fate concept was still a bit fuzzy for me. So far, I'd banished a whole boatload of unnamed djinn, and one particularly nasty djenie.

"I can't stand this thing one moment longer. You've got to get rid of it—right now!"

Sure enough, a grey-brown toad-like creature with three yellow eyes crouched at her feet. It's only human nature to start referring to a creature who accompanies you everywhere by name; people can't help themselves. And once a djinn has a name, they are forever attached to the person who names them. And once you've named it, it's nearly impossible to stop yourself from talking to them or giving them commands.

Before you know it, they've become a permanent part of your life. Until death do you part.

I wanted to change out of my uniform. "Just give me a minute--."

"I've waited long enough! You have to help us." Others in the crowd echoed her frustration.

I held up my hands. "Okay, okay."

I'd been in exactly the same spot not so long ago, and remembered how desperate I'd been to get rid of Blix. Demon masters are legally required to register with the government. They track the size of your demon annually, and any signs of growth indicate you've been using it for presumably nefarious purposes. Say good-bye to air travel, and probably your job, too. And unless your spouse files for divorce, child protective services usually moves to remove children from the homes of demon masters. In the eyes of the federal government, anyone who consorts or otherwise engages in naming, harboring, or summoning a djemon is guilty of terrorist activities. You can be arrested and imprisoned. And if they discover an unregistered demon of any size, you could be arrested and held without bail—or even executed.

Nobody wants that kind of trouble, which is why they go to the Hand of Fate.

And now, that's me. I am the last direct descendant of the goddess Morta, Queen of Death. Not exactly a super power, but having power over the non-living gives me the ability to banish pesky djinn and djemons.

I eased my way through the crowd to my front door. "I'll take care of each of you as soon I can."

There was a typed sheet of paper taped to my front door. An eviction notice. Great. The property had just been sold at auction, and I had to be out in 30 days. Not so surprising, really. My landlord had been jailed last month for having an unregistered demon, and no doubt needed to sell the property to pay for legal fees.

An old man peered over my shoulder. "I'll bet Mad Otto bought it. He's been buyin' ever'thing between Third and Bayshore. Gonna tear it down to make room for that blasted new Marina."

The old guy must've had chili with onions for lunch.

"Let's get on with it, girlie," chili breath grouched.

I crumpled up the notice and opened the door to my apartment. "The first two of you can come inside with me. The rest of you, please wait out here until it's your turn."

I climbed the stairs, accompanied by a pounding headache. After dropping my purse and helmet at the top of the stairs, I turned to face my first two clients. The first, a soccer mom, had a clear aura and deep maroon lifeline—sign of a normal human. On the other hand, chili-breath's lifeline was black. Curious, but not beyond my experience. It meant he was either not-human, or not-alive. Or maybe both.

My about-to-be new boyfriend, Rhys Warrick, didn't have a lifeline either. In his case, he was a djenie; a former djemon that had outlived his master. When his master died, Rhys was released from servitude and assumed a human form.

"Have either of you ever brought a djinn or djemon to Madame Coumlie to be banished before?"

They both shook their heads.

"Will it hurt?" Chili breath wore his long silver hair in a single thin braid that trailed down his back, past his waist.

"No," I bragged, "Doesn't bother me a bit. Piece of cake."

"I'll go get Mimsy," the soccer mom said, and she left

before I could protest. Great.

Lying at his feet, the old man's djemon looked like a horned slug, and was about the size of a chocolate éclair.

"Come here little guy." When I reached out to it, it reverse halumphed away from me, out of reach. Golden eyes glared at me from atop dark eye stalks.

"Are you going to kill it?" The old man looked worried.

"No, no. It's not alive. It can't die. All I'm going to do is banish it." I took a deep breath, and shook out my sweaty hands. "Wait a second. What's its name?"

Chili breath reddened. "I swear I didn't name it on purpose. It—I started thinking of it as a Snot-wad, and before I knew it, that was 'er name."

Okaaay.

"Hear me and obey, Snot-wad. I am the Hand of Fate. I hereby banish you from all physical and metaphysical earthly planes, never to return." I clapped my hands.

Nothing happened.

"I command it." I clapped again. Again, nothing happened.

"You have to hold his hand." Mimsy came into the room, accompanied by soccer mom.

"What?"

Mimsy grabbed my left hand and put it into the old man's bony right. "Now say it again. You don't need to clap."

"How would you know?" I felt like I'd just been scolded my one of my teachers, and it came out all huffy and pissy. I already felt like a stupid cow next to Mimsy, and having her tell me I was doing it wrong didn't help.

"Because that's the way Madame Coumlie did it for me the last two times."

She must have seen something in my face. "I'm just trying to help."

"Hey, you gonna fix this thing or not," the old man said. "I've gotta go to the can. I've been sittin' around waitin' for you all afternoon. I can't wait much longer."

"Sorry." I gripped his hand. "Okay then. Snot-wad, I banish you from all physical and metaphysical planes, never to return."

Immediately, an earth-shattering scream pierced the air. The windows rattled. We all put our hands over our ears, but Snot-wad's shrill wails and convulsions went on for several seconds before she finally blinked out. The old man snatched his hand away from me and grabbed at his chest. The echoes of the djemon's toe-curling squeals reverberated off the walls of my apartment for several long moments.

"Jaysus Mary of Morgantown. I thought you said it warn't goin' ta hurt. What in tarnation did you do? You some kinda sadist or somethin'?"

I stared openmouthed at the empty spot on the carpet where Snot-wad used to be. "I had no idea that would happen. They're not supposed to be able to feel anything."

"Feels like a piece been torn right outa me." The old man hunched over, his eyes watering.

Maybe he was having a heart attack. "Are you all right?" I reached for him, but he pushed me away.

"Don't know what yer tryin' to pull, here. Miz Coumlie never hurt anybody." He stumbled toward the stairs, muttering. "She never did no harm. Kept me comp'ny; me livin alone and all."

Soccer mom and Mimsy stared at me with wide-eyed apprehension.

"I didn't mean to hurt anybody," I protested.

"That never happened when Madame Coumlie banished my djemons."

"I don't think you're doing it right," said soccer mom. She had a death grip on her purse.

"Do you want to come back later?"

"I don't think that's a good idea." She pulled a scrap of newspaper out of the pocket of her jacket. "Have you seen this? It's from today's paper."

FBI Announces New Security Monitoring Measures for Selected US Cities

AP/UPI The Federal Bureau of Investigation announced that their Anti-Terrorism Task Force is beefing up homeland security efforts with specially-trained dogs to detect invisible threats such as demons, hexes, curses, and in some instances, compulsions. The dogs will be used at major transportation hubs such as airports, major rail stations, and subways to inspect travelers, pilots and engineers for psychic interference.

"We've known for years that dogs could be trained to detect drugs, explosives, and even diseases such as cancer. It wasn't a big stretch to train them to detect inhuman interference and demonic presence," stated an FBI insider on the anti-terrorism task force, who spoke on the condition of anonymity.

New York Senator Bob Wise (R) agreed. "The safety of the American public is of critical importance. These dogs can detect psychic and demonic interference at comparatively little cost to the taxpayer. The public is already used to seeing these dogs at airports, so it's not a big change. No one wants another incident like what happened in Europe two years ago. I for one, would feel much safer knowing that my pilot is not under the influence of some curse or demonic compulsion"

The first paranormal detection dog-handler teams were rolled out at the major international airports last year, but the FBI is also sending these specially-trained teams to selected cities where higher-than-normal incidents of supernatural activities have been reported. The FBI would not confirm or deny which cities have been targeted, but there are several small towns in Louisiana, Missouri, New Mexico, and upstate New York reporting recent spikes of supernatural activity.

I glanced to the top of the bookshelf, where my two own demons, Blix and Larry perched invisibly. They watched me with frightened expressions, their bulbous yellow eyes nearly popping out of their heads. So far, I'd managed to keep them hidden, but I wasn't so sure they'd be safe from a demon-sniffing dog. Maybe I should have banished them when I banished all the other djinn, but they'd saved my life, and I didn't want them to go.

"You think they're coming here?" I asked.

"My husband is a realtor. Two weeks ago he was contacted by the FBI field office in Rochester. They're looking for short-term rentals that will allow dogs."

"Maybe it's for something else," I said. "Like search and rescue training or something."

"I'm not going to argue with you. I want this thing banished right now."

"Yes, but—."

"If the authorities find out, I could lose everything! I have children. I can't spend the rest of my life in hiding."

I could feel the heat of her fear radiating off her. Her eyes shone with anxiety. "Are you sure?"

She stiffened. "Whatever it takes. Just do it."

I looked at the lizard-thing crouched at her feet and swallowed hard. It had a single horn in the middle of its forehead. It was the first one I'd seen that really looked like a demon ought to. "What's the name?"

"No names," soccer mom said. "I don't want anyone to know who I am. And if you see me on the street, act like you don't know me. No one can know about this." She wrung her hands.

"No, I meant, what's your djemon's name?"

"Oh." She wouldn't look at it. "It's Barnaby. Can't we just get this over with?" Already Barnaby was looking a little uncertain. His big yellow eyes flitted around the room, as if looking for a place to hide.

Poor guy. "Take my hand."

As soon as she touched my hand, Barnaby started to squeal like a puppy. As I began to speak the words to banish him, the volume rose to an ear-splitting howl. A seizure gripped Barnaby, and a sour, scorched smell filled the air as he began to bite at himself, writhing in torment before he disappeared. It was an ugly, disturbing scene. Mimsy and soccer mom were both pale and trembling by the time the screams stopped. If there hadn't been a crowd outside, I would have run away right then.

Soccer mom snatched her hand back like she'd been burned.

"I'm so sorry," I gasped. I felt as if I'd just killed her pet. "Are you all right?"

She clasped her hands to her chest; tears streaming down her face. "It feels as if you ripped my heart out through my throat. It's like he was connected to me, somehow. Oh this is horrible!" She glared at me. "You murdered him, you evil witch!"

I tried to explain that Barnaby wasn't ever alive, but she only shook her head.

"I hope I never have to see you again." Her voice held the quaver of near-tears. She couldn't get away from me fast enough.

A moment later, the next client climbed the stairs and the traumatic scene was repeated. Each person as desperate as the last, each banishment an exercise in pain and anguish for both demon and master. And in the end, every one of them left furious with me.

I felt like a monster. I tried everything I could think of to avoid hurting the little guys, but nothing worked. Only two people showed up who had not yet named their djinn, and those were the only ones which disappeared silently, like they were supposed to. Maybe the mere act of naming a djinn somehow hooked the creature into its new master. It was the only thing I could think of, because banishing the djemon seemed to cause too much agony for both of them. I wasn't sure if I could stand one more tortured scream.

If this was what being the Hand of Fate was all about, I wanted no part of it.

www.ingramcontent.com/pod-product-compliance
Lightning Source LLC
Chambersburg PA
CBHW020404260626
47156CB00007B/2232